CHARLES WATERMERE
CRUISING ALONG

I0685380

AGATHA PENNYFEATHER

SERIES TITLE

DEDICATED TO

To everyone who's been on this
ride since Book One:
I was aiming for a trilogy,
but then you kept showing up.

So really, this is your fault.

Thank you!

CONTENTS

CONTENTS

GOODBYE MERASHIRE

Charles Watermere and his wife, Elli, stood at the window of their luxury compartment on the Heronpool train and waved to their extended family until the station was out of view. Their compartment resembled a traditional yet lavish sitting room, complete with all the necessary facilities. Charles had booked it because Elli had been abducted from a train a few months earlier, and—as you can well imagine—she was understandably uneasy about spending any length of time on a train. Charles had reassured her that they would not have to leave their compartment until they arrived in Heronpool. The nearer they got to their destination, the more relaxed Elli became.

As they arrived in a bustling Heronpool Station, their luggage was unloaded and stacked on a trolley by a porter, who then loaded it into a taxi. A short journey later, they arrived at Heronpool docks and got their first glimpse of the ocean liner—the *Queen Euphorbia*.

'My goodness! That is a *huge* ship!' Charles exclaimed, shaking his head in disbelief.

1

'It certainly is. From what the taxi driver said, it's brand new,' Elli replied.

They could not help but think of Heather—a good friend and Charles' father's ladyfriend, who just happened to be Queen Euphorbia.

A porter met them at the taxi, loaded their luggage onto a cart, and escorted them to the ship. Charles showed a crew member their tickets, who then called the concierge (a curlew) over. 'I am Aves Numenius. If you would like to follow me, I will show you to your suite, Your Graces.'

Charles and Elli were stunned at being addressed thus. 'May I ask how you knew who we are?' Charles inquired. 'I booked the cruise as Mr and Mrs Watermere.'

Aves Numenius looked at his clipboard, then said, 'It simply states, VIP plus and telephone.' He escorted them to the Royal Suite.

'What does VIP plus and telephone mean?' Elli asked.

'I would imagine someone called to inform us of your arrival, Your Grace.'

Charles and Elli gave each other a knowing look.

'If you don't mind, we would prefer to be addressed as Mr and Mrs Watermere,' Charles stated. 'We're on our honeymoon, and want to relax.'

'I completely understand, Mr Watermere, Mrs Watermere. If you need anything, please call me.' The concierge took out a business card and handed it to Charles. 'I hope you have a delightful cruise,' he said, then he left the suite.

Charles and Elli's suite was luxurious indeed, with a king-sized bed, a sitting area with a large

2

sofa and two armchairs, a coffee table, wall sconces, and even a crystal chandelier. A dining table with four chairs, a refreshment area, and tea-making facilities completed the package. There was also a generous balcony with dining and relaxing areas. After having a little look at their temporary home, they set to work unpacking.

'This suite is lovely, Sweetie,' Elli said. 'It's fit for a queen.'

'As it's the Royal Suite, I would expect so, Ell. This would be the suite Heather would use if she were on the cruise.'

'Speaking of Aunt Heather... '

'Were you thinking it was Heather who called and told them who we were?' Charles asked, interrupting his wife.

'Yes, that's exactly what I was thinking. I mean, who else could it be?' Elli asked. 'How many people knew which cruise we'd be on? Besides, you never use your title.'

'Only our family knew,' Charles answered.

'Well, we're here now, and the suite is lovely.'

'Shall we go to the balcony, and take in some fresh air?' Charles asked.

'Let's.'

They made their way to the balcony and stood at the rail for a while. They could see people on the dockside wishing bon voyage to loved ones.

A little while later, Charles asked, 'Do you want to stay here or explore?'

'Won't it be busy out there?'

'You're probably right. Let's stay here and take a nap.'

QUEEN EUPHORBIA

CRUISE
IN LUXURY

SETTING SAIL

Charles and Elli were awakened by the blare of the ship's horn.

'We must be underway,' Elli said with a stretch.

'Shall we venture out now and find somewhere to dine this evening?' Charles asked.

'There's a directory on the coffee table if you prefer to see what our choices are,' Elli stated. 'Or, we could just go for a walk and see what's out there.'

'Let's just stroll,' Charles said as he picked up the key to their suite. They left the suite, Charles locking the door behind them. The couple strolled down a passageway where they saw a sign for the dining room, bar, and shops.

'Shops?' Elli asked in surprise.

'Yes, my love. This is, in essence, a floating city. If you need something, you can't exactly head into town.'

'That's true. I hadn't really thought about it.'

As they strolled, they encountered other passengers and wished them a good evening as they passed by. Charles and Elli stopped at an eatery called The Ocean Grill.

4

'How about this one, Ell? It's a seafood restaurant.'
'Perfect!'

They entered and found it had an intimate, quiet atmosphere, which suited their mood.

'Good evening, sir, madam. Table for two?' the maître d' (a seagull) asked.

'Yes, please,' Charles replied.

'Name and cabin number, please,' the maître d' requested.

'Watermere, the Royal Suite,' Elli answered.

They were shown to a table and asked if it would suit. They replied in the positive. He left them with a menu each, told them their waiter would be with them momentarily, then headed back to his post.

The Watermeres perused the menu and Elli asked, 'Sweetie, would you like to share the seafood platter? It's too big for me.'

'It does sound good. I think I can force myself to help you out with that,' Charles replied with a silly smile.

The waiter (an avocet) arrived. Charles and Elli placed their order of a bottle of lemon fizz and a seafood platter for two. As the waiter left, a couple (badgers) walked in and acknowledged the Watermeres with a nod. Charles and Elli returned the greeting with a slight wave, then resumed chatting about their wedding photographs and the ones they would like copies of.

'I love the one of Daddy and Aunt Heather dancing.'

'I do, too. I want the photograph of you walking

down the stairs, in a frame next to my side of the bed,' Charles said.

'For my desk at work, I want the one of you, Sweetie, with Archie straightening your cravat. I also want one of you on your own, next to the bed.'

'How about getting copies of all of them?' Charles asked.

'*All of them*?' Elli asked, completely surprised. 'There are so many of them!'

'It's a record of the whole day with people we love.'

'I agree. All of them, it is then!'

The waiter returned, poured their lemon fizz, and then served their meal.

After dinner, Charles and Elli strolled up on deck. They did a full circuit and then went back to their suite. It had been a long day, and all they wanted to do was relax on the sofa, listen to some music, do a crossword, and perhaps have a little cuddle.

Charles and Elli woke early the next morning and called room service for a breakfast of kippers and toast, which was served on the balcony. They then showered and dressed—Charles in navy shorts, a white polo shirt, and a pair of deck shoes, Elli in a very pretty, pale yellow halter-neck sundress and wedge-heeled sandals.

'Shall we, Mrs Watermere?'

They left the suite, locked it, and went to explore the shops and entertainment areas, even peeking inside the Grand Dining Room. They stopped on deck near the swimming pool and lay down on two

6

sun loungers. The area started to get extremely busy and quite noisy, so they headed inside to find a tea shop.

'Where's our first port of call, Sweetie?'

'Lancaset.'

'Lovely! Have you been there before, Sweetie?'

'No, Ell. Have you?'

'Yes, but not with you,' Elli answered with a sweet smile.

As they strolled paw-in-paw back to their suite, members of staff kept congratulating them.

'Do we have signs on us saying "Just married"?' Charles asked Elli.

'I'm sure it's just that we hold paws, and look so happy.'

'You mean, we look lovey-dovey?' Charles asked.

'Does that bother you, Sweetie?'

'Absolutely not! I'm proud to be married to you. I love you. I hope we're always like this.'

Elli kissed him. 'I hope we are, too.'

They made themselves a cup of tea and were about to sit down on the sofa when Elli noticed an envelope on the coffee table. She opened it.

'We've been invited to join the captain at his table for dinner, Sweetie.'

'Do we *have* to go?' Charles asked.

'I think it may be rude if we don't,' Elli replied with a shrug.

'Ell, did you pack any evening wear?'

'Of course I did. Did you?'

'Yes.'

'Is it your deep, dark blue suit?' Elli asked.

'It *is* my deep, dark blue one. Why do you ask?'

'You look absolutely *gorgeous* in that.'

'I'm glad you think so,' Charles said with a wink.

'What are you wearing tonight, Ell?'

'I brought my midnight blue gown with the tiny sparkles.'

'Ooh! I love that one. You wore that in Heronpool when we went dancing.'

Elli thought for a moment or two, then said, 'Yes, you're right. I did wear it then. Has it been that long?'

CATPTAIN WHETMORE

Cordially Invites You
to
Dine With Him
at His Table

7 p.m.

Grand Dining Room

8

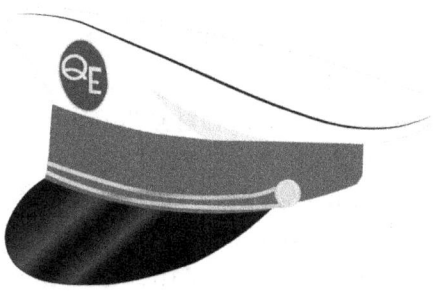

A BAD TASTE IN THE MOUTH

Around six p.m., Charles and Elli showered, then dressed for dinner. Eager to stay in their cosy suite alone together, they reluctantly left and locked the door behind them. Arm-in-arm, they strolled along the passageways. They looked incredibly elegant as they entered the Grand Dining Room. Charles showed the maître d' (a rabbit) their invitation, then Elli popped it in her clutch bag.

'If you would like to join your dinner companions at the table in the middle of the room,' the rabbit instructed.

'Thank you,' Elli said, then she and Charles strode across the room to join two couples who were already seated at the table. As Charles pulled out a chair for Elli, one of their dinner companions (a badger), introduced himself and his wife. Like the other gentlemen at the table, he was wearing a traditional black evening suit, whilst his wife was wearing a black sequinned top and skirt. 'Good evening. I'm Clay Dachs, and this is my wife, Rose.'

'Good evening,' Charles said. 'We're Charles and Elli Watermere.'

The other couple (rabbits) introduced themselves, 'I'm Kevin Conill.'

'And I'm Kevin's wife, Maxie.' She was wearing a long, lime green, short-sleeved dress.

Another couple (martens) approached the table and joined them. 'Good evening, all. We're the Snetrams. Shane and Angie,' the male marten announced.

As the others were about to introduce themselves, the captain— an avocet— joined the table. He wore his white dress uniform, which had so much gold braid it looked like a plate of scrambled eggs.

'Good evening, ladies and gentlemen. I am Captain Whetmore. I do hope you are enjoying the cruise so far, and that the crew are looking after you.'

One member of each couple introduced themselves and their partner. People then started asking each other what they did for a living and where they were from. Charles and Elli exchanged uneasy glances, giving polite but vague answers to the probing questions regarding their private life. By the end of the evening, as Charles and Elli headed back to their suite, they vowed they would politely decline any further invitations to formal dinners in future. It was not that their dinner companions were unsavoury characters; it was just that it was not particularly relaxing or enjoyable.

'Ell, my love, I would have preferred to have had dinner with just you. It was exhausting being asked so many questions all evening.'

'I know people were trying to be friendly, but a

10

lot of those questions were pretty personal, and with Mereland being a village… ' Elli stalled.

'I understand. I think we were invited because we're in the Royal Suite.'

'It's probably protocol for the captain to invite dukes and duchesses to his table,' Elli said.

'At least the captain did not address us as Your Graces,' Charles said. 'I just want us to be Mr and Mrs Watermere.' He sighed. 'It is our honeymoon after all. Would you like a glass of something, Ell?'

'Let's sit on the balcony with a glass of sloe lemonade under the stars.'

'Sounds lovely. Will you not be chilly in that gown?'

'I'll be fine. I'll just snuggle up to you.'

'I like that idea! I'll get the drinks.'

Charles woke early for some reason. He thought it was probably not being in his own bed. He got out of bed, looked at his sleeping wife, and gave her a gentle kiss on the cheek. He threw on a pair of shorts and a T-shirt and went to the balcony with a fountain pen and a crossword book. It was a beautiful morning, the sea was as calm as a mill pond, and the air was cool and refreshing. It was a while later as Charles was just entering the last word of his crossword when Elli appeared, wearing a cream silk robe.

'Good morning, gorgeous!'

'Good morning, Sweetie,' Elli responded, then stifled a yawn.

'You didn't need to get up.'

'Why didn't you wake me?'

CHAPTER 3

'You looked so peaceful, I didn't want to disturb you.'

Elli nestled herself on Charles' lap, sleepily putting her head on his shoulder.

Charles wrapped his arms around her. 'My love, you're still tired. You should go back to bed.'

'I... am... alright,' Elli said through a yawn.

'You can't keep your eyes open, Ell. It's only six o'clock.' Charles stated after a glance at his wristwatch.

'But you're up and dressed.'

'I only threw on a pair of shorts and a T-shirt,' Charles said, as Elli yawned again.

'I want to spend time with you,' Elli stated.

'Ell, we have a lifetime to spend together. You need your sleep. You've been through so much over the last few months,' Charles said, then kissed her on the forehead.

'Okay, you're right. I'll sleep for another hour,' Elli relented, as she got up off Charles' lap and headed back to bed.

A little before noon, Elli woke up and put on her robe. Charles was sitting on the sofa reading a book by Caraway Cynge - *On the Wing - A Travel Guide to the Wider World*.

'Sweetie, it's lunchtime! You let me sleep that long,' Elli said, startled by how much sleep she had had.

'You evidently needed it, Ell,' Charles said, as he put his book down. 'You're on holiday, there's no need to keep to any schedule.'

'What do you want to do with what's left of the

12

day?' Elli asked. 'I just need to get showered and dressed.'

'How about going to sit by the pool? We can take a swim if we feel like,' Charles suggested.

'I just need to brush my teeth, then pop my swimsuit on,' Elli said, as she rummaged in a drawer. She went to the bathroom, brushed her teeth and put on a hot pink swimsuit, then wrapped a white sarong around her waist.

'You look fabulous, Ell! You ready?' Charles asked as he picked up his sunglasses.

'Yes. Just let me get my beach bag.'

They left the suite, and using the signs on the walls, they made their way to the pool. It was fairly busy, but they managed to find two sun loungers together. Elli put her beach bag next to her seat and then lay down.

'I fancy a swim. How about you?' Charles asked.

'I'll sit here, whilst you swim.'

'Don't you feel like swimming, Ell? You not feeling well?' Charles asked with a frown of concern.

Elli reflexively moved her paw to her leg. She didn't want to be reminded of the scars, didn't want anyone to notice them.

'Is your leg bothering you, Ell?'

'Well, it has scars on it, and the fur hasn't grown back where the scars are,' Elli whispered with a little grimace.

'Does your leg hurt?'

'No. It just doesn't look very nice. I don't want people looking at my scars,' she said in a low voice.

'Ell, you're gorgeous! Those scars are a mark of

how brave and strong you are. Besides, nobody will be looking at your scars, they'll be looking at your beautiful face and that stunning swimsuit.' Charles gave Elli a quick kiss.

'You are wonderful! Okay, let's take a swim!' As Elli took off her sarong, Charles undressed to reveal a pair of bright green swimming shorts with ladybirds all over them.

Elli laughed. 'They're new! I now have to agree with you about people not looking at my scars. They'll be looking at *those* shorts!' Elli took Charles' offered paw, then they both walked to the pool edge and, in perfect unison, they dived gracefully into the pool. The moment they hit the water, Elli's leg was the last thing on her mind as they twisted through the water. When they had finished swimming and leapt out of the pool, Elli grabbed her sarong quickly to cover her leg.

'Ell, you're *gorgeous*, a strong, confident woman, and there's no need to cover up. I love everything about you.'

'I don't want people to see my scars, Sweetie.'

'So, you'll never go swimming with the family?'

'Of course I will,' Elli answered immediately. 'Why wouldn't I?'

'Why would the opinions of people you don't know bother you? People you will probably never meet again. I'm not trying to force you, I just want to understand. If you want to cover up, that's your choice. Nobody's opinion of you should make you want to cover up. There's no shame in your scars—that's all I'm saying.'

Elli gave Charles a kiss, untied her sarong and

waved it like a flag. Charles chuckled. 'That's my wife! *She is gorgeous*!' Charles said fairly loudly.

A male badger who was passing said, 'She certainly is, mate!'

Elli blushed a little and put her face against Charles' shoulder.

'That's my wife,' Charles said with a grin. 'I'm the lucky one. Come on, missus. Do you want to swim more or sit on the loungers?'

'Actually, I'm very hungry. Let's go to lunch.'

MM MERASHIRE MARINE

PORTS OF CALL

Elli sat bolt upright in bed, wide-eyed with excitement, 'We make our first port of call today!' She leapt out of bed, showered, and dressed in a pair of white trousers and a pale blue bikini top, with an open white shirt knotted at the front.

Charles dressed in navy shorts and a white polo shirt. When Charles exited the bathroom, he found Elli sitting on the balcony.

'Look out there, Sweetie! It's Lancaset,' Elli said excitedly.

'Not long, we'll be there. Do you want to go on the guided tour?' Charles asked.

'I thought we could do our own thing. I've been to Lancaset many times, and Lawseh is *beautiful*.'

'Ell, I should have realised before I booked the cruise, you've been to these places before.'

'Most of my visits have been for business to Prewtna, it being the diamond centre. Sweetie, I've never been to these places with *you*.'

When they dropped anchor in the port of Lawseh, Elli and Charles made their way to the centre of the town. Charles was captivated by the white-

16

rendered buildings topped with brightly coloured roofs. Elli watched Charles' reaction—as he had never travelled abroad before.

'Ell, I love this place. The cobbled streets, the buildings, the wonderfully colourful roofs. It must be quite a sight from above.'

'I'm sure it must be. I'd never thought about it until now,' Elli said, looking up.

Elli and Charles meandered the cobbled streets, Elli delighted in showing him all the sights, taking in the familiar views with fresh eyes as she shared the memories with her love. They went to the marketplace, spoke to locals, and bought a few items, including some souvenirs, a pair of cerise-coloured beach pyjamas for Elli, and a pair of funky, silk boxer shorts for Charles. Elli said she would steal them, as they were her favourite colour—turquoise— and had teacups all over them.

Paw in paw, they wandered down the narrow streets until, in the late afternoon, they found a quaint tea shop with a few tables outside. The couple entered the shop and ordered the local speciality—bergamot and lavender tea—along with two lemon and ginger fancies. They took their tea and pastries and sat outside at one of the small tables.

'Sweetie, this is fantastic!'

'What? The tea? The pastries? Or sitting outside?'

'All of it. Also, being able to share it with you,' Elli responded.

'I love this tea,' Charles enthused.

'We should take some back with us, Sweetie.'

They watched fellow passengers go by on their guided tour, and Charles commented on how he had his own personal tour guide. When they had finished their tea, they went to the counter and purchased an enormous package of loose-leaf tea to take home with them. The shopkeeper wrapped the tea, then placed it in a beautifully ornate box. They paid, said thank you, and made their way back to the ship.

That evening, Elli said she would like to go dancing.

'Do you want to dress up again?' Charles asked.

'Why not?'

They had a light dinner in their suite, then dressed to go out—Elli in a little black dress with a sweetheart neckline, and Charles in a navy suit and white shirt. They found a dance hall called Sway. They entered and were pleased to see it had subdued lighting, which gave it a very romantic atmosphere. The walls were bathed in light, which made you feel as though you were up on deck, with the sea all around. The ceiling looked like a romantic, starry night. The band was on one side of the room, with a dance floor surrounded by tables with candles.

The band started to play, and people got up to dance. Charles and Elli joined the throng. They danced to a few songs, took a break, then danced some more. They had a drink or two in between dances.

Around eleven o'clock, they decided to head back to their suite. They unlocked and entered the Royal

Suite, and had just snuggled up on the sofa when they heard a commotion in the passageway outside their door.

Charles went to see what the problem was—he was not naturally a nosy person, he just thought someone might be in need of help.

He popped his head out of the door and saw Aves Numenius, the head concierge, attempting to calm down a couple of irate barn owls.

'It's alright, sir. If you would like to return to your suite. I have everything in hand,' Aves said to Charles.

Charles slowly put his head back inside the suite, and as he did, he heard someone say, 'Stolen.' He shut the door and returned to Elli, who was still sitting on the sofa.

'What was it, Sweetie?'

'I'm not entirely sure, but the couple in the next suite were blazing mad. The only thing I heard was the word "stolen".'

'No!' Elli blurted out.

'We don't have much to steal—unless they like evening gowns,' Charles joked. 'Thankfully, your real pendant and engagement ring are in the safe back at home.'

'Just make sure the door is locked, Sweetie,' Elli requested.

'I did. It's locked.'

'It's after midnight. I think it's time for bed,' Elli said, exhausted.

On Sunday, the ship made its next stop in the port of Shroptyn, in the country of Surset. The town was filled with stone buildings with red-tiled roofs. With all those terracotta roofs, it was no surprise to find out that the town specialised in pottery. What was astounding about Surset was that there was a mountain covered in snow. The shops and homes were nestled at the foot of the mountain. When they disembarked, Charles and Elli quickly realised they should have brought coats. They hurtled into the town and found the first shop that sold outerwear—Winterspawt, where they purchased a padded jacket and a pair of gloves each.

A number of the passengers were well prepared, and had brought skiing gear with them. The skiers headed to a cable car that would take them all the way up the mountain, whilst Elli and Charles decided to take the cable car to its first stop—a small area with a ski lodge and tea shop. They made themselves comfortable at one of the outside tables, even though it was cold, because it was so beautiful with a snowy cliff above them. They could hear in the distance the whoops and cries of skiers having fun on the slopes.

With gloved paws, they sipped their tea and chatted. Charles was just asking Elli where she would like to go after they finished their warming beverages when a ski boot fell from the sky and crash-landed on their table, causing them to leap back. Without missing a beat, Charles looked up and bellowed, '*IS THE LEG FOLLOWING?*'

Elli could not stop laughing, and almost spilt the last of her tea. 'I jolly well hope the leg *isn't* following!'

'I wonder how this happened?' Charles asked, holding up the ski boot.

'What do we do with it?'

'Look for a one-booted skier?' Charles replied.

'Should we leave it on a chair with a note?' Elli asked.

'Sounds like a plan. Hopefully, the owner will find it.'

After tea, they boarded the cable car and headed down to the town, where they purchased a few gifts for friends and family back home. They found a wonderful traditional toy shop, where everything was handcrafted. They bought items for Isaac, Charlotte, Pippo, Olive, and Keen and Acanthus' twins, Lille and Acacia. Mid-afternoon, laden with packages, Charles and Elli returned to the ship.

As they were about to enter their suite, they met their next-door neighbours, the barn owls.

'Good afternoon,' Charles and Elli said politely.

'Good afternoon,' the barn owls replied. 'Just a word of caution, if you leave your suite, don't leave any valuables in it. Our suite was broken into,' the male owl said.

'How awful!' Elli exclaimed.

'They took my jewellery and some cash,' the female owl added.

'You don't expect that on a ship like this,' Charles said.

'No, you don't,' the male owl agreed. 'By the way, we're Birch and Nula Tyto.'

'Tyto? Do you happen to have family in Mereland, by any chance?' Charles asked.

'Yes, my cousins live there,' Birch replied.

'We know them,' Charles said. 'Albie and Quinn.'

'That's them!' Birch said in surprise.

'We're Charles and Elli Watermere,' Charles said with a smile.

'You're on honeymoon, aren't you?' Nula asked.

'Yes, we are, Nula,' Elli said, blushing a little.

'How did you know?' Charles asked.

'You look like newlyweds. You're glowing,' Nula answered.

'We're here for our anniversary,' Birch said.

'How many years?' Elli asked.

'Ten,' Nula answered.

'Happy anniversary,' the Watermeres said together.

'We remember what it was like to be newly married. But if you ever want to have dinner one evening, just let us know,' Nula said. 'Don't feel pressured. We'll understand if you want to spend time on your own.'

'Thank you. We'll let you know,' Charles said.

'Thank you for understanding,' Elli added.

'We'll let you get on with your evening,' Birch said.

They all wished each other a good evening, then they entered their respective suites.

Upon entering the Royal Suite, Elli said, 'Sweetie, I think someone has been in here.'

'I'm sure it was housekeeping,' Charles responded.

'No, things have been moved,' Elli said determinedly.

22

'Ell, has anything been taken?'

'Not that I can tell.'

Charles checked the bathroom to make sure nobody was hiding in there. He then checked the balcony.

'Ell, nobody is here, and nothing has been taken.' Charles pulled her close and held her tightly.

'You're safe, Ell.'

Elli exhaled at his touch.

The evening was spent having an intimate dinner in their suite, then a leisurely after-dinner stroll on deck.

ABSOLUTE STUNNER

The next afternoon, Charles and Elli made their way to the pool area. Elli chose to wear a pretty pink sundress and flat slip-on sandals. Charles wore khaki-coloured shorts and a white polo shirt. They selected two sun loungers and made themselves comfortable.

They had been sitting there for ten minutes or so when a couple of hares walked up and sat on the two loungers next to them. The female hare was wearing a bright orange bikini, and around her neck, she wore a heavy gold chain with a heart dangling from it. The male hare was wearing a pair of shorts in an eye-watering shade of chartreuse, and on his wrist was a thick gold chain. The female hare smiled at Elli, who politely smiled back.

'Bright, look at her pendant. It's *gorgeous*!' the female hare enthused, turning to her partner.

The male hare, Bright, leant over and stared at Elli's pendant. 'Yes, it's an absolute stunner... So is that engagement ring.'

'Thank you,' Elli said. 'But to be honest, they're fake,' she whispered.

24

'No way!' the female hare cried, stunned.

'Absolutely,' Charles added.

'I would never bring these on a cruise if they were the genuine article. Seriously,' Elli said.

Just then, a family of three squirrels—mother, father, and teenage son, took the sun loungers on the other side of the Watermeres.

'Well, your jewellery is stunning!' the female hare said. 'Bright, I want a ring just like hers.'

'Ell, we should go. I just remembered we made arrangements to meet Birch and Nula,' Charles said, giving Elli a look which clearly said, '*Let's just go.*'

Elli, realising Charles just wanted to get away from further questions, responded, 'You're right! I forgot.'

They said goodbye to the hares. As they stood up Charles said in a low voice, 'Ell, you shouldn't wear that jewellery, it attracts too much attention.'

'I think you're right, Sweetie.' Elli glanced at Charles as they walked. 'I know you did make arrangements with Birch and Nula this morning, but that isn't until this evening.'

'I know, but we wanted to go up there to relax.'

'I know what you mean. I was beginning to feel a little uncomfortable with my jewellery being eyed up.'

Early that evening, Charles and Elli showered and dressed for dinner. Charles wore a navy suit, and a magenta shirt with no tie. Elli chose her new, cerise silk beach pyjamas.

Charles gave Elli a kiss and said, 'You are so beautiful.'

25

Elli replied, 'You're not bad, yourself!'

'This old thing? I just threw on the first thing in the wardrobe,' Charles joked.

They left their suite, and Charles locked it, just as Elli realised that she was still wearing her pendant and ring.

'Don't worry, Ell, I'll put them in my inside pocket,' Charles said. He then knocked on the Tyto's suite door. They were greeted by Nula and Birch. Nula was wearing a long, mauve gown, and Birch was wearing a dark grey suit with a navy tie.

'Good evening, folks,' Birch said with a warm smile. 'You both look fabulous.'

'You do!' Nula added. 'I love that suit. Is it silk, Elli?'

'Thank you, Nula. It is silk.'

'Shall we?' Birch asked.

The couples chatted as they walked towards the Grand Dining Room—a place that Charles and Elli had never expected to enter again. They were escorted by the maître d' through the softly lit dining room to a table for four near the window, offering a view of the stars. At a nearby table, Charles and Elli noticed the family of squirrels they saw earlier up on deck.

The waiter arrived and asked what they would like to drink.

'Do you like lemon fizz?' Elli asked.

'We've never tried it, Elli,' Nula replied.

'You must. It's lovely,' Charles said, then asked the waiter for a bottle.

'Name and suite, sir,' the waiter asked.

'Watermere, Royal Suite.'

26

The waiter thanked Charles, then returned with a chilled bottle of lemon fizz and four glasses. He proceeded to serve the beverage.

Birch raised his glass with a grin, 'A toast! Newlyweds and anniversaries!'

Charles, Elli, and Nula echoed, 'Newlyweds and anniversaries!' and took a sip.

'Ooh! I do like this stuff!' Nula trilled.

'It is lovely. Nice choice, Elli,' Birch said.

The waiter returned and took their food order. Charles and Elli ordered garlic and lemon salmon with asparagus and roast potatoes. The Tytos chose cod with lemon butter, parsnips, and boiled potatoes.

As they ate, they chatted about Mereland and Heronpool, where the Tytos were from. Birch said he was an accountant, and Nula was a kindergarten school assistant. When asked what Charles did, he said he was in marketing but had not worked since moving to Mereland, which was true. Elli said she worked in a jewellery shop, which was also not a lie. Though they liked the Tytos, they did not want eavesdroppers to hear their business.

Just before dessert, the ladies excused themselves and headed to the loo. They were just about to go back to the table when Elli noticed her trousers were slipping down a little, and said, 'Nula, I need to fix these. You head back to the table. I won't be far behind you.' Elli tightened the drawstring, opened the door and stepped out—only to be bowled over by a teenage squirrel. As she was getting up off the floor, he called out, 'Sorry,

Missus!' and kept running.

Elli dusted herself off, fixed her clothes, rubbed her hip, returned to the dining room, and sat back down at the table.

'Are you alright, Ell?' Charles asked because she looked a little stunned.

'I was just knocked down by a teenage squirrel. I think it was the one from that table over there,' she said, gesturing over her shoulder.

'Are you okay? You weren't hurt, were you?' Charles asked, noticing she looked a little stunned.

'I'm fine, Sweetie. Just a little shocked.'

They each ordered a dessert of raspberry and blackcurrant sorbet. Afterwards, they sat a while longer, sipping the last of their lemon fizz and chatting. Charles whispered to the waiter that he would take care of the bill.

Once finished, they strolled back to their suites. As they passed the squirrel family's table, Elli caught the teenage son sneering at her as if to say, *Who are you looking at*? The two couples continued, stopping outside their suites, where they wished each other goodnight. Birch and Nula thanked Charles and Elli for a most enjoyable evening and said they hoped to do it again before the end of the cruise. Then they entered their respective suites.

As the Watermeres entered their suite, Elli said, 'Sweetie, someone's been in here *again*.'

'Ell, come on!' Charles said, a little exasperated.

Elli looked around the suite. '*Look*!' she said

28

firmly. 'Look at my undies drawer.'

'Yes, I know you have some lovely undies,' Charles said playfully.

'I don't mean that, plant pot! Look at the mess.'

Charles looked at the drawer. Indeed, Elli's intimates were in a tangled mess.

'Okay, you're right! Someone *has* been in here,' Charles said, picking up the telephone. He took the business card next to the phone and called Aves Numenius, the head concierge. 'This is Charles Watermere in the Royal Suite—yes, our suite has been broken into, and my wife's intimate apparel drawer has been rummaged through—Yes, we're absolutely sure—Is that all?—*Goodnight.*' Charles hung up the phone and turned to Elli.

'What did he say?'

'He asked if we were sure that the room had been broken into. He did say they'd put another lock on the door, though I'm not sure how that helps.'

Elli tidied her underwear drawer, then put on a beautiful white silk nightgown. She chatted to Charles as he undressed. 'Ooh! You're wearing *my* boxer shorts,' Elli joked, noticing the turquoise ones with the teacups on.

'No, these are mine,' Charles said, opening a drawer and pulling out another pair. 'These are *yours*. I sneakily bought you a pair.'

Elli giggled. 'You are the best, Sweetie!' Elli gave him a big hug. 'I think I'm ready for bed. I'm tired this evening,' Elli said as she rubbed her hip.

'Ell, are you sure you're alright?' Charles frowned.

'I think I'm alright. I just feel a little bruised, that's all.'

'If you need to see the doctor... '

'If I do, I will.'

As they got into bed, Elli asked, 'Where's our next port of call?'

'Kroy in the country of Erihskroy. The day after tomorrow.'

'I've never been to Kroy before,' Elli said.

'What shall we do tomorrow?' Charles asked.

'I'm not sure. Let's decide in the morning. But for now, just cuddle me.'

SHOPPING AND SUSPECTS

Charles woke early, his gaze drawn to his sleeping bride. He watched her gentle breathing, a quiet rhythm that grounded him in the stillness of the morning. For a minute or two, he simply stayed there, marvelling at how lucky he was to be married to her. He quietly slipped out of bed, and noticing the jacket he wore the previous night draped across the back of a chair, he grabbed it and hung it on a coat hanger. He then remembered Elli's pendant and engagement ring were still in the inside pocket. Taking them out, he held the engagement ring up to the light, turning it over thoughtfully, *Ell truly is a master jeweller.* He then placed the two pieces of jewellery on Elli's bedside table, stepped out onto the balcony, and closed the door behind him.

He thought about the days since their marriage. They were halfway through their cruise, which meant they had been married almost three weeks. *How is it almost three weeks?* At that moment, Elli came out onto the balcony, her white silk nightgown fluttering in the sea air.

'Good morning, early bird,' she said as she sat

31

herself on his lap.

'Good morning, my sleepy head. I left your pendant and ring on the bedside table. I forgot they were in my jacket pocket.'

'I found them. I hid them in my undies drawer.'

'Why, Ell? We've been broken into once.'

'Well, I'm not going to wear them, because you said they drew the eye. Besides, they've already been through my undies drawer and found nothing.'

'Fair comment,' Charles said. 'How is your hip feeling today?'

'It's a little sore,' Elli replied.

'Do you need to get checked out by the doctor?'

'I don't think so. I'm just a little tired.'

Charles raised an eyebrow.

'We've just had a lot of late nights, Sweetie.'

'If you think you need to see a doctor, please see one.'

'I promise I will, Sweetie. Stop worrying.' She kissed Charles on the nose.

'As we're docking in Kroy tomorrow, do you just want to relax today?'

'Yes, I think so. But, if you want to do something, don't let me stop you,' Elli said.

'I want to spend time with you,' Charles stated.

'Sweetie, we have a lifetime together. Don't feel you have to stop being you. I don't want you to change. I don't want to change you. So many people get married, then spend years changing or trying to change their partner. They then turn around and say, "You're not the person I married." No kidding!'

Charles laughed. 'You are such a wise lady.'

'I don't want to change you, Sweetie.'

'Even when I'm a plant pot?'

'Even then. Being a plant pot at times is who you are. It would be like trying to stop you being a sweetie. I love you as you are.'

Charles kissed Elli. 'I love you, Elli Watermere.'

'I love you, my sweet plant pot.'

'I fancy having a stroll around. Would you like to join me?'

'No, Sweetie. I think I'll just sit on the balcony, and read.'

Charles showered and then dressed in navy shorts, a magenta polo shirt, and deck shoes. He gave Elli a kiss, then left the suite.

Charles made his way to the shopping area, where he saw a silk evening gown that happened to be a Canire Couture design. He just knew Elli would love it. A turquoise silk slip-dress, full-length, with shoestring straps, and a daringly deep scoop back. Charles bought the gown, then left the shop. He continued to browse in shops. There was a little jewellery shop, which Charles passed by, thinking, *You don't buy your master jeweller wife jewellery from another jeweller.*

There was a shop called Sea Scents that sold perfume, and Charles decided Elli might like a new fragrance, because sadly, the last perfume she used, was the one she was wearing when she was abducted. Memories, good and bad can be triggered by scents and smells. Charles chose a

33

fragrance by Elli's favourite brand, Mac & Monty, that was fresh and clean, with the scent of rain, roses, and freesias.

Charles headed back to the Royal Suite. He could not wait to see what Elli thought of his purchases. Arriving, he found Elli asleep on the bed. She stirred when she heard the door close, and sat up blinking sleepily. 'Sweetie!'

'Hello, gorgeous! You tired?'

'I was, but I'll get up and shower.'

'In a minute. I have something for you,' Charles said handing her the packages.

She opened the gown first. 'Oh my! Oh my! It's *gorgeous*!' It's one of Thia's designs!' Elli held the gown up to admire it a little more. 'I should shower and try it on.'

'Open the other package.'

Elli did as she was asked. She saw the Mac & Monty box, and Charles could see her hesitate slightly.

'It's a new fragrance, Ell. Smell it.'

Elli opened it with some hesitation, her mind stalling when she saw the bottle. She took a breath, sprayed a little on her wrists, then took a sniff. '*My word*! It smells like our wedding flowers.' Elli held her wrist up for Charles to smell.

Charles smiled.

'Sweetie, you are the best husband!' She kissed him. 'I'm going to shower so I can try on my new gown.'

'Do you want to wear your new gown tonight? How about dinner and a little dancing?'

'That would be nice,' Elli said, gave Charles another kiss, then went to shower.

Elli appeared later wearing a long white, wrap-around skirt and a turquoise strapless top.

'That gown's changed since I bought it,' Charles joked.

'Plant pot. I hung it up.'

'Why? Doesn't it fit? Don't you like it?'

'I *love* it!'

'Then why didn't you show me?'

'Because...'

'You want me to see it tonight?'

She simply gave him a cheeky smile.

'Do you feel like something to eat, Ell?'

Elli thought for a moment, then said, 'Yes, I think I could eat something.'

Charles called room service to order a brunch of smoked salmon with a green salad. They chatted whilst they enjoyed the particularly tasty meal.

'Sweetie, I was thinking about our room being entered twice. I remember the second time was the night we went to dinner with Nula and Birch.'

'You don't think *they* had anything to do with it, do you?' Charles asked somewhat startled by the suggestion.

'No, no, no. Earlier that day, we were on deck, where the...'

Charles cut her off, 'Where the hare couple were overly interested in your necklace and ring.'

'Yes! Exactly,' Elli said.

'We did say we had to go because we had plans. They knew we would be out of our suite, also, you

35

said I should leave my jewellery off. They could have heard you.'

'It's my fault. Sorry, Ell,' Charles said.

'No, Sweetie. It's not your fault. I wasn't blaming you. What I meant was, they knew we'd be out.'

'Ell, you told them the jewellery was fake.'

'Perhaps, they didn't believe me,' Elli said with a shrug.

They're incredible replicas, Charles thought. 'You may well be right, Ell. Perhaps the hares... I don't know. I guess we'll never know.' Charles glanced at the door, just to make sure it was locked.

'You may well be right, Ell. We'll never know.'

Seas the Day

CAUSING TROUBLE

That evening, Charles showered and dressed in black trousers, white shirt, and black shoes. He sat down on the sofa and waited for his wife to finish getting ready. When Elli walked out of the bedroom, she looked sensational. The fit of the gown was so perfect, it looked like Thia had made it for her. Charles put his paw to his heart and said, 'Ell, are you trying to kill me? I think my heart just stopped. Is that a split at the side?'

Elli giggled. 'Yes, it's a split.'

'Really, Ell, that is a heart-stopping gown. There will be males dropping dead all over the ship when they see you.'

'You are silly!'

'No, I'm not. You are drop-dead gorgeous!'

'Thank you, Sweetie. By the way, I adore my new fragrance. It reminds me of our wedding day.'

'That long ago!' Charles jested. 'I take it you like the gown.'

'Are you kidding?' Elli asked. 'I *love* it! I would have thought Thia had sent it with you.'

'Well, Mrs Watermere, let's go to dinner.'

'Where are we going?' Elli asked.

'I noticed a restaurant called Sea Breeze, whilst I was out earlier. Apparently, the menu includes dishes from all our ports of call.'

'Sounds interesting,' Elli said.

They locked the suite and then made their way down the passageway. Charles and Elli arrived at the restaurant, which was bright with lots of glass and stainless steel. As they were being shown to their table, Charles and Elli noticed the hare couple at another table, but the hares were so deep in conversation, they were oblivious to anyone. Charles and Elli perused the menu, then ordered a glass of sloe lemonade each, then salmon with dill pesto wrapped in a flaky pastry case. For their main course, they selected spicy monkfish with a green salad. They were just tucking into their lemon fizz sorbet when the hares approached.

'It's lovely to see you again,' the female hare said. 'That's a lovely gown you're wearing.'

'It really is,' Bright said, which earned him a filthy look from his partner.

'Thank you,' Elli said.

'We're going dancing at Shimmy,' the female hare announced.

'What's that?' Elli asked.

'It plays lots of modern music,' the female hare replied. 'Join us if you like.'

Charles answered, 'We have plans, but thank you for asking.' Elli played with her sorbet.

The hares got the hint, as they could see Elli's sorbet melting.

'Have fun!' Elli said.

'You too!' the hares said, then left.

Charles and Elli finished their dessert.

'Do you want to go to Shimmy or Sway?' Charles asked.

'Sway. Shimmy doesn't sound like a place we can dance close together,' Elli said.

'I like your reasoning.'

They left the restaurant, and just as a couple were being shown to a table, the male turned around and looked at Elli, which earned him a slap from his ladyfriend.

At Sway, all eyes were on Elli.

'Ell, I told you. Heart-stopping!'

Elli giggled.

'Come on missus, dance with me.'

They danced and laughed. An otter, about Lionel's age tapped Charles on the shoulder and said, 'She's a keeper!' Charles responded with, 'She most certainly is!'

Elli asked what the otter had said.

Charles replied, 'He said, if he was thirty years younger, he'd steal you from me.'

'Really?' Elli asked.

'No. He asked me where he could buy that gown.'

'You are a plant pot.'

'Actually, he said you're a keeper. I agreed with him.'

'I think I'll keep you too!' Elli said. 'My feet are aching, Sweetie.'

'No wonder! You insist on wearing skyscrapers. Want me to carry you?'

'Don't be silly!' Elli replied.

'Stay here, then, and I'll go back and get you

some flat shoes,' Charles offered.

'It's okay, Sweetie. Let's just walk back slowly.'

They walked and talked, Charles with his arm around Elli's waist.

When they unlocked and entered their suite, they were horrified. Elli's underwear was scattered all over the floor.

'*That's it*!' Charles yelled. He picked up the telephone and called Aves Numenius, but he was told that he was unavailable. '*Then put me through to the captain.*'

'I'm sorry, sir, you will have to go through the concierge,' Charles was told by the person on the other end of the line.

'This is Charles Watermere, Duke of Mereland and Ashlowe, and my suite has been broken into for the *third time*! I am *appalled*!'

'I will give Captain Whetmore your message.'

'*I don't want him to get my message, I want him to do something about it.*' Charles said firmly, his hackles rising. He slammed the phone down.

Elli kicked off her shoes, then started picking her intimates off the floor. A minute or two later, there was a tap on the door, and Charles opened it. It was Captain Whetmore, who looked a little puzzled when he saw Charles.

'Your Grace?'

'Yes, I am Charles Watermere, Duke of Mereland and Ashlowe. I'm on honeymoon with my wife, and we'd prefer to be known as Charles and Elli Watermere to other passengers.

'I understand, Your Grace.'

Charles ushered the captain into the suite, where he saw Elli with an armful of underwear.

'My wife and I just got back from dinner and dancing, and for the *third* time, our suite had been broken into. They rummaged through my wife's intimate apparel drawer—*again*.'

'Was anything taken?' the captain asked.

Elli thought for a moment. 'Oh no! My pendant and ring have been taken!'

'What are they like?' the captain asked.

Elli described them. 'They aren't hugely expensive, but they are handcrafted.'

'Ell, it doesn't matter how much they're worth. They not only violated our space but went through your underwear drawer,' Charles said, most disgruntled. 'From what we've been told, it isn't the only suite that's been broken into, and I'm sure it won't be the last.'

'I would move you to a different suite, but we only have one empty single cabin. I am so sorry,' the captain said, clearly distressed.

'The thief needs to be caught,' Charles pressed.

'Did you tell anyone you would be out this evening?' Captain Whetmore asked.

'No. I would imagine someone is getting to know who people are and then breaking in when they see them out and about. Unless, of course, it's pure chance, which I don't believe for one moment. The thief or thieves must have known we would be out. *Three times*.'

'I will see what we can do,' the captain said.

Charles and Elli thought, that probably meant, *'There isn't much I can do.'*

'Well, it is late, and we're tired,' Charles stated.

The captain bade Charles and Elli a good night and left. Charles locked the door.

'Sweetie, what if they come back in the middle of the night?'

Charles shoved an armchair in front of the door.

Elli put her things back in the drawer, then walked over to Charles, who wrapped his arms around her.

The next morning, after a fitful night's sleep, Charles and Elli decided they would go ashore. After all, what else could the thieves take? They showered and dressed, and made their way to join other passengers ready to head down the gangplank. Elli kept glancing around, wondering if one of these people could be the thief. With reservations, Charles and Elli stepped ashore.

The town buildings were all red brick with flat roofs. All the streets met at circular paved areas, which had beautiful planters and benches in the middle. Charles had read that the town's local drink was an orange mead, which neither of the Watermeres liked when they tasted it. Kroy was also famous for its seafood, which Charles and Elli loved. It did not take long to visit every street in the town, it being small. They headed back to the ship early. Thankfully, their room appeared to be unmolested.

The couple decided to spend the rest of the day and evening relaxing in their suite.

Sunday morning, they were eating breakfast on the

balcony, where they could see the port they would be docking at off in the distance.

Elli asked, 'How far do you think we are from Erest?'

'A couple of hours. I'm not sure. Do you want to go ashore, Ell?'

'Yes. Erest is famous for spectacular glass.'

'You going to buy a lot of glass?' Charles asked, flexing his muscles.

Elli laughed. 'Not a huge amount. Perhaps a piece or two.'

'Let's get dressed.'

Charles wore black shorts, white cotton shirt, and deck shoes. Elli opted for black cotton, wide-legged trousers, a loose, white silk shirt, and a pair of wedged-heeled sandals.

When the ship docked, Charles and Elli made their way around all the glass shops. Every one of them had beautiful pieces, but one artisan's pieces were exquisite. They watched the artisan work for some time, then they purchased a few pieces for themselves that they had fallen in love with, and a couple of gifts for people back home. Charles said he would take the packages back to the ship, rather than them carrying them all day. Elli said she would grab a cup of tea from a tea shop and wait for his return.

On the way to his suite, Charles saw a teenage male squirrel in one of the passageways.

'Good morning,' Charles said, but the teenager did not reply.

43

Charles continued to the suite and deposited the packages. After double-checking the door was locked, he returned to Elli, who was sitting outside the tea shop with a cup of tea and a lemon and lime slice.

'Sweetie! Sit down, I'll get you a cup of tea.'

Elli went into the tea shop, returning with tea and a pastry. 'You were quick, Sweetie.'

'Not many people going back. I only saw that teenager that knocked you down.'

'You couldn't have. He's over there with his parents. He's been there since you left for the ship.'

'Really?'

'He's been there the whole time, I swear,' Elli confirmed emphatically.

'What's wrong, Ell?' Charles asked, noticing her furrowing her brow.

'Hmm? Do you remember when I got knocked over, I told you the teenager said, "Sorry missus.", then ran on?'

'Yes, I remember.'

'When we left the restaurant with Birch and Nula, the teenager at the table looked at me as if he'd never seen me before.'

'What are you getting at, Ell?'

'Let's go back to the ship, then I'll tell you. Drink up!'

They left the town and strolled back to the ship, unlocked their suite and settled on the sofa.

'You were going to tell me something,' Charles said.

'Well, there must be two of them!'

44

'But, Ell, we've seen that family a few times, and there's only ever been a mother, father, and one son.'

'True,' Elli agreed, but appeared deep in thought. She suddenly blurted out, 'Sweetie!'

'What? What's wrong?'

'Remember we were on deck by the pool, and were leaving the hare couple?'

'Yes, vividly. And?' Charles asked, a little bemused. 'Ell, I'm not sure what station you're train of thought is going to pull into.'

'Don't you remember, that squirrel family was there when you said I shouldn't wear my jewellery?'

'So, you think it's that squirrel family that have been doing the break-ins? It can't be. They were sitting in front of us when one of the break-ins occurred.'

'Could be,' Elli shrugged.
'Then it is my fault. I'm sorry, Ell. Old big mouth, me.'

'Not your fault, Sweetie. Not at all.'

'So, what shall we do about it?' Charles asked.

'Call the captain. I have an idea.'

Charles called a number and asked for the captain to visit their suite as a matter of urgency.

Captain Whetmore arrived a few minutes later, completely confused by being asked to visit, but listened to Elli's theory about the break-ins. The captain mulled it over, and agreed to give Charles and Elli any and all the assistance they needed, if it meant catching the thief. They discussed a plan and who would be involved.

DOUBLE TROUBLE

Charles and Elli dressed for dinner—Charles in navy trousers, a white shirt, and black shoes—Elli in a pair of navy beach pyjamas. They left their suite and were a little way down the passageway when they stopped and Charles said, 'Ell, I forgot to put on my good watch. The one you got me.'

'We can go back and get it, Sweetie.'

'It's okay, I left it in my bedside table. It'll be safe. I'll get it when we get back after dinner.'

'Okay then, let's go to dinner,' Elli said, and they strolled to the Grand Dining Room.

They were shown to a table by the maître d'. As they crossed the dining room, they noticed the squirrel family sitting at the captain's table. They were glad to have not been invited and would be dining alone. They took their seats at a table for two, and the waiter approached to take their order.

'Lemon fizz, please,' Charles ordered, glancing at the menu.

Charles and Elli were looking at the menu together, discussing each dish when the teenage squirrel left the captain's table. A few minutes later,

46

a crew member approached the captain, leant forward, and whispered something. The captain appeared to excuse himself from the table, and then left the dining room.

Charles and Elli chatted about their last port of call, which would be in two days. They were just about to order when Aves Numenius approached.

'I do beg your pardon, Mr and Mrs Watermere, but please return to your suite.'

Charles and Elli stood up, returned to the Royal Suite, and unlocked the door.

'Sweetie! My undies are all over the place *again*. Why do they have a thing about my delicates?'

'They're pretty?' Charles called from the living room. Elli put her things back in a drawer, undressed, put on a pair of jeans and a T-shirt, and returned to the living room just as there was a knock on the door. Charles answered it. There stood Captain Whetmore along with the Tytos.

'Please come in,' Charles requested.

The Tytos looked completely nonplussed as to why they would be summoned to the Royal Suite by the captain.

'Please take a seat,' Charles said. He then went to the balcony, collected a chair, and offered it to Elli.

'You take it, Sweetie,' she said, as she sat herself down on the floor next to Charles' legs.

'So, Mr and Mrs Tyto, I know you're probably wondering why you're here,' the captain said.

'We were thinking along those lines,' Birch answered.

'Mr and Mrs Tyto, Mr and Mrs Watermere

47

noticed something earlier today, that they shared with me. They believe we have a stowaway,' the captain said.

'A stowaway!' Nula said.

Elli continued, picking up the conversation, 'Our room had been broken into multiple times... '

'*Multiple!*' Birch exploded, completely disgusted.

Elli continued, 'We knew that someone must have overheard us saying we were going to dinner with you.'

'No way!' Nula gasped.

'Remember me getting knocked down by that teenager?'

'Yes, the teenage squirrel,' Nula said.

'Yes. He said "Sorry, Missus," when he did it, but later when we passed the table, he glared at me as if he had never seen me before.'

'That is odd,' Birch said.

'I thought so, too. Earlier today, when we were in port, Charles said he'd run back to the ship to drop some heavy gifts off. When he returned, he said he had run into the teenager who knocked me down on the ship. The thing was, the teenager was sitting with his parents at a table outside a cafe all the time Charles was away.'

'Oh!' Nula said.

'Then Charles said, "I'm sure it was him,". That made me think that perhaps there *were* two of them.'

'So, we contacted Captain Whetmore and told him we had an idea,' Charles said.

The captain spoke. 'Thank you, Mr and Mrs Watermere. With all the disturbance of this suite, I

48

would have relocated the Watermeres to another suite, but we only have one empty, a single, a little down the passageway from this suite. I checked the number, then told Mr and Mrs Watermere. On the way to dinner this evening, they stopped outside it, and in loud voices, talked about a valuable item being forgotten in their suite, and that it should be safe, as it was in the bedside table.'

Nula was on the edge of her seat, listening.

'The Watermeres went to dinner in the Grand Dining Room. I had invited the squirrel family to dine with me, having been told about Mr and Mrs Watermere's suspicions about their teenage son.'

'I see,' Birch said, wondering where the captain was heading with the story.

'I had a crew member watch the teenage squirrel, and when he left the table, which we were sure he would, the crew member would inform me. That meant the plan was underway. I excused myself, and hurried down the passageway to the Royal Suite, where a squirrel was caught outside with lockpicks.'

'No!' Birch exclaimed.

'Absolutely, Mr Tyto,' the captain stated.

'As this passageway is a dead end, there was no reason for the miscreant to be outside this suite, and he had no way out.'

'You said there were two of them,' Nula said.

'Well, one of my crew was in this suite before Mr and Mrs Watermere left. The crew member hid, and when the squirrel entered the suite, and went straight to the bedside table, the crew member caught him.'

'Wow!' the Tyto's said in unison.

'So, how were they working together?' Birch asked.

'From what we know so far... ' the captain said. 'we believe, they are twin brothers, and one of them said he was going on holiday with friends. He got on board by pretending to be his brother. We don't know how he found the empty cabin. One of them would mingle and find out information, then let the other know which guests were out of their cabins. One would break in, then hand the items to the other.'

'That's why there was one ashore and one on the ship. The one on the ship relied on nobody realising it was another teenager, but Elli worked it out,' Charles said, admiringly.

'So, where is he now?' Birch asked.

'They are both in the brig,' the captain said.

'So, what happened to the stuff they stole?' Nula asked.

'I unlocked the single cabin and found it in an absolute mess, with a large quantity of cash and jewellery scattered about.' The captain reached into a box he had with him, and said, 'I believe these are yours, Mr and Mrs Tyto.' He handed them Nula's jewellery, and a quantity of cash they had reported stolen.

'Thank you Captain Whetmore, I thought I would never see my jewellery again! The necklace belonged to my mother,' Nula said.

'You are welcome. I am glad you have them back. I have these, Mrs Watermere.' The captain handed Elli her replica pendant and engagement ring. As the captain lifted Elli's jewellery out of the box, Elli spotted a heavy gold chain with a heart dangling from it, and realised the hares had also been victims of theft.

'You two are very clever!' Nula said to the Watermeres.

'They certainly are, Mrs Tyto,' Captain Whetmore agreed. 'Now you have a few days to relax before our final port of call, Alexham in Glodur. I have also arranged for you, Mr and Mrs Watermere, to return for a cruise with us. The same for you, Mr and Mrs Tyto. You will be given the Royal Suite, unless of course, you choose to come on the cruise together. You would then have to decide who got the Royal Suite. I know it doesn't make up for any upset on this cruise, but perhaps we can make up for it in the future.'

'I have a question, Captain,' Nula said. 'Could we give the cruise to our daughter? She's getting married, and it could be a honeymoon for her and her husband.'

'Of course, Mrs Tyto. They will be your tickets. You may transfer them if you wish.'

'Thank you,' Birch said.

'Well, I will leave you to relax. Thank you very much for your assistance and patience,' the captain said, as he stood up. 'I believe your dinner was interrupted, Mr and Mrs Watermere.'

'Yes, it was,' Charles said.

'Let Aves Numenius know what you would like to eat, and it will be brought here for you.' the captain said.

'We would appreciate that,' Elli responded.

Nula and Birch stood up, and Birch said, 'Thanks again, Charles, Elli. We'll see you. Goodnight.'

The captain and the Tytos left, and Charles ordered a piping hot dish of pesto pasta for two.

'Ell, you aren't just gorgeous, you're also really smart. Maybe not for choosing me, but in other areas.'

Elli stood, sat on Charles' lap, and then kissed him. 'The smartest thing I ever did, was steal your crossword book.'

MAGIC GEMS

The morning of their last port of call, Charles and Elli got up early, breakfasted on the balcony, showered then dressed. Charles wore navy shorts, a white polo shirt, and deck shoes. Elli had on a pair of stone-coloured, wide-legged trousers, a white halter-neck top, a wide-brimmed hat, and a pair of slip-on sandals.

Elli was excited to be visiting Alexham, because this town was not only famous for its architecture, stone buildings with slate roofs, but also for gemstones.

'Ell, you're buzzing with excitement,' Charles said, as they grabbed their sunglasses before they left their suite.

'Alexham is famous for alexandrite,' Elli said, sounding a little like a giddy schoolgirl.

'Showing my ignorance, what is alexandrite?'

'It's a fabulous gemstone that can do a little magic trick,' Elli explained to him.

'In a top hat and with a magic wand?' Charles asked, with a smirk.

'No, plant pot. It's one colour by day and another under artificial light,' Elli told Charles.

'You're pulling my leg, Ell.'

'No, Sweetie, I'm not,' Elli replied with a warm smile.

'It sounds lovely. Let's go see some!' Charles said, taking his wife's paw. Elli was so eager, she practically dragged Charles off the ship.

When they stepped off the cruise liner, they went from shop to shop looking at gems. Charles loved watching Elli examining gemstones. She was in her element. She was like a pup in a sweetshop. A very smart pup that knows every single sweet and how it is made.

Elli showed Charles a piece of alexandrite. He marvelled when the shopkeeper showed him the colour change using a lightbox, which simulated daylight.

'Ell, that's mesmerising!'

Elli examined stones and purchased some from different shops. Charles noticed that Elli was picking out some rather dull-looking stones.

'Ell, why are you buying those dull ones, not the shiny ones?'

'I cut my own stones, Sweetie, depending on the piece I'm making.'

'Stupid me! Of course, you do,' Charles said, feeling like a complete and total nincompoop.

'Not stupid, Sweetie. It's not your field. I wouldn't expect you to know. I'm sure you're bored by all this wandering from gem shop to gem shop. Let's go get a cup of tea.'

'I'm alright, Ell. I'm not bored.'

'It's been *two hours*, Sweetie.'

'How about I go get a cup of tea across the road, and you can meander and shop a little more?'

Elli gave Charles a kiss, and then Charles crossed the road. As he crossed, he saw a shop that sold silk fabric and wandered inside. The whole shop was lined with a mind-boggling array of coloured bolts of silk. He chatted with the shopkeeper, a chaffinch. Charles told her he would like some fabrics, and she told him to select the colours he liked. Charles thought about Elli and the colours she loved, and picked sixteen bolts in a variety of colours, patterns, and shades. He asked for twenty metres of each colour, as he was not sure how much he should buy. The shopkeeper of course was thrilled, and wrapped the fabric into a nice secure package.

After thanking the chaffinch, Charles stepped next door and bought a cup of tea and a strawberry layered pastry. It was another half an hour later, Elli showed up.

'Have fun, Ell?'

'So much fun, Sweetie,' Elli said with a glint in her eye. 'What have you been buying?' she asked pointing to the rather large package sitting on a chair next to her husband.

'I'll tell you when we get home,' Charles answered mysteriously. 'How about you, Ell? Buy much alexandrite. Did you buy so much it'll sink the ship?'

'Not quite that much.'

'We'll be back in Heronpool in a couple of days. What would you like to do tonight, Ell?'

'It would be great if we could just have fish and

chips, and listen to some music,' Elli mused.

'That sounds perfect.'

'I think we're both ready to be home, Sweetie.'

'I agree. I'm really looking forward to seeing everyone. I miss them,' Charles said, a distant look in
his eyes. 'Shall we head back to the ship, or do you want to shop some more?'

'Let's go back to the ship, Sweetie.'

That evening, Charles called Aves Numenius and arranged for fish and chips to be sent to their suite. The captain had given Aves strict orders to make sure the Watermeres and the Tytos got exactly what they wanted or needed. Elli sat looking out to sea, appreciating the beauty of the stars on the water. But even with the stunning view, she couldn't help but long to be home.

56

JUST ONE MORE NIGHT

The next morning, Charles and Elli breakfasted on the balcony, where they discussed how to spend the day. They decided to take it easy—a dip in the pool, wander around the onboard shops, and read a bit.

When they returned later that afternoon, they found an invitation on the coffee table.

CAPTAIN'S GALA

Captain Whetmore cordially invites

Mr and Mrs Charles Watermere

to join him at his table for
an evening of dinner and dancing

57

'Sweetie...'

'Yes, Ell.'

'There's an invitation to the Captain's Gala. I know we said we would politely decline, but... he personally invited us.'

'I guess we should go then,' Charles said resignedly.

'Are you going to wear your deep dark blue tuxedo?'

'I think so. How about you?'

'I don't have a tuxedo. I'll have to wear a gown.'

'Now who's the plant pot?' Charles chuckled.

That evening, as they left their suite, they met Nula and Birch, who evidently had also been invited to the Captain's Gala Dinner, as Birch was wearing a tuxedo, and Nula was wearing a pale blue, sleeveless evening gown.

'Good evening, folks,' Birch said. 'You on the way to the Captain's Table?'

'Good evening. Yes, Ell and I are on our way there.'

'That is a stunning gown, Elli,' Nula said admiringly.

'It's a showstopper alright,' Birch added.

'Thank you. Nula, Birch.' Elli took hold of Charles' paw, and the four of them strolled down the passageways and made their way to the Grand Dining Room. Much to their surprise, it was dimly lit with mood lighting, candles on each table, and a band at the back edge of the dance floor. The maître d' checked their invitations, then directed them across the room, where Captain Whetmore was seated at a much smaller table than the one they had previously sat at.

'Good evening, Mr and Mrs Watermere, Mr and Mrs Tyto. Please join me.'

The Watermeres and the Tytos took seats around the table.

Birch said, 'I thought you would have been on a bigger table, with a few more guests, Captain.'

'I decided to have a smaller table this evening. I am sure with all that has gone on, you would appreciate an evening with fewer strangers, possibly asking questions.'

Elli and Charles thought the captain must be a mind reader.

'We certainly appreciate it, Captain,' Charles said.

'We do, too,' Nula agreed.

'We got sick of people asking if our suite was broken into,' Birch admitted.

'This evening is about having an enjoyable time. Please relax,' the captain said. 'I must say, ladies, you both look stunning this evening.'

'Thank you,' Elli and Nula said at once.

Drinks were served, and they chatted a little about their trips ashore, what interested them in the ports they visited, and what they would suggest other passengers visit in the future.

The fragrant meal of roast turbot with potatoes, fennel and tarragon was scrumptious and enjoyed by all.

'My goodness! That was delicious,' Elli said. 'I think I need a break before dessert though.'

'That is certainly understandable,' the captain said.

The music started playing, and a few people headed to the dance floor.

'Please excuse us,' Charles said, as he offered his paw to Elli to take. She took hold of it, and they stepped onto the dance floor. Charles noticed how all eyes seemed to be on Elli. Birch was right, Elli's turquoise gown certainly was a showstopper. Charles held Elli in his arms, and they swayed together, lost in the moment. After a dance or two, they were making their way back to their table when a couple of people stopped Elli and told her she looked enchanting in her gown. They had just returned to their seats when dessert arrived—a creation of meringue, raspberries, and mint.

'I hate to bring the mood down, but what will happen to the two thieves when we get back to Heronpool, Captain?' Birch asked.

'I have radioed ahead, and there will be people to hand them over to.'

'Let's not dwell on that, Birch,' Nula said. 'Let's just enjoy the evening.'

Despite having been a little reluctant to go to the gala, Charles and Elli thoroughly enjoyed the evening. They laughed, chatted, and danced. At the end of the evening, Charles and Elli excused themselves, said goodnight to all at the table, and took a final stroll on deck under the stars. The next day they would dock in Heronpool.

During the night, the sea became rough, and Charles and Elli had a less-than-restful night. By morning, Elli was feeling very unwell.

'Good morning, Ell,' Charles said when he woke.

'It's an...' Elli said, put her paw over her mouth, and ran to the bathroom.

'Ell, are you alright?' Charles called through the bathroom door.

'Swee...tie. I feel...dread...ful,' Elli mumbled, attempting not to vomit.

'I'll get the doctor, Ell,' Charles called out.

'No... need. It's... just sea... sickness.'

Charles sat himself down next to the bathroom door. 'I'm here outside, Ell, if you need anything.'

Elli opened the door. She looked as bad as she felt. If an otter could turn green, Elli would have been emerald. Charles helped her to the bed.

'How long before we get to land?' Elli asked weakly.

'A couple of hours,' Charles replied. 'We don't have much to pack, as you've been packing for the last few days.'

'I'll help pack,' Elli said as she attempted to get up.

'*No*! *Stay there*! You rest until we get to port.'

SILENT

61

GREATER MERASHIRE RAILWAY

THE LAST LEG

As soon as Charles mentioned he could see Heronpool from the balcony, Elli got up off the bed and grabbed a couple of bags. She was getting off that ship as soon as possible.

'Ell, leave those bags. I've arranged for a porter to take all our luggage off the ship. You just head off the ship and sit down, and I'll find you.'

'Okay, Sweetie—I'm sorry. I still feel pretty iffy.' Elli hurried down the passageways and was standing ready to be the first person off the ship the minute it docked.

Elli found a bench, sat herself down, and breathed some slow deep breaths. *It feels good to be on dry land at last*, she thought to herself. It was about ten minutes before Charles approached with a porter pushing a luggage trolley.

'How are you feeling, Ell?'

'A little better, thank you,' Elli said with a sigh.

'According to the porter, Captain Whetmore has arranged for a limousine to take us to the station.'

'That was nice of him,' Elli said a little half-heartedly.

The porter informed them that the limousine was ready, then went to load the luggage. Charles thanked and tipped the porter, then got in next to his wife.

When they arrived at Heronpool Station, another porter hurried to the limousine and helped with the luggage.

'Ell, we have a ten-minute wait for our train, let's call home.'

'What about all our luggage? We can't drag that with us, Sweetie.'

'It's okay. We have our porter. He'll look after our luggage.'

'Let's tell him where we're going, at least,' Elli said.

'We don't need to.'

Elli dialled the number for The Cottage and handed Charles the receiver.

'Hello, Dad!'

'Son! How are you? How's our Elli?'

'I'm fine, and Ell is fabulous. Just a quick call. We're in Heronpool. We should be home around half past one this afternoon. Any chance you could ask Arch to drop my car off? We have loads of luggage.'

'Of course, Son.'

'Got to go, Dad! The train's pulling in. We love you.'

'*I love you, Daddy*!' Elli shouted down the phone.

'I love you both,' Lionel responded.

Charles hung up the telephone, and then he and Elli followed their porter to their luxury compartment.

As they were making themselves comfortable, Elli asked Charles, 'Does the porter stay with us all the way to Ashlowe?'

'Yes, Ell. It's a new service the railway offers. I thought it was a good idea to have some help to transfer all our luggage. We do have quite a lot of packages as well.'

'We did go a bit mad, didn't we?'

'Some of us did,' Charles said with a wink.

'You stinker, Charles Watermere! You bought quite a bit, including that huge heavy mystery package.'

'You're right, Ell. We did go a bit mad, but how many times do you go on honeymoon? Once, twice in a lifetime?' Charles joked.

'Hey now! You planning wife number two already?'

'I think I'll keep the fabulous one I have,' Charles said, then he kissed Elli on the nose. 'Do you know what the best thing I'm taking home is?'

'What? That mystery package?'

'No. You, Mrs Elli Watermere.'

They put their feet up, snuggled up next to each other and did a crossword or two.

When they arrived in Ashlowe, their porter collected their luggage and removed it from the train. There was a short wait, and then they were onto the last leg of their journey to Mereland.

'I wish we were home already,' Elli voiced.

'Not long now, Ell and we'll be in Mereland,' Charles said, as he looked out of the window of their train compartment.

Charles and Elli collected their belongings and stood up before Mereland Station came into view. Once their luggage was taken off the train and piled onto a trolley, Charles thanked the porter, shook his paw, and then handed him a rather generous tip.

Charles and Elli grabbed hold of the trolley's handle together. It certainly would take two of them to move the mountain of luggage and packages. It was piled so high, neither of them could see the way ahead. They directed the trolley as best they could towards the exit, but the trolley came to an abrupt halt. They tried to move it, but it still would not budge.

'Ell, I think we may need one of us in front to guide the way.'

'I'll go to the front,' Elli said, as she let go of the handle, and edged her way to the front of the trolley. 'OH, MY!' she yelled.

Charles ran around to see what was wrong, only to find their family and friends were the reason they could not move forward.

'*Welcome home*!' the family and friends cried as one. Then Charles and Elli were hugged and kissed by all.

'We're glad you're home,' Lionel said.

'It is wonderful to have you both back,' Heather added.

'It's so wonderful to *be* home and see you all again,' Elli squealed as she gave Heather another hug.

'It is great to be home, but I think we should get this trolley out of the way, we're blocking the station,' Charles said, returning to the handle side of the trolley. Lionel guided the front, and they made their way outside.

When they had manoeuvred the heavily laden trolley outside, they found five cars parked—Charles', Elli's, Archie's, Lionel's, and Flynn and Willow's.

'Wow!' Charles exclaimed when he saw all the vehicles.

'Looks like you'll need them all for the amount of luggage you have, Son,' Lionel said, chuckling a little at the expression on Charles' face. 'Have you been shopping, Petal?'

'A little, Daddy. Most of it was Charles' doing.'

'Granddad, why don't you and GH go with Uncle and Auntie Squish, and we can share all the luggage between us,' Ermgarde suggested. 'I can drive your car back.'

'GH?' Charles frowned.

'We'll explain at home,' Ermgarde said with a little grin, as she took the offered keys from Lionel.

Everything was loaded, everyone got into vehicles, and a little convoy began to wend its way back through the village, up Bushelbee Lane, finally pulling up on The Holt's driveway.

Archie unlocked The House, but before any luggage was moved inside, Charles scooped Elli up and carried her over the threshold.

'Sweetie, you've already done this.'

'I don't care. It feels so long ago, I wanted to do it again.'

As soon as Charles had set Elli on her feet,

everyone grabbed bags and packages and started ferrying them into the hall.

Elli exhaled, *It's so good to be home again*. She had not realised just how much she had missed The Holt, and the people who lived there. She inhaled deeply.

Once everything was inside, Archie asked, 'Would everyone like a cup of tea?'

'Arch, hold that thought a moment.' Charles started to dig in the pile of packages. 'Here you go, use this,'
Charles said, as he handed Archie a box.

'What is it?' Archie asked.

'It's some wonderful tea we tried in Lawseh. It's bergamot and lavender,' Charles replied.

Archie looked a little suspiciously at the box.

'Seriously, Archie, it is lovely,' Elli reassured.

'That is if people want to try it,' Charles said.

Everyone said they would give it a go, so Archie took the box to the kitchen to make some tea.

'LP, where are the pups?' Charles asked.

'With Daisy. We'll bring them over tomorrow when you're rested.'

Elli chuckled. 'I'm sure we'll manage.'

'Isaac has been driving us up the wall since you left. He's been asking "Is Uncle and Auntie Squish coming home from the ship soon?" every five minutes,' Ermgarde said.

'He doesn't know you're home yet,' Rupert said.

'Where does he think you are?' Elli asked.

'Working,' Ermgarde said with a light laugh.

'Let's go to the drawing room,' Lionel said. 'We haven't sold your furniture.'

'LP, I have a question about something you said at the station,' Charles said as they entered the drawing room.

'What is it?' Ermgarde asked.

'You said something about GH.'

'Oh!' Ermgarde said. 'Isaac saw Granddad and Heather holding paws, and asked, "Is Auntie Heather Pop-Pop's girlfriend?" I told him that she was. Isaac thought for a moment, then said, "Now she's Gran-Gran Heather."'

'How adorable!' Elli cooed as she smiled at Heather.

'I *know*,' Heather said with a slight squeal. 'I feel so honoured.'

'That's lovely,' Charles added.

'So, how was the cruise?' Flynn asked.

'One minute,' Elli said, then she ran to the hall, grabbed a few bags and packages, and returned to the drawing room just as Archie was pouring tea. The air was wonderfully fragrant. Charles and Elli awaited a reaction to the tea.

The first to react was Willow. 'Ooh! This stuff smells *incredible*.'

There was a lot of exhaling, then Heather said, 'I love this. I genuinely want to take a bath in it.'

Everyone laughed.

'It is lovely,' Ermgarde said.

Lionel said, 'It's different. I think I'd have one once in a while.'

Charles laughed. 'Dad, you don't like it, and you're just being polite.'

'Well, Son... yes.'

Everyone laughed.

'Daddy, are you thinking it will change the taste of your Garibaldi biscuits?'

'Exactly, Petal!'

'I will make you a *regular* cup of tea, Dad,' Archie said, then bustled off to the kitchen.

Charles opened one of the bags that Elli had brought into the room. He pulled out a gift for Ermgarde and Rupert and handed it to them. Ermgarde unwrapped the package to reveal a large hand-painted, terracotta serving platter.

'Thank you,' Rupert said. 'I love the colours, they're so vibrant.'

'It is lovely. Thank you,' Ermgarde added.

Elli handed Flynn and Willow a gift of a hand-painted terracotta salad bowl, similar in style to Ermgarde and Rupert's gift.

'Thank you!' Flynn said.

'I love it!' Willow enthused. 'I want to use it tonight at dinner.'

'Where did they come from, Uncle Squish?' Ermgarde asked.

'They were handcrafted in Shroptyn,' Charles replied.

'We're sorry, but we need to go,' Willow said a little reluctantly. Sorrel's watching the pups, and she needs to get back to work. Hopefully, we'll see you soon.'

After saying goodbye to the Rohans, Elli dug in another bag and pulled out a package. 'This is for you, Aunt Heather,' Elli said, handing over a beautifully wrapped gift.

'The wrapping isn't paper,' Heather said, rather astounded.

69

'It's silk,' Charles said.

'Silk! How beautiful,' Heather said, as she carefully opened up the gift to find a silk nightgown and robe in a shade of pale aqua. 'Oh my! This is absolutely stunning. Thank you.' Heather stood up and then kissed both Charles and Elli.

'This is for you, Dad,' Charles said, as he handed Lionel a box.

Lionel opened the gift to find a collection of tiny packages with tags attached. 'What are these?' Lionel asked.

'They're a range of plant seeds from every port we went to,' Charles replied.

'Wow! That is *fantastic*!'

'The little tag tells you what the plant is, and the planting and care instructions,' Elli informed.

'Do you two know what you have done?' Heather asked.

'No. What have we done?' Charles asked.

'Lionel is now replanning the garden we spent the last few weeks planting,' Heather said with a chuckle and a shake of the head.

Lionel sat there with a mischievous grin on his face. 'Thank you, both of you.'

'Arch, this is for you,' Charles said as he handed over a heavy box.

'Careful when opening it, Archie. It's fragile,' Elli warned.

Archie opened the box to see a pair of handcrafted, glass bookends that looked as though the artist had captured a galaxy inside the glass.

'How do they do that?' Archie asked as he handed

70

one to Lionel who asked to take a closer look.

'It looks like magic,' Heather commented.

'We watched them make those bookends, Arch, and I still don't know how they did it,' Charles admitted.

'Thank you, so much, both of you. I *love* them,' Archie said, as he hugged the one he was holding.

'So, tell us about the cruise,' Lionel said, eager to hear all.

Elli gave Charles a sideways glance.

'What's wrong? Did you not enjoy it?' Heather asked with concern in her voice.

'We loved every minute of being together,' Charles said evasively.

'But?' Lionel asked.

'We're just so glad to be home,' Elli said. 'I'm thoroughly exhausted.'

'You poor dear,' Heather said. 'You could probably do with a nap.'

'I forgot to tell you,' Archie said. 'Your photographs were delivered this week.'

'We'll sort them out once we're settled back in,' Charles said. 'Thanks, Arch.'

'You two go take a nap, settle in.' Lionel said. 'We'll catch up soon, and you can tell us where you went on your cruise.'

'How about dinner tomorrow night?' Elli suggested.

'If you two are up to it,' Lionel replied. 'Don't decide now, we'll see you tomorrow. Just see how you feel.' They all hugged each other, then Lionel and Heather left as Archie cleared away the tea things.

71

'I think I do want to take a nap, Sweetie,' Elli said. 'I didn't get much sleep last night.'

'I know. You spent most of it on the floor of the bathroom. Okay, let's go upstairs.' Charles loaded the lift with luggage and packages, sent it upstairs, and he and Elli took the stairs to meet it on the landing. After taking the luggage to the bedroom, Elli said, 'We can sort out the luggage after our nap.'

Elli slept until the next morning. When she woke, she noticed Charles was not there. She put on a robe and some slippers, then ventured downstairs to find him chatting with Archie over a cup of tea.

'Good morning, Mrs Watermere,' Charles said.

'Good morning, Sweetie. You're up early.'

'Not really. It's nine a.m.'

'Nine? No! It isn't nine o'clock. You're pulling my leg.' Elli looked at Archie for confirmation.

'It certainly is nine o'clock, Elli.' Archie said, answering her look.

'I've slept since four yesterday afternoon! Surely not!'

'You have, my love. There's nothing quite like your own bed.'

'Travelling can be tiring,' Archie mused. He was also thinking, *With all Elli has been through—the abduction, organising a wedding, and travelling for three weeks, it was no wonder she was tired.*

'I should get dressed. I am sorry, Archie, for coming downstairs in my robe.'

'You are the lady of the house. You are always

beautifully dressed,' Archie responded with a smile.

'You don't say that to me, Arch,' Charles pouted.

'Yes, but... ' Archie started.

Charles interrupted, 'I know, I know. Ell's prettier.'

'This is also true, but she also does not wear outrageously questionable boxer shorts,' Archie said, raising his eyebrows.

Charles gave Elli a significant look. They were both thinking about the turquoise silk boxer shorts with teacups all over that Charles had bought Elli.

'What would you like to eat?' Archie asked.

'Anything you would like to make. I will enjoy whatever you choose,' Elli said gratefully.

'Ell, you just made Arch very happy.'

'Will I have time to shower and dress?'

'Yes, of course, Elli,' Archie replied, then went to the kitchen. Of course, he already had decided what he as going to make for Elli.

Elli went upstairs, whilst Charles stepped out onto the terrace, and sat down at the table. Lionel and Heather were sitting on the garden bench outside The Cottage, Lionel had his arm around Heather's shoulder. They noticed Charles and wandered over.

'Good morning, Son.'

'Good morning, my dear,' Heather said.

'Where's our Elli?'

'Showering and dressing,' Charles replied. 'She was so tired, that when we went for a nap yesterday afternoon, she slept all the way through until this morning. She's just got up.'

'Is she sickening for something?' Lionel asked.

'I don't think so. I think she's just tired, though a rough sea journey back to Heronpool upset her quite a bit.'

'How was she on the train?' Heather asked. Remembering what happened the last time Elli was on one.

'She was anxious on the Ashlowe train, but on the Heronpool train, we had a private compartment, so, no need to leave it.'

'How was the cruise?' Heather asked. 'You seemed a little reticent to tell us. Did something happen?'

'The suite was lovely,' Charles said. 'Thank you for calling and speaking to them, Heather.'

'I didn't, my dear,' Heather said, truly perplexed.

'We were given the Royal Suite. I wonder who did call, because they knew we were the Duke and Duchess of Mereland.'

'How odd,' Lionel said.

'The people in the next suite were Albie and Quinn's cousin, Birch, and his wife, Nula. Nice people.'

Elli stepped out onto the terrace. She was wearing navy silk trousers and a loose-fitting, hot pink silk shirt.

'Here she is! Darling Girl, you look *beautiful*.'

'Thank you,' Elli said, then gave Lionel and Heather a kiss on the cheek. 'I bought the shirt and trousers whilst we were away.'

'We came over, because we wanted to let you know, Maldon's coronation is at the end of July,' Heather said.

74

'So, you'll be away for a while?' Charles asked.

'We'll be away a couple of days, but you will be invited.'

'We'll be invited?' Charles queried.

'Yes, my dear. You are the Duke and Duchess of Mereland and Ashlowe. You certainly can decline if you so wish,' Heather stated.

Charles said, 'I would never dream of declining, Heather. It means a lot to you.'

Heather smiled, patted Lionel's paw, and said, 'Your son.'

'Who else is going, Aunt Heather?'

'I spoke with Maldon and Basil Comfrey, and was told that Lionel and Archie are invited.'

As if he had heard his name, Archie approached the table with a tray of food, and as expected, he had prepared enough for everyone—fish sausages, mushrooms, tomatoes, baked beans, and toast.

'Archie! This is amazing!' Elli enthused. 'It smells delicious. Thank you.'

'You are most welcome.'

'Heather, does Archie know?' Charles asked.

'Yes, Archie does know.'

'Do I know what?' Archie asked suspiciously.

'About the coronation, dear,' Heather replied.

'Yes, I know. I have had the morning suits cleaned, and top hats brushed.'

'Of course, you have! Thanks, Arch,' Charles said, ever astounded by his friend's efficiency and foresight.

'That is, mine and Dad's top hats,' Archie stated.

Charles gave Archie a puzzled look, which was answered by Heather.

'As the Duke and Duchess of Mereland and Ashlowe, the two of you will be wearing robes with coronets.'

'Aunt Heather, what do I wear under my robe?' Elli asked.

'I would suggest a simple dress. I will arrange for your robe and coronet, Darling Girl.'

'Ell, just don't wear the dress I bought you on the cruise,' Charles said with a wink.

'Why not, Son?'

'She caused quite a stir. There were a few males slapped by their partners when she walked by. She had admirers from all over the globe, and could stop traffic in it.'

Lionel, Heather, and Archie laughed. 'That sounds like quite a dress,' Lionel said.

'Charles is exaggerating. Though I remember a couple of slapped faces. They weren't admirers.'

'Yes, they were, Ell. One man said, "She's a keeper". I told him she most certainly is.'

'What is this sensational gown like?' Heather asked.

'It's Canire Couture,' Elli stated.

'Well, we know Thia's work is fabulous,' Heather said, and Archie smiled.

'It's a turquoise silk slip-dress full-length with shoestring straps and a daringly deep scoop back, and a split up the side,' Elli said. 'Charles bought it for me on the ship.'

'I see why it caught attention,' Heather said.

'It looked like the gown was *made* for her,' Charles added.

'I think I will ask Mrs Bauson to make me a dress

for the coronation. I would ask Thia, but... '

'It's a long way to travel?' Heather asked.

'That, Aunt Heather, and the fact Thia has already done so much for me,' Elli responded.

'Thia told me, she loved designing and making gowns for you. The gown Charles purchased for you, you were probably the original model for it.' Archie stated. 'Thia told me, you have always been her favourite model.'

'Hey, Ell! If you ever give up jewellery making, you could become a model,' Charles said.

'You certainly could, Darling Girl,' Heather agreed wholeheartedly.

'It's a pity Thia doesn't live nearer, Archie,' Lionel commented.

'It certainly is, Dad,' Archie said with a heavy sigh.

'I guess she needs to be in Norchester for work,' Lionel supposed.

Much to everyone's surprise, Archie admitted that he and Thia had discussed it; then again they had been together for over a year.

'And?' Charles pushed.

'Thia said she could move from Norchester as long as she had a good main link to get to her workshop once a week. Lots of things have been discussed, including Thia not wanting to compete with the Bausons.'

'Surely she wouldn't be competing,' Elli said.

'Also, a major design company has made overtures,' Archie informed them.

'They want to buy her brand?' Charles asked in surprise.

'Yes, Charles,' Archie replied.

'That's wonderful, but a huge decision,' Lionel said, rather impressed.

'That is true, Dad, but it has to be her decision,' Archie said. Archie changed the subject, obviously not wanting to discuss it any further. 'So, how was the cruise? Where did you go?'

As Charles and Elli were about to answer, Ermgarde and the pups walked up the stairs to the terrace.

'Good morning, all,' Ermgarde said cheerily.

'*Squish-Squish, Auntie Squish*! *You're home*!' Isaac shrieked. He ran first to Charles, and hugged and kissed him, then Elli. 'I missed you!'

'We missed you, pup,' Elli said.

'Was your boat nice?'

'The ship was gigantic,' Charles said animatedly. 'It had shops, restaurants, and a swimming pool!'

Isaac's eyes were huge, 'A swimming pool! *Wow*!' Isaac waved at Archie, 'Hello, Uncle Archie.'

'Hello, young Isaac,' Archie said, as he waved back.

Isaac then went over to Lionel and Heather. 'Good morning, Pop-Pop, Gran-Gran Heather.'

Lionel returned the greeting and ruffled the top of Isaac's head. Heather smiled. She loved being called Gran-Gran. It really did make her feel accepted by the whole family, but most of all, it meant their relationship was not an issue.

Charlotte was toddling around.

'Hello pretty one,' Elli said.

'Mummy, drink time,' Charlotte said.

'She's saying more words, LP,' Charles commented.

78

'She is. She can say quite a few words now.'

'Hello, Charlotte,' Charles said.

'Love Squishy,' Charlotte replied.

Charles' heart melted. 'That's a new name.'

Isaac turned to Heather and said, 'Person loves Squish-Squish.'

'Squish-Squish loves her and you very much,' Elli said.

'I do, little man. I love you both so very much. In fact, I love you oodles,' Charles said.

'Oodles? That's a lot,' Isaac said.

'I will go get some refreshments,' Archie said, and left for the kitchen.

Ermgarde lifted Charlotte up and placed the pup on her lap.

'Mummy, drinky time.'

'In a moment, Sweet Pea. Uncle Archie is getting some for you.'

'I'll be back in a minute,' Elli said, then dashed indoors, returning a minute or two later with two big bags. 'One for you, Isaac,' Elli said as she placed one bag on the terrace floor. 'And, one for you, sweet girl.' Elli placed the other bag next to Ermgarde.

'Thank you, Auntie Squish. Thank you, Squish-Squish,' Isaac said as he sat down on the terrace floor and dug into the bag. Ermgarde set Charlotte down and then helped her lift items out of her bag. In Isaac's bag, there were wooden building blocks that locked together, along with a beautifully crafted wooden map of the world puzzle. Isaac immediately dumped the pieces out, read the name of each country out, and then started putting it back together. Charlotte was playing with balancing blocks of different shapes.

Archie returned and served lemonade to all. Of course, Charlotte's was in a sippy cup. Archie then joined everyone at the table.

'I'm stupid,' Ermgarde said. 'What is this?' She was holding a curved piece of wood she had pulled out of Charlotte's bag.

'It's a balance board,' Elli replied.

Charles added, 'It can be sat on and rocked, used as a reclining reading chair, turned over and walked across like a hill. It helps with balance, coordination, and imagination. It can also be used as a see-saw.'

'Wow!' Lionel and Heather exclaimed.

'That sounds fantastic! Thank you,' Ermgarde said. She placed the board on the floor, and Charlotte instantly sat herself down and started to rock it like a rocking chair. 'I may not have known what it was, but clearly, my pup is smarter.'

Everyone laughed.

'How was the cruise?' Ermgarde asked.

'We were just about to tell Dad and Heather about the cruise,' Charles replied.

Charles and Elli starting talking about the countries they visited, and a little about each port.

'I bet it was really relaxing,' Ermgarde said.

Charles and Elli looked at each other.

'What is wrong?' Archie asked.

'Well, there was a bit of ... ' Charles hesitated.

'Trouble?' Lionel asked, attempting to read the expression on Charles' face.

'A little,' Elli replied. 'A few suites were broken into.'

'*No!*' Heather exclaimed.

Charles and Elli assumed it was a little personal for Heather, as the ship was named the *Queen Euphorbia*.

'Was *your* suite broken into?' Archie asked.

'Yes. Multiple times,' Elli replied.

'*That's awful!*' Lionel said fiercely.

'Our next-door neighbours, Nula and Birch Tyto,' Charles said. Noticing that both Archie and Ermgarde looked as if they were about to speak, he held up a paw and added, 'Yes, Albie and Quinn's cousin, and his wife, Nula. They had jewellery and cash stolen.'

Charles and Elli continued to tell them the whole story of the thieves, and how they were caught.

'I'm not sure I would want to go on a cruise now,' Ermgarde said.

'Don't let it put you off, Ermgarde,' Elli said. 'Were you thinking of going on one?'

'We thought that perhaps we'd go on one for our tenth anniversary, but I'm not too sure about taking the pups on such a long trip.'

'We'll look after them,' Heather and Lionel responded, barely beating Charles and Elli to it.

'We don't need to worry about that for two years,' Ermgarde said.

'Mummy, I'm hungry,' Charlotte said. 'Food, please.'

'We should go back. Rupe is putting up some shelves in the pantry.'

'Not enough room, LP?' Charles asked.

'We have enough, just organising it differently,' Ermgarde answered, knowing her uncle would have an extension built at the speed of light if he thought they needed more space. 'Say thank you and bye-bye, pups.'

The pups dropped their toys, then went to Lionel and Heather first, and gave them a kiss. 'Bye-bye, Pop-Pop. Bye-bye Gran-Gran,' Isaac and Charlotte said. They then went to Archie, 'Bye-bye Uncle Chi,' Charlotte said.

'Person, it's Uncle *Archie*,' Isaac corrected. 'Bye-bye, Uncle Archie,' Isaac said.

The pups then turned to Charles and Elli and said thank you and bye-bye. Elli took hold of Charlotte's little paw, kissed it, and said, 'Bye-bye baby girl.'

'Isaac, pick up your toys, please,' Ermgarde requested as she helped Charlotte with hers. Once Isaac had picked up his toys, the Staff family said another goodbye and strolled back to The Lodge. Lionel and Heather decided to return to The Cottage, Archie cleared the table, and Charles and Elli went to unpack their luggage.

In their bedroom, Elli nudged the mysterious heavy package with her foot, then asked, 'Sweetie, where do you want this package to go?'

Charles took the package, placed it on the bed, then opened it up.

Elli looked at the assemblage of colours. '*Flipping heck*! Did you buy the entire stock of silk?'

'No. I did leave a little in the shop,' Charles responded cheekily.

'What's it all for?' Elli asked, completely stumped

as to why her husband would need a mountain of fabric.

'I know you love silk clothing. You can have whatever you want made from this. Possibly another gorgeous gown, one in every colour, if you want, nightgowns, blouses, undies, whatever your heart desires. You could get some ties and pocket squares made for Archie, out of the offcuts.'

Elli kissed Charles. 'You are so thoughtful.'

Charles entered his dressing room, and Elli called out, '*You may want to hang your robe up.*'

'*It's already hung up, Ell.*'

'Archie!' they both said.

'*Ell! Talk about Arch. Look at this!*' Charles called out.

Elli entered the dressing room and looked in the direction Charles was facing. 'There's a door!'

'Yes, Ell. It's the door to your dressing room. Arch and I talked about getting it put in. He must have just gone ahead and had it done whilst we were away.'

'He is a love,' Elli said, eager to open the door. She opened it, and they entered what had been the west suite.

'This is going to be some dressing room, Ell.'

'I'm so excited. This really is an enormous dressing room. Where did the bed go?'

'No doubt, Arch had it moved upstairs,' Charles replied.

They made their way back to the bedroom, just as there was a knock on the door.

'Come in!' Charles and Elli called out.

Archie entered and was kissed on one cheek by Elli, and the other cheek by Charles.

'Thank you, Arch! You have made my lovely wife incredibly happy—thanks for hanging up my robe.'

'Thank you, Archie. You are such a sweetie,' Elli said with another kiss on the cheek.

'You are most welcome. I wanted you to feel at home when you got home, if that makes sense,' Archie said proudly.

'It makes complete sense,' Elli said, beaming. 'It's part of our bedroom now, not another suite.'

'Precisely,' Archie said. 'Come to think of it, if you had put your clothes in Charles' dressing room, you may have pushed out some of his less dignified items of clothing.'

'It's a good job you have your own space, Ell,' Charles said with a goofy grin.

HONEYBEES AND HOLIDAYS

Monday morning Elli was dressed in a navy trouser suit and white silk blouse, all ready to go back to work. Charles got up so he could breakfast with her.

'You don't need to get up, Sweetie.'

'I want to see you before you go to work, because I won't see you all day.'

'I can give up working if you want me to,' Elli said.

'No, Ell, you love your work. It's part of who you are—a master jeweller. If *you* want to stop working, that is *your* choice. Don't do it for me.'

'Okay, Sweetie.'

After breakfast, Elli said, 'Well, I'm off to work.'

'Don't forget to visit the Bausons,' Charles reminded her.

'I almost forgot. I'll pop in, and sort out a dress for the coronation. I'll see you this evening, H.'

'It's a while since you've called me that,' Charles said.

'It just felt right, and H could stand for husband too!' Elli said, giving him a kiss. She then grabbed her shades, headed out of the terrace doors, strode across the lawn, and went through the gate behind The Guest House.

Elli unlocked the shutters of her shop, Daresbury and Co. It felt strange to be back there after such a long break. Once her little shop was unlocked, she went straight to her workshop and took out the box of alexandrite she had purchased in Glodur. Elli tipped the gems out onto the protective padding that covered her workbench, then examined the gemstones. Once she had sorted them, she locked them in the safe. Elli then got out her sketchpad, hoping to design some pieces using alexandrite, but her mind started to wander. *Daresbury and Co. Maybe it's time for a name change. I only kept it because I was new to the village, and the Daresbury name was well known. But what to*? Elli stood up, left the shop, locked it up, pulled the shutters down, and crossed the road.

When Elli entered The Country Set, Mrs Bauson appeared from the workshop upon hearing the tinkle of the bell above the door.

'Good morning, Duchess. How may I help you?'

'Mrs Bauson, you can call me Elli.'

'I couldn't do that. You're the Duke's wife,' Mrs Bauson said, emphatically.

'Then call me Mrs Watermere,' Elli suggested.

'I would prefer to call you, Duchess.'

'Very well,' Elli acquiesced, remembering what Charles had said; *They'll call you what they want to*; 'I need a dress for a formal occasion.'

86

'Do you have something in mind?' Mrs Bauson enquired.

Elli thought, *It has to go with a red robe.* 'How about something white or cream?'

'It's entirely your choice, Duchess. Please excuse me one moment,' Mrs Bauson said, then nipped into the workshop and brought back a few bolts of white and cream fabrics, and set them down on the counter.

Elli handled the fabrics and instantly fell in love with one in particular. 'This is the one, Mrs Bauson.'

'Now the style.'

'Long, V-neck, and simple, please, Mrs Bauson.'

'With a simple shift style full-length dress, it would need a split to allow you to walk.'

'A split at the back, please.' Elli thought that as she would be wearing a robe, the split would not be seen.

'Let me take some measurements.'

Elli stepped into the fitting room, and a few minutes later she exited. 'I need it for the end of July. Is that doable?'

'Yes, of course, Duchess.'

'Thank you, Mrs Bauson. Would you like paying now?'

'When it's finished, and you're happy with it.'

'I'm sure I will be happy with it. I'll let you get on. Thank you, once again.' Elli left the shop, but did not want to go back to work. She made the decision to head home to The Holt.

When Elli entered The House, Archie appeared. 'Elli!' he said, completely surprised by her appearance. They entered the drawing room, where Charles was sitting with Lionel and Heather.

'Ell, what's wrong?' Charles asked.

Lionel and Heather would have said hello, but were too concerned by Elli's early appearance.

'Nothing. Why?' Elli asked.

'You're home less than two hours after leaving for work.'

'I was sitting there trying to sketch, but couldn't concentrate.'

'Why? What's on your mind, Petal?' Lionel asked.

'I just wanted to be home, that's all.'

Charles smiled.

'I went to see Mrs Bauson—she's making me a dress for the coronation. It's cream and full-length. It's simple with a back split, so I can walk in it. The robe will cover the split. Is that okay, Aunt Heather?'

'Perfect, Darling Girl.'

'So, what are you going to do today?' Lionel asked.

'I need to design my dressing room,' Elli said, sounding exactly like a small child excited over a new toy.

'Are you taking over Charles' dressing room?' Lionel asked.

'No, Daddy. Archie arranged for a door to be put in, so I can go through Charles' dressing room to the west suite, which is now my dressing room,' Elli squealed.

'*That is some dressing room*!' Heather gasped.

Archie made some tea and returned.

'So, how are you?' Elli asked Lionel and Heather.

'We're fine, Petal.'

'Lionel, my dear, I think she means *us*' Heather emphasised the last word.

'It's like we've been together years,' Lionel said.

'That's nice,' Elli said with a warm smile.

'You both do look happy,' Charles said.

'Talking about how people are. How are you, Petal?
Are you just tired or are you giving up work?'

'I'm tired. I have thought a bit about giving up work.'

'Don't make a decision now, Darling Girl, let yourself adjust to things. A lot has gone on over the last few months.'

'Why not try working two or three days a week for the next few weeks?' Lionel suggested.

'Hmm?' Elli mused.

'That's not a bad idea, Ell,' Charles said.

'What would *you* do?' Elli asked the group.

'It is your decision, Elli, but may I suggest... If you took Monday and Friday off, you would have long weekends,' was Archie's suggestion.

'That is an *excellent* idea, Archie!' Elli replied.

That afternoon, Charles and Elli went for a short drive in Elli's car. When they returned to The Holt, Isaac approached them on the driveway, followed by Ermgarde, who was holding Charlotte's paw.

'Hello, People!' Charles said cheerfully.

'Hello, Ermgarde. Hello, lovely pups,' Elli said.

'Everything alright, LP?'

'Isaac has something to ask you,' she responded.

Charles crouched down so he was nearer the

pup's height. 'What is it little man? What did you want to ask me?'

'Squish-Squish, before you and Auntie Squish went on your honeybee, you said we could go to the seaside.'

The adults had to smile.

'Honey*moon*, Sweet Pea,' Ermgarde corrected.

Charles asked the pup, 'What did your mummy and daddy say about going on holiday?'

'Mummy, Daddy, *and* Person want to go,' Isaac said categorically.

Elli was now holding Charlotte's paw, and walking around the driveway with her. Charlotte was saying, 'Auntie Squishy!'

'How about we go and see Pop-Pop and Gran-Gran Heather, and see if they want to go?' Charles had barely finished the last word, and Isaac was hurtling down the side of The House towards The Cottage as though his trousers were on fire. He stumbled, but picked himself up unperturbed and carried on. Ermgarde, Charles, and Elli, who was now carrying Charlotte, followed.

Isaac banged on the door, and Heather opened it. 'What's wrong, pup?' Heather asked. Lionel appeared over Heather's shoulder.

'Gran-Gran, can we go on holiday with Squish-Squish and Auntie Squish to the seaside, please?'

Charles answered Heather and Lionel's confused looks. 'Before Ell and I went on honeymoon, Isaac asked if we could go to the seaside again. I said we could before school restarted, if everyone wanted to go.'

'I see,' Heather said.

'It would be nice to go on a family holiday,' Lionel said as he put his arm around Heather's shoulder. 'And Thia could join us.'

'Great idea, Dad.'

'The answer from us, is...' Lionel looked at Heather.

'Yes,' Heather said with a smile.

Isaac was literally jumping for joy. '*Yippee!*'

'Where are we going?' Lionel asked.

'We could go back to Heronpool or somewhere different,' Charles said.

'Perhaps Trebmal Bay,' Elli suggested. 'It's a decent-sized town, and it's growing.'

'I have not been to either on holiday,' Heather said. 'You decide.'

'They have a new hotel in Trebmal Bay,' Lionel said. 'I heard about it on the radio.'

'Trebmal Bay isn't as far either,' Elli pointed out. Despite Elli appearing to not mind where they went, the adults could tell she was not looking forward to another long train journey.

'Son, you could drive to Trebmal Bay in our Elli's car.'

'Trebmal Bay isn't that far, all the cars should be able to make it,' Charles said. 'The journey by train means you have to go to Norchester and change to the Trebmal Bay train. Though, if you prefer to go by train...'

'I agree, Son. Trebmal Bay is less than one hundred miles away. The SilentCarts should all be able to make it there.'

'LP, if Ell and I go in her car, you and Rupe can take mine.'

'That's a plan, Son!' Lionel said.

'I'll check with Arch, to see if Thia will join us, but I'm sure she'll want to. Once I know how many of us there'll be, I'll book the hotel,' Charles said. 'What's the hotel called, Dad?'

'Trebmal Tides or The Bay. I'm not sure.'

'No matter. I'll check the phone book.'

Elli put Charlotte on the ground, and the pup ran to Heather, who picked her up.

'Gran-Gran, Pop-Pop,' Charlotte said.

Heather exhaled. How she loved this family.

'When will we go on holiday?' Ermgarde asked.

'We have the coronation at the end of July, then we can go,' Lionel said.

'The weekend after the coronation, then.' Ermgarde suggested.

'Sounds good to me, LP. What does everyone else think?'

'Yes. That sounds good,' Heather replied.

'What about work, ladies?' Lionel asked.

'I'll work three days a week until we go, then I'll shut up shop for the duration,' Elli decided.

'You giving up work, Elli? Or should I say, "Auntie Elli"?'

Elli smiled, and responded, 'Ermgarde, you can call me whatever you like, as long as you're not calling me rotten.'

Ermgarde laughed. 'I want to call you Auntie Elli.'

'That's fine. Whatever makes you happy. As for giving up work. I'm not giving up work, just working fewer days for the time being. I just need to get back to it slowly after such a long break.'

'I see,' Ermgarde said. 'I'll make sure everything

92

is done at the studio before we go. I should get the pups back for dinner. We'll see you tomorrow morning, Granddad, Gran-Gran.' Lionel no longer walked Isaac to school, because Ermgarde just crossed him over Bushelbee Lane, and from there, he walked through the wildflower field to the manor on his own. Lionel did, however, take Charlotte to Totsie Tails. Since Heather had lived in The Bower, she had accompanied Lionel twice a day on his trips to and from the nursery.

Isaac said goodbye to everyone, gave them all a kiss, then Ermgarde and her youngsters walked along the garden path back to The Lodge. Charles and Elli bade Lionel and Heather a good evening and returned home to see Archie.

When they returned, Archie met them in the hall. 'Good evening, Charles, Elli. I am terribly sorry, I have not prepared dinner, as I was unsure of the time you would be home. I will prepare something straight away.'

'Arch, Isaac wants everyone to go on a family holiday, and Ell suggested Trebmal Bay. Dad says there is a new hotel there,' Charles said. 'We hoped you and Thia could join us.'

'When?'

'LP suggested the weekend after the coronation,' Charles replied. 'I guess we could leave Friday evening.'

'We would have to leave Sunday or Monday,' Archie stated. 'You have a commitment on the Saturday.'

'What commitment?' Charles asked, completely

befuddled by Archie's comment.

'You are holding a tea party on the fifth.'

Elli gaped. '*A what*? A tea party?'

'Yes, Elli. Lord Bushelbee traditionally held a village tea party annually on the fifth of August,' Archie replied with raised eyebrows.

'It's not something Arch made up, Ell. It was in the newspaper archives. If I don't do it, the villagers will be after me with pitchforks.'

Elli howled with laughter.

'What's so funny, Ell?'

'I'm imagining you, running down the High Street in your duck swimming shorts, pursued by villagers with pitchforks and lanterns,' she said through muffled laughs.

'You have a *mean* streak I didn't know about, Elli Watermere,' Charles said with a sideways glance and a frown.

Elli kissed Charles on the nose. 'Not really, Sweetie. I wouldn't let them get to you.'

'Okay, Arch, I'll do the tea party, and we can leave on Sunday. Let's all go out to Enivid, and discuss plans for the holiday. That way, you don't have to worry about dinner.'

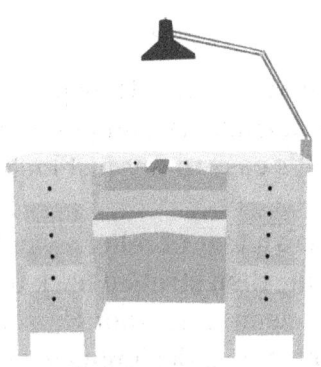

NEVER VOICED

The next few weeks, Elli worked three days a week, or at least tried to work. She was distracted by thoughts she had not voiced to Charles. She just could not settle. One afternoon her mind was whirring so fast, she had to do something about the invasive thoughts. She locked up her shop and walked to the Police House.

Fortunately, Keen was there, and seeing the look on Elli's face, he asked her to take a seat and tell him why she looked so concerned. He noticed she was trembling like a leaf.

'Elli, I'm sure you'll feel better getting it off your chest, but tell me in your own time,' Keen said kindly, then waited in silence for Elli to speak.

She took a deep breath, exhaled, then told Keen her concerns. 'Will I have to go to court and face my abductors again?' she asked.

Keen calmly said, 'Elli, take another deep breath. Don't worry about that. You won't need to face them again.'

'Are you *sure*, Keen?' she asked plaintively.

'I am *absolutely positive*. They pled guilty, so, there won't be a trial. Try and put it out of your mind. I know it's easy to say, just look forward now.'

Elli had to dab a tear of relief away. She thanked Keen with a hug, then strolled back to work. With her mind now clearer, she thought she might be able to concentrate on designing jewellery once more.

When Elli got home that evening, Charles noticed a marked difference in his wife's mood. She seemed more relaxed. 'Did you have a good day, Ell?'

'Yes, Sweetie. I was designing again.'

'I didn't know you were having problems designing,' Charles said, wondering if that was the real reason Elli had cut back on her days at work.

'Yes. I couldn't design a thing.'

'Not able to get back into it after the wedding and honeymoon?' Charles asked.

'No. There were things on my mind,' Elli told Charles a little tentatively. She then proceeded to tell him about her trip to the Police House, and what Keen had told her.

'Ell, my love, why did you carry that worry alone? Why didn't you tell me what was on your mind?'

'I didn't want to worry you with my troubles,' Elli said in a very small voice.

'*Remember* when we made our vows, we said— "In *good times and bad.*" Ell, talk to me if you're worried. I may not have the answers, but I'm here to listen.'

'I'm sorry, Sweetie. I should have talked to you.'

'No need to apologise. Just remember, I'm here for you. You're not alone any longer. You have family. I hope you can talk to me, but if you need someone else's opinion or ear, you have Dad, Heather, Archie, and LP.'

'I know it sounds silly, but I keep forgetting I have family, even though I love the bones of them.'

'You were on your own for so long, Ell. It isn't silly at all,' Charles said, putting his arm around her.

SITTING PRETTY

The last week of July rolled around, and Charles, Elli, Archie, Lionel, and Heather all packed for the trip to the capital. Heather would be staying at the palace until after the coronation, whilst the rest of the party would be staying at their hotel of choice in Norchester, The Regency. Even though Elli knew going by train to Norchester would bring back horrendous memories, she said they should all go by train together.

On the journey to Norchester everyone chatted almost non-stop in an attempt to keep Elli's mind off passing through Muttleby. Charles thought it was working, until he felt her squeeze his paw as they pulled up at Muttleby Station. She released her hold slightly as the train continued on its journey towards Norchester.

As soon as they arrived at Norchester Station, they all got into taxicabs to the hotel. Charles checked the party in, and everyone went upstairs to their suites. Heather went with Lionel to his suite, so she could call the palace in private, and inform Basil

Comfrey of her arrival. Basil said he would send a vehicle straight over to collect her.

Lionel gave Heather a kiss and a hug, then he picked up her luggage, escorted her downstairs, and waited with her until her driver arrived. After waving farewell, Lionel went back upstairs and tapped on Charles and Elli's suite. Elli answered.

'Hello, Petal.'

'Come in, Daddy.' Elli could tell Lionel was feeling a little lost without Heather.

'Hello, Dad!' Charles said as Lionel entered the suite.

'Hello, Son.'

'Dad, are you okay?'

'Yes, Son. Just saw Heather to her car. She took your robe box with her. She said your things will be at the palace, Petal.'

'Are you worried about her? Worried she's missing palace life?' Charles asked.

'No, Son. She loves Mereland. She loves The Bower and the family.'

'And you, Dad,' Charles said honestly. 'It won't be long, and you'll be heading home to Mereland together soon.'

They had a cup of tea, then decided to stroll around the city shops together. Archie did not go with them; they knew he would want to spend time with Thia. Lionel went into a shop and returned with a large box in a bag.

'You been treating yourself, Dad?' Charles asked, gesturing to the big bag.

'No, Son. It's a gift for Heather.'

'Daddy, how thoughtful,' Elli said.

After they had wandered enough and their feet were tired, they wended their way back to the hotel.

Back in Charles and Elli's penthouse suite, they all sat down, exhausted.

'What do you want to do for dinner, gentlemen?' Elli asked.

Lionel was surprised to be asked. 'Petal, I thought you'd want to have a quiet dinner together.'

'We will be having a quiet dinner together— with you,' Charles said, and patted Lionel on the back.

'You two decide,' Lionel said. 'Is Archie joining us?'

Charles leapt out of his seat, and called Archie's suite. 'There's no answer. Arch must be out with Thia.'

'That's understandable,' Elli said.

'Good for him,' Lionel said. 'She's a nice lady. Nearly as nice as our Elli.'

Elli smiled, then looked miles away.

'You alright, Ell?' Charles asked, noticing her expression.

'Yes. Fine. Just thinking,' she responded.

'Getting back to dinner, how about ordering room service?' Charles suggested.

'Sounds good to me,' Lionel said. 'Unless Petal wants something different.'

'Room service is fine by me. Let's order.'

The next morning, they breakfasted in their own suites. Charles showered, then dressed in his morning suit—his coronet and robe would be waiting for him at the palace. His morning suit brought back memories of their wedding day—the last time he had worn it.

Elli was dressed in the cream, silk cashmere dress Mrs Bauson had made for her.

'Ell, that dress is beautiful! It has tiny sparkles on it,' Charles said, a little surprised.

'It does, and thank you, Sweetie. I *love* this fabric.'

'Are we ready?' Charles asked.

As Elli was about to reply, there was a knock on the door. It was Lionel and Archie, both looking incredibly dapper in their morning suits and top hats.

'Good morning, beautiful people!' Lionel said cheerily.

'Good morning, Daddy. Good morning, Archie,' Elli said. As they left, Charles locked the suite door.

'I have to say, wearing this suit again brings back memories of walking our Elli down the aisle,' Lionel said with a broad smile.

Elli rubbed Lionel's arm affectionately.

'Shall we go?' Charles asked.

They had just entered the hotel foyer when a badger in a dark grey suit approached the party and quietly said, 'Your Graces, this way please.'

Charles and party followed the badger to the waiting limousines. Charles and Elli were directed to the first vehicle, Lionel and Archie to the one behind.

Arriving at the palace, Charles and Elli were greeted by Basil Comfrey. 'Your Graces, this way please.' They followed Basil up the red, plush carpeted hall they had walked along on previous visits. They passed large gold doors, gilt-framed paintings, and exquisite chandeliers. Basil stopped at a door, and ushered them in. 'Your Graces, Her Majesty has arranged for you to ready yourselves here.' he said, indicating the robes, chains, and coronets.

'Thank you, Mr Comfrey,' Charles responded.

Basil bowed his head slightly, and then left the room.

'Sweetie, I have a coronet!' Elli said, quite taken aback.

'Of course you do. You're a duchess.'

They helped each other with their robes and chains, then Charles placed his coronet on his head. Elli picked her one up, and examined it. She noticed the hallmark on it, and gasped.

'Ell, what's wrong?' Charles asked, thinking it was damaged.

'My granddad made this coronet!'

'Really? How can you tell?'

'In Merashire, the assay mark shows the maker's initials or personal stamp. This is my granddad's stamp.'

'How lovely. That means he's with you, Ell.'

Elli's eyes started to fill up. 'Sweetie, don't make me cry,' she said, flapping her paws in front of her face, in an attempt to stop the tears from flowing. Elli took a deep breath, and composed herself.

Charles helped her put on her coronet, just as Basil Comfrey returned. He then spent the next five minutes briefing them on what was to happen, and what they would be doing. 'Her Majesty, Queen Euphorbia will meet you in this room after the coronation.'

Charles and Elli thanked Basil, then as requested, followed him up the red carpet to two doors almost twice the size of the other doors in the hall. Charles and Elli thought, *This has to be the throne room.*

Once Basil opened the doors, they got their first look at the throne room, which was a sight to behold. The ceiling was so high, it seemed as though it was not there at all. The only indication that the room had a ceiling was the many substantial crystal chandeliers suspended below it. The walls were panelled and held gold sconces. In the centre of the room was what looked like an enormous, two-tiered, red wedding cake, with two elaborately carved gold thrones, upholstered with dark red velvet upon it. Off to the sides of the thrones were large carved chairs, which were for the royal family.

Basil escorted Charles and Elli to one of the two seating areas for guests, where other nobles were already seated. There were a couple of swans, a badger or two, and a pair of puffins. Charles and Elli returned nods of greeting as they made their way to their designated seats on the front row. From their seats they could see Lionel and Archie sitting in another area, where everyone was formally dressed—the gentlemen in morning suits, and the ladies in dresses and hats.

Elli squeezed Charles' paw, and he squeezed it back. They were both clearly a little nervous, having never attended an official event as the Duke and Duchess of Mereland and Ashlowe before. And what an event to start with! It was not as if they had to do anything, just be themselves. They were terribly excited, and understandably so. After all, this was history in the making.

Royal trumpeters in their red and gold uniforms played as guests continued to arrive. A short while later, a fanfare was played, and all present stood. From two large gold doors Prince Norton and his wife, Tansy, entered, each dressed in red robes with white sashes, followed by Princess Saffron and her husband, Moreton. Last, but by no means least, was Princess Marjoram—or as the Watermere family knew her, Marjy. She wore a red robe and white sash, and was adorned with the tiara Elli had made for her.

After the royals had taken their seats at the side of the very large red platform, another fanfare was played. King Maldon and Queen Angelica, her paw gently resting on his, appeared at the door. Both wore exceptionally long red robes edged in gold, along with white sashes adorned with jewelled brooches and medals. The King and Queen stately made their way to the platform and seated themselves on the gold thrones.

The trumpeters sounded another fanfare, as the doors opened a third time, and Queen Euphorbia entered. She was dressed in a beautiful full-length white gown, with a long red robe over it. Across her body, she wore a white sash decorated with a number of jewelled brooches and medals. On her head, she wore the heavily jewelled state crown of

Merashire. She made her way gracefully to the platform and stopped at the foot of the steps just as Maldon stood up. She ascended the steps as Maldon bowed his head. Heather removed the crown from her own head and placed it on her son's. This was a different kind of coronation—one that had never happened before because, the crown had never before been passed from living predecessor to successor.

Basil Comfrey approached Heather with a purple velvet cushion, from which she took a ring. Basil left the platform. Heather placed the ring on Maldon's paw, kissed him on both cheeks, then curtsied before taking a seat near the rest of the royal family.

Maldon spoke in a clear voice, 'I Maldon Wilberforce Lutridae, promise and pledge to serve Merashire with honesty, loyalty, love, and kindness. This I vow to my country with all my heart.'

As The King finished, the royal trumpeters began the opening notes to the Merashire national anthem, and everyone sang:

From sandy shores to mountains high,
We sing with voices strong,
Your winds and waves will never cease
To you our hearts belong.

This land we love, from coast to coast,
Its spirit sets us free,
In storm or calm, it's where we belong
Our island in the sea.

CHAPTER 14

We lift our gaze to the sky above,
And let our voices ring,
Our hearts are true to only you,
We vow to you, our King.

Once the national anthem had concluded, everyone took their seats—except Maldon and Angelica.

Basil Comfrey returned with the purple cushion, which carried a small crown. He held out the cushion. Maldon took the crown, turned to his wife, placed it on her head, then kissed her on both cheeks. She then curtsied. The trumpeters played the recessional music, and The King and Queen left the platform, and the throne room. Heather followed, then the royal family. The area Charles and Elli were sitting in was next to leave. Basil Comfrey appeared, took Charles and Elli aside, and quietly said, 'This way Your Graces.' He then led them to the room they had been taken to on arrival. Basil assisted in removing their coronets, robes, and chains. He packed them into chests and told the Watermeres that they would be placed in the limousine for their return to the hotel. Basil then asked Charles and Elli to take a seat, saying he would be back momentarily. A few minutes later, Basil returned, and said, 'If you would please follow me.'

As they walked down the hall, they met Lionel and Archie, who joined them. Basil led the party to an open door, where Basil announced, 'The Duke and Duchess of Mereland and Ashlowe, and party.' He then ushered the Watermere group inside and left. Charles, Elli, Lionel, and Archie froze on the spot. They were standing before the entire royal family. Immediately, Charles, Lionel, and Archie bowed their heads, and Elli curtsied.

Maldon said warmly, 'Welcome!'

Marjy rushed over and hugged them all. 'It is so lovely to see you all again!' she chirruped.

Maldon continued, 'I know this is a very unusual situation, but please relax. Mummy and I have spoken—and I speak for us all—we have not seen Mummy this happy for many years. It is lovely to see her smile again, and it is all because of Mereland. But I think it is mostly because of you and your family.'

Maldon looked directly at Lionel. 'When Mummy speaks of her life at The Holt, she sounds so alive.'

Lionel looked at Heather, who smiled back at him.

'All I want to say is, thank you,' Maldon said, shaking Lionel's paw. 'Thank you, Lionel.' He then shook paws with both Charles and Archie. Turning to Elli, he added, 'Mummy told me how special you are to her, Elli.'

Elli smiled, tiny tears forming in her eyes. She dropped her head. Maldon raised her chin with his finger, then kissed her on the cheek. 'Please all of you, take a seat,' Maldon said warmly.

Marjy chimed in, 'I believe congratulations are in order, Charles and Elli. You were recently married.'

'Thank you. Yes, Marjy,' Elli replied without thinking about formality. 'We were married in May.'

Charles and Elli sat on one of the overstuffed

sofas, and Archie chose an armchair. Looking around, Charles realised they were in the monarch's private sitting room, a room they had been in before, when Heather was queen. Lionel sat next to Heather on a sofa, looking exactly like a naughty schoolchild sitting outside the headmaster's office.

I don't believe you have met my son Norton, his wife Tansy, my daughter Saffron, and her husband Moreton,' Heather said. Each person she mentioned, stepped forward and shook paws with the guests. Heather noticed Lionel was visibly nervous. 'Lionel my dear, relax,' she said comfortingly.

'Yes, Lionel, relax,' Maldon added. 'I want for Mummy what Mummy has always wanted for us— to be happy. Now, if you break her heart... I'll have your head chopped off.'

Lionel almost fainted.

'Lionel, *Lionel!*' Heather said, slightly panicked. 'Maldon didn't mean it, my love. Besides, I know my heart is safe with you.' She gave him a peck on the cheek.

'Of course it's safe with me,' Lionel said, as he took her paw and patted it.

Charles, Elli, and Archie were all a little amused and delighted by the situation. It was clear that the entire royal family now knew about Lionel and Heather's relationship—and were as happy about it as the Watermeres.

'Let us have some tea,' Maldon said, pressing a button to summon Basil. When Mr Comfrey appeared, Maldon arranged for tea for everyone, and Basil left. The ladies had started chatting together about fashion, weddings, and Elli's work, whilst the gentlemen discussed gardening and SilentCarts. Apparently, Maldon loved driving, though rarely had the chance, due to his current position. Once the tea was served, everyone continued chatting.

'When not in public, please use our first names,' Maldon told the guests. 'It is silly not to, especially since you call Mummy, "Heather" and Marjoram, "Marjy". And of course, Mummy considers you family. Mummy said your estate has magical properties, Charles.'

'Maldon, my dear, it certainly does. It's called The Holt effect. Isn't it, Archie?'

'Yes, Heather. That is what I call it.'

'Mummy said it is the only place she can completely relax,' Maldon said with a smile.

'It does sound magical,' Angelica added.

'You're always welcome to visit,' Charles offered. 'We have a guest house, or you could stay in The House.'

'Thank you, Charles,' Maldon and Angelica said.

Heather beamed. She was absolutely thrilled to see her two families finally meeting—and getting along famously.

Basil entered the room, bowed his head, then said, 'Your Majesty, the call you were expecting has just come through.'

'Thank you, Basil. I will be right there,' Maldon said, then turned to his guests. 'I must apologise, please excuse me. It was lovely to meet you all. Mummy, take care.' He kissed Heather on the cheek, then he and Angelica left the room.

Heather chatted for a few minutes with Norton and Tansy, Saffron and Moreton, and finally Marjy. She then kissed each of them on the cheek. Everyone shook paws, or hugged and kissed, then Heather pressed the button for Basil.

'We are ready to leave, Basil,' Heather said when Mr Comfrey appeared.

'Your vehicles are waiting,' Basil stated, then he opened the door.

Everyone said a final farewell, then Watermere party left.

Heather took hold of Lionel's arm as they walked to the back entrance of the palace. 'I am sorry it's the back entrance, but there will be too many people at the front.'

'That's perfectly fine, my dear,' Lionel said with a wink. 'None of us like publicity.'

The limousines whisked them back to the hotel, where they changed into travelling clothes. Charles paid the bill, then they made their way to the station in taxicabs. Charles and Archie pushed the luggage and the regalia chests on trolleys, whilst Lionel escorted the ladies to their reserved train compartment.

As they were making themselves comfortable, they heard Heather chuckle to herself.

'Want to share the joke, my dear?' Lionel asked.

'I'm just remembering the expressions when you entered the room. You all looked like you needed a blackcurrant mead—or something stronger.'

'Heather, you could have warned us,' Charles said.

'What would be the fun in that?' Heather chortled.

'It was hard enough entering a room and seeing you, Marjy and Ell, chatting like old friends. Walking into a room with the whole royal family almost finished us off.'

'You very nearly had to scrape us off the floor, my love,' Lionel said.

'Would you have felt any better knowing you were about to meet the whole family?' Heather asked.

'Probably not,' Charles replied honestly.

'I am sure we would have been just as nervous,' Archie added.

Elli just shook her head. 'Well, we've all met, and it's lovely that your family got to meet Daddy.' Heather smiled as she rubbed Lionel's arm.

'Maldon has a *wicked* sense of humour, my dear,' Lionel stated.

They all laughed.

'Yes, he does, Dad,' Charles said with a light laugh. 'Your face, when he said he would have your head chopped off. I thought you'd faint.'

'I don't know about faint, Son. I thought I was about to die on the spot,' Lionel said.

Heather kissed Lionel on the cheek. 'I was worried about you for a minute or two.'

'My dear, how does it feel to officially hand over the crown?' Lionel asked.

'I thought I would feel a little melancholic, but I was happy. Maldon is a good man. He has a good mind and a kind heart.' Heather looked directly at Charles when she said this. 'He will make a good king, and he is ready.'

'Your last official duty, Aunt Heather,' Elli stated.

'Yes, pretty much, my dear. I'm a Merelander from now on.'

'I have to say, you looked splendid in your robe and coronet,' Archie said.

'Thanks, Arch,' Charles said.

'I was speaking to Elli,' Archie said with a smirk, knowing full well Charles would respond.

'Thank you, Archie,' Elli said with a giggle.

'You also looked splendid, Son,' Lionel said. 'But, Archie's right, our Elli looked like...'

'A princess,' Heather finished.

'That is high praise indeed, Aunt Heather.'

'Son, I was just thinking—did you book the hotel for the family holiday in Trebmal Bay?' Lionel asked.

'I certainly did,' Charles answered.

'Charles, dear, I will settle up with you when we get home,' Heather said.

Lionel said, '*He won't take it.*'

Charles raised his eyebrows, and shook his head with a cheeky smile.

Heather chuckled.

'My love, you should know him by now,' Lionel said.

'I know, but I would never *assume*. You have already had a beautiful home built for me, Charles.'

'Yes, I did, and it was my pleasure. It's also my pleasure to pay for my family to go on holiday together.'

'Heather, you may as well accept it,' Archie said. 'There is no arguing with him.'

As they approached Muttleby, Elli tensed up.

Noticing this, Charles grabbed hold of her paw. Heather also noticed and started a conversation to take Elli's mind off things. 'Isn't it Charlotte's birthday soon?'

'Yes, it's on Monday,' Elli replied.

'Is she having a party?' Heather asked.

'Not a big party,' Lionel answered. 'Erm and Rupe said a two-year-old doesn't really need one.'

'But we can still have a family one, can't we?' Elli asked.

'Of course, Petal. I'm sure Erm won't mind.'

'Are we sure Ermgarde has not organised anything?' Archie asked, eager to get to work.

'I'm sure she would have told us,' Lionel responded.

'I can arrange a cake as soon as we get to Mereland,' Archie said. 'I will cater.'

'I'm sure you already have a menu in your head, Arch,' Charles said with a smile.

'As a matter of fact—I do, Charles.'

'I'll check with Erm and Rupe, but I'm sure they'll be okay with it,' Lionel said.

'I wonder if Eileen at Dough Wise will be able to make a cake at short notice,' Archie mused.

'I'm sure she will. She'll do anything for The Duke,' Elli said, raising her eyebrows.

A while later, Elli announced that they were about to pull into Mereland Station. Everyone could tell she wanted to get off the train as soon as possible. They gathered their luggage and the chests with the robes inside. They alighted the train quickly and headed to their cars.

PERSON'S PARTY

Monday afternoon, Lionel, Heather, and the Staff family arrived at The House and entered the usual way—through the terrace doors. Elli had decorated the hall and dining room with pretty pink bunting.

'*Happy birthday, Charlotte*!' everyone sang when the Staff family entered. Charlotte, who was wearing a very pretty blue dress, squealed with delight when she saw the pink decorations.

Everyone went to the dining room and Archie served baked cod, green beans, and new potatoes with lemon and garlic. Everyone ate, except Isaac who was talking non-stop about the forthcoming holiday. 'We're going to the beach, Person. I'm going to teach you how to build sandcastles. And I'm going to swim, and I'm going to kite. You can watch me kite, Person. When you're bigger, you can kite too, but not with my kite. I'll buy you your own kite.'

'Isaac, please eat your food,' Rupert urged.

'Okay, Daddy.' Isaac said. He picked up his knife and fork and started eating.

When they had finished their main course,

Archie excused himself, left the room, and wheeled in a large butterfly birthday cake. Everyone gasped when they saw it. Charlotte was clapping her hands excitedly. Archie lit the two candles on top of the cake, and everyone sang a birthday song.

'Blow the candles out, Person,' Isaac said.

'Be careful!' Ermgarde warned.

'You have to puff like this.' Isaac blew the candles out, and Charlotte giggled. Archie lit the candles again, and Isaac blew them out again.

'That's enough blowing out candles,' Ermgarde said firmly.

Archie cut and served a little piece of cake in a toddler bowl to Charlotte. She picked up the cake, and most of it made it to her mouth. After everyone had finished their piece of birthday cake and Charlotte's face had been cleaned, it was time to open cards. Ermgarde let Isaac open the envelopes and then he showed them to Charlotte.

'Let's go to the drawing room,' Charles suggested.

'Archie, leave the dishes. I'll help you in a while,' Elli said. Archie agreed to join the family.

In the drawing room, Elli started things off by giving Charlotte's birthday gift to Ermgarde, who tore the corner of the wrapping paper so Charlotte could get her little paws in and finish the job. After Elli and Charles' gift was opened, the rest of the family started handing their gifts to Ermgarde. Charlotte had quite a pile of gifts, which included an activity board (with buttons, bells, counting beads, and other things to keep a toddler occupied) and a story-a-day book. When Isaac saw it, he said,

'I'll read you a story each day, Person, until you're big enough to read it yourself.' There were some pretty dresses, a plush butterfly, and a sit-on unicorn rocker. However, she fell in love with the otter doll Isaac had bought her with his own money. He had absolutely insisted on paying for it himself, and had raided his money box.

They all sat there watching Charlotte play with her gifts, mostly her otter doll. The family listened to Isaac read the first story in the story-a-day book. By mid-afternoon, Charlotte was asleep on the floor, and Heather put a blanket over her.

'Thank you, Gran-Gran,' Ermgarde said. 'The minute I move her, she'll wake up. I'll let her sleep a little while. I was wondering — what day do we leave for Trebmal Bay?'

'I would have booked the hotel from Saturday, but Arch reminded me, I have a commitment on that day,' Charles replied.

'Yes, Ermgarde, he has to hold a village tea party on the green,' Elli said, a note of amusement in her voice.

'We haven't had a tea party before,' Rupert said.

'Remember when we were searching through the archives, Rupe? Well, Arch found a piece in one of the old newspapers that stated Lord Bushelbee historically held an annual tea party on the fifth of August.'

'Not only that, but Lord Bushelbee serves the tea,' Archie said with a smirk.

Ermgarde laughed.

'LP, what are you laughing at?' Charles asked.

'You in an apron, with your teapot,' she replied.

116

'That's it! Let them come after me with pitchforks!' Charles joked.

'I'll get you a very dignified apron,' Elli said. 'What about a chef's toque?'

'No thanks, Ell. I don't need a big white chef's hat making me stand out even more.'

'We'll help,' Heather offered, volunteering Lionel at the same time.

'I would appreciate that,' Charles said.

'Is it just tea you'll be serving?' Ermgarde asked.

Archie answered, 'I will make sandwiches and cakes.'

'That's an awful lot, Arch,' Charles said.

'Charles, my dear, there's no arguing with him,' Heather said with a smirk.

'In that case, thank you. Whatever you need put it on my account.'

Elli said, 'I'll help if you need help, Archie.'

'Thank you for the offer, but I am sure I can do all the catering.'

'We can at least ferry things to the village green,' Elli offered.

'Does everyone know about it?' Ermgarde asked.

'I haven't spread the word,' Charles said.

'I think it would be a good idea to let people know, Son. We would be eating cake and sandwiches for months if nobody showed up.'

Heather chuckled. 'I don't think there would be enough space in the freezer.'

'Don't worry, I'll make flyers,' Ermgarde offered. Just the time, place, and event—Is that okay?'

'Thanks, LP. That's a great idea.'

'I can distribute them,' Elli said eagerly.

'I can put it in the newspaper,' Rupert said.

'Thanks, Rupe,' Charles said.

'We should go, folks,' Rupert said, pointing to his daughter, who was still sleeping. 'We'll see you during the week.'

'See you tomorrow, Erm,' Lionel said. As the school year was over, Heather and Lionel had offered to look after Isaac and Charlotte, so Ermgarde could finish her work before they went on holiday.

'See you tomorrow, Granddad, Gran-Gran.'

Rupert lifted his sleeping daughter, bade everyone farewell, then the Staff family made their way back to The Lodge.

Heronova
Interiors

Cendra Ardeus

118

TEA AND CAKE

Saturday morning, the Watermere household was abuzz. Archie was loading his and Charles' cars with trays and boxes of cakes and sandwiches. At Ermgarde's suggestion, Archie used the kitchen at Willow Tail Designs to make the tea. He then wheeled it down the High Street to the village green.

The Duke's Tea Party

The Village Green
1 p.m. Saturday, 5th August

Bring a chair or a picnic blanket

CHAPTER 16

The village green was full of deck chairs and picnic blankets. The air was filled with chatter and laughter, and all seemed to be having a very good time, even before the festivities started. Elli, Ermgarde, and Heather had gone mad, and decorated all the tables with tablecloths and bunting.

At one o'clock, Charles donned the very dignified apron Elli had acquired for him—it looked exactly like a tuxedo front, complete with shirt and bow tie. Charles suspected Mrs Bauson had something to do with it, as it was exquisite. Elli, Ermgarde, and Heather were serving sandwiches. Archie served tea alongside Charles, whilst Rupert shuttled urns of tea between the studio and the village green. Charlotte was in her pram, playing with her otter doll, and Isaac was having a whale of a time handing plates to people. He did a little jump for joy when his best friend Pippo and his parents approached.

'Mummy, may I please go play with Pippo?' Isaac asked Ermgarde.

'Ermgarde, he can come with us, if it's okay with you,' Willow said.

'Pleeease, Mummy,' Isaac pleaded.

'Alright, but stay with Auntie Willow and Uncle Flynn.'

Isaac nodded, then after the Rohan family and Isaac got tea and cake, they went off to sit down on a picnic blanket. The villagers were thoroughly enjoying themselves. Some of the Watermeres' favourite people stopped by—Avril and Lyle Pica,

120

Archie's Aunt Gerti, Keen, Acanthus, and their twins, and Athena and Albie Tyto.

Athena spoke, 'I just wanted to let you know, the new school has just been finished.'

'That is fantastic news!' Charles cheered.

'I discussed it with the staff, and we decided, the two of you should open it,' Athena said.

'That is quite an honour,' Elli said. 'When is the opening?'

'The sixteenth of September. We set back the start of school, because we wanted to start the year in the new building. We open to students on the eighteenth,' Athena said quite excitedly.

Even though Charles had gifted the land to the school, paid for the build, battled to stop the destruction of the old school, and offered the manor as a temporary school, Elli believed Charles was likely to refuse to be centre stage at the opening, so she headed him off. 'What do we need to do?'

'Say a word or two, and cut a ribbon,' Athena said plainly.

'We can do that, Sweetie,' Elli said, smiling at Charles.

'Very well, Athena, the wife has decided,' Charles joked.

Athena gave a chuckle, then said, 'Thank you, both of you. How is married life?'

'Wonderful!' the Watermeres said at once.

'Nula and Birch said they met you. They send their best,' Athena said.

Archie approached. 'Excuse me,' he said as he handed Athena a plate with the last slice of cake.

'Thank you, Archie,' Athena said, as Charles

poured her a cup of tea. 'Thank you, once again,' Athena said, then wandered off.

'Charles, it is now four o'clock, and all the food has been served,' Archie announced. 'Shall we pack everything up?'

'I think so, Arch.'

As they were clearing everything away, the crowd on the village green cheered.

'*HAPPY BIRTHDAY, DUKE*!' Then they gave him three cheers.

'*HIP HIP HOORAY! HIP HIP HOORAY! HIP HIP HOORAY*!' The roar was deafening. Charles was rather embarrassed by all the attention. Lionel turned to his son, and said, 'Just bow, Son.'

Charles did as his father suggested, and the crowd went bonkers, cheering all over again. Charles, Elli, and the family waved, then went back to packing up. A large group of villagers stepped forward to help.

Back at The House, everyone helped unload the vehicles, the result being, they were all pooped. Lionel and Heather said that they would go back to The Cottage, as they needed to put their feet up. Ermgarde, Rupert, and Isaac returned to The Lodge. Meanwhile, Archie drove to the station, to meet Thia. Charles and Elli went upstairs to their private sitting room and flopped onto the sofa. In no time, Charles was asleep.

Around six o'clock that evening, Charles was awakened by Elli. 'Wake up, sleepy head. Time for dinner.'

'I think I'll just take a quick shower to wake myself up a bit.'

'Okay, Sweetie. I'll tell Archie, you'll be a few minutes.' She gave Charles a kiss, then hurried downstairs.

Charles arrived in the hall dressed in a pair of jeans and his favourite band T-shirt, Mammalogy. Archie and Thia were standing there. 'Hello, Thia. Lovely to see you!' Charles said. He kissed her on the cheek.

Archie announced, 'Dinner will be in a little while. Why not join Elli in the drawing room. You have time for an aperitif.'

'Sounds good. Thanks, Arch.' As soon as Charles opened the drawing room door, his family cheered, 'HAPPY BIRTHDAY!' Archie and Thia had entered the room quietly to join them.

'Happy birthday, Sweetie,' Elli said, then gave him a kiss.

'I thought you were all tired,' Charles stated.

'We wanted you to *think* we were,' Lionel said with a mischievous grin.

'Squish-Squish, this is for you,' Isaac said, as he handed Charles a gift he had clearly wrapped on his own.

'Thank you, little man. I love the wrapping paper,' Charles said.

'I wrapped it all by myself,' Isaac said proudly.

Charles opened the wrapping to find a crossword book. 'This is fantastic! Thank you! I *love* it!'

Isaac looked very pleased with himself. 'I bought it myself.'

'*You did a lovely job, pup,*' Charles praised enthusiastically, with a big smile.

'It's okay to share it with Auntie Squish if you want to.'

'I think I might just do that. Good idea,' Charles said.

Heather and Lionel bought Charles a valet box, with space for sunglasses, wallet, cash, and car keys. Archie bought him a pair of plain, navy blue cashmere pyjamas.

'I may steal those,' Elli said.

'They are gorgeous, Arch.'

Ermgarde and Rupert had bought a book about ciphers and codes.

'Ooh! I love this! Thanks, LP, Rupe.' Charles turned the book over and read the blurb on the back.

'I should have bought you some invisible ink, but I got you this,' Elli said, as she handed him a small box.

Charles unwrapped the box, believing it was a piece of jewellery. Inside the box was a small photograph of a key. Charles looked baffled, and scratched his head. 'I love it, Ell,' he said, not really having a clue why she would give him a photo. 'Lovely photograph of a key.'

Realising Charles was clueless about the gift, she said, 'It's for your new SilentCart, Sweetie. It comes out next month. It's bigger, can go more than two hundred miles on a single charge, has room for six people, and it also has a radio.'

Charles reeled. 'Oh, Ell. You really didn't need to.' He shook his head in dazed amazement.

'A radio!' Lionel exclaimed. 'In your car?'

'Yes, Daddy, a radio in the car.'

'Ell, I have a car. You bought me one,' Charles said.

Elli leant over, kissed Charles on the cheek, and whispered, 'Someone else may like an upgrade.'

'Dad, would you like my car?' Charles asked Lionel.

'I have a car, Son. You bought me one. I don't need two.' Lionel said.

Charles caught his father's eye, and then quickly flicked his eyes towards Ermgarde and Rupert.

'Come to think of it, I could upgrade, Son. Then Erm and Rupe can have mine. If they want it.'

'Yes, please, Granddad!' Ermgarde and Rupert crowed in unison. They were clearly elated at the thought of having their very own SilentCart.

'You can have it after the holiday. How is that?' Lionel asked.

'Dad, Ell and I can go in her car. You take mine, then... '

'You can have your car today, Erm, Rupe. Great idea, Son!'

'Thank you, Ell. You never cease to surprise me,' Charles said, then he kissed her.

Last, but by no means least, was Thia's gift, which was a beautiful, cornflower blue, Canire Couture shirt.

'Thank you, Thia. This is *gorgeous*!' Charles enthused.

'Excuse me, but dinner is ready,' Archie informed the room. After dinner, which included a slice or two of birthday cake, everyone went to pack and load their vehicles.

About nine o'clock that evening, there was a telephone call. 'Watermere residence,' Charles said when he picked up the receiver. 'Hello, LP. You sound worked up. What's wrong?'

'Charlotte has lost her favourite otter doll, and is *inconsolable*. Did she drop it there?'

'I haven't seen it, but I'll put out a search party for it. I'll call if I find it.'

'Thanks, Uncle Squish. See you tomorrow.'

Charles and Elli almost dismantled The House searching for the otter doll, but it was nowhere to be found.

The next morning, Charles and Elli showered, then dressed in jeans and T-shirts. When they made their way downstairs, they found Archie and Thia putting the finishing touches to breakfast. They all said good morning to each other, and Archie asked everyone to take seats in the dining room.

'Sorry, Archie, I'll just have a cup of tea,' Elli said tiredly.

'You not feeling well, Ell?' a concerned Charles asked.

'I think it's just a combination of the journey ahead, and worrying if Charlotte's otter doll was found.'

'Charlotte lost her doll?' Archie asked, concerned.

'Yes. LP called last night, and said that Charlotte was inconsolable. Ell and I looked everywhere, and we couldn't find it.'

'I wonder if a new one could be bought,' Elli mused.

'I'll run over to Picot's Toys as soon as they open, and see if they have one.'

'A very good idea, Elli,' Archie said.

After breakfast, Elli jogged down the terrace steps, down the lawn, and took the shortcut behind Ermgarde's studio, and was in Picot's toyshop in minutes. Sadly, they did not have any other otter dolls. The one Isaac bought was a one-off item. A disappointed Elli returned to The Holt. When she got back, she found most of the family on the driveway checking their luggage.

'Ermgarde, I ran over to Picot's, to see if they had another D-O-L-L-Y,' Elli spelt the word, as she did not want to upset Charlotte.

'We found it!' Ermgarde trilled.

'It was in a plant pot next to the back door of The Lodge,' Lionel said. 'I was going to check to see if it'd been found, and bumped the empty pot by the door with my big feet. I went to put the pot back in position, and there was the doll inside the pot.'

'Charlotte must have dropped it when we got back last night. We didn't notice until she started screaming the house down,' Ermgarde said, as she picked Charlotte up to put her in their vehicle.

'All present and correct, dolly included,' Lionel said.

'All doors are locked,' Archie added.

'Let's get on the road!' Charles said bracingly.

'*No racing!*' Lionel warned.

'Don't worry, Dad. We'll just be cruising along.'

127

TREBMAL TIDES

CRUISING ALONG

Charles and Elli led the way to Trebmal Bay, the four vehicles snaking their way down the roads and lanes. It was an interesting route, one that none of the party had been on before. They drove through Clattermere—a hamlet that consisted of a post office, a corner shop, and a few homes, Whistmarch—a village, but considerably smaller than Mereland; and Holly Patch—a tiny settlement in the middle of nowhere.

When they arrived in Trebmal Bay, Elli commented on how much the town had grown since she was last there. It now had a few restaurants, shops, and other amenities. There was also a library and a natural history museum.

The little convoy of vehicles made its way down the lane towards the beach, where they could not fail to see the new hotel, Trebmal Tides. Once parked up, everyone got out, and Heather's comment was, 'Wow! This is quite a place.'

Everyone had a little smile on their face, evidently they were all thinking the same thing. *Heather lived in a palace, and is impressed by the hotel.*

128

'It is rather splendid,' Archie stated.

'That wasn't a bad journey. Let's get checked in,' Lionel said.

'It wasn't a bad journey, at all. Thanks for the SilentCart, Granddad,' Rupert said.

'Well, it's Charles you should be thanking,' Lionel said humbly.

'Thanks, Uncle Squish,' Ermgarde said.

'Thanks, Uncle Charles,' Rupert echoed as he got Charlotte out of her car seat. Isaac was out of the car the moment they parked.

'It was Dad's car, after all,' Charles stated modestly.

'Shall we?' Lionel urged, shaking his head.

The party entered the Trebmal Tides, which was white-rendered, had curved walls, black window frames, and was elegantly chic both outside and in. The reception area was bright and light, with splashes of colour.

Charles and Archie approached the reception, which was attended by an oystercatcher whose name badge read Bianca Lustre.

'Good morning, gentlemen. Welcome to the Trebmal Tides. How may I help you?'

Charles took the lead, 'Good morning. We're the Watermere party.'

Bianca slid the register towards Charles. 'Here are your keys,' Bianca said after Charles had signed.

'You have four beachfront suites. The Driftwood, Sea Spray, Seafoam, and Sea Glass. All have two bedrooms.'

'Thank you, Bianca,' Charles said, as he accepted

the suite keys.

As they approached their suites, Heather seemed excited. 'They all face the sea!' she exclaimed.

Lionel realised that Heather had never before been on a regular holiday with her family, and he smiled at her.

Lionel and Heather took the Seafoam Suite, Ermgarde, Rupert, and the pups—the Driftwood Suite, Archie and Thia— the Sea Spray Suite, and Charles and Elli took the last one—the Sea Glass Suite.

The minute each couple entered their suite, they noticed two things—the first was a patio door that opened onto a large courtyard, where there was access to a restaurant, bar, pool, and other parts of the hotel. The second was a set of stairs that led to the bedrooms. Each bedroom had a door to a joint balcony overlooking the sea, and the distant isle of Lissof.

When Charles and Elli exited their bedroom and stepped out onto their balcony, they noticed the rest of their party checking out the view from their balconies. Everyone waved to each other. Charles and Elli unpacked, and then decided to check out the town.

As they left their suite, they met Archie and Thia.

'The suite is fantastic!' Thia said. 'Thank you, Charles.'

'They are lovely, and you're most welcome, but it was Ell who suggested Trebmal Bay, and Dad, who suggested the hotel. I can't take credit for it.'

'Well, it's lovely. And it will be wonderful to spend this time with my Archie,' Thia said, then kissed Archie on the cheek.

'Where are you two heading?' Elli asked.

'We were thinking of walking into the town,' Archie responded.

'That's what we were going to do,' Charles commented.

'We could all go together, and grab lunch,' Thia suggested.

'Surely, you and Archie want time alone together,' Elli said with a smile.

'We have two weeks,' Archie chipped in.

'If you're sure,' Charles said.

The two couples strolled around the side of the hotel, then up the road to the town. It was a pretty road, with small shops on both sides of the road— Saltmarsh (a florist), By the Bay (a restaurant), Trebmal Titles (a bookshop), and Samphire (greengrocers), amongst others.

'This town is delightful,' Thia enthused.

'It really is, Thia,' Elli agreed. 'I was just thinking the same thing.'

'Should we lunch here?' Archie asked as they got to a restaurant called By the Bay.

'We don't know anywhere, so it's as good a place as any,' Charles replied, then turned to open the door for his companions to enter.

The restaurant had obviously been there for a number of years, but was in very good condition, and tastefully decorated. The owner of the restaurant (a duck) greeted them as they entered.

'Good afternoon, folks. Welcome to By the Bay. Table for four?'

'Yes, please,' Archie replied.

'This way, please. May I get you something to drink?'

'Lemonade, please,' Thia said, and Charles and Archie said they would have the same. Elli said, 'Water for me, please.' Her stomach was churning.

Charles gave Elli a concerned look.

The waiter gave them each a menu, then left to get their drinks.

In a quiet voice, Charles asked, 'Are you alright, Ell?'

'Why do you ask?' Elli responded.

'You didn't have much for breakfast, and...'

'I just feel like water, Sweetie.'

Thia looked at Elli, and asked, 'Do you really want to walk into town? I hope you don't mind me saying, but you do look a little peaky.'

'I didn't sleep very well last night, and we had an early start this morning,' Elli responded with a sigh.

'Ell, we can go back and you can have a nap,' Charles said.

'Can we look around the bookshop a little first?' Elli asked with a small smile.

'Of course,' Charles replied.

'We'll head back too,' Archie said.

'No, don't let me stop you. You go into town. Let us know what it's like,' Elli said.

'We'll have plenty of time to go,' Thia said.

'Please don't change your day. It's your holiday

too. I should be fine tomorrow.'

Archie looked at Thia. 'Okay, but if you need us to pick anything up, tell us,' Archie said firmly.

The waiter returned and asked what they would like to eat.

They all ordered the same, salmon, broccoli, and new potatoes. When the food arrived, Charles, Archie, and Thia tucked in, but Elli pushed her food around her plate. It was not the food she was avoiding, it was the churning inside, along with the waves of nausea. Charles noticed immediately, leant over, and whispered, 'Ell, are you sure you're alright? You don't look well at all. Do you want to go back now?'

With a pained expression, Elli replied, 'Yes, please.'

'Sorry folks, we're going back,' Charles said apologetically.

Elli said, 'I'm so sorry, but I really don't feel well.'

'No need to apologise, Elli. I hope you feel better soon,' Archie said his voice warm with concern.

Charles pulled out his wallet, to leave money for the whole meal, and Archie attempted to stop him. 'No, Arch. Allow me. I insist. Have a lovely afternoon. We'll see you later. We hope.' Charles helped Elli to her feet, put his arm around her, then they left.

They slowly made their way back to the hotel, where they met Heather and Lionel sitting outside on a bench, watching Ermgarde, Rupert, and the pups on the beach. Ermgarde was sitting with

Charlotte, and Rupert was playing ball with Isaac.

'You alright, Petal?' Lionel asked with a frown of concern.

'Just feeling a little off, Daddy.'

'You poor dear,' Heather said. 'What's wrong? Upset tummy?'

'A little,' Elli answered.

'You need some soda water and ginger snaps,' Heather advised.

'We'll get you some, Petal. You go take a nap,' Lionel said.

GINGER SNAPS

Charles opened the suite door and they made their way upstairs. Elli decided to take a cool shower, then dressed in a pale yellow silk nightgown. Still feeling queasy, she climbed onto the king-size bed. Charles placed a sheet over her, then opened the window slightly and closed the curtains, at Elli's request. 'How are you feeling, Ell?'

'As if I have sea sickness,' Elli responded.

'Try and get some sleep. If you're no better tomorrow, I'll call a doctor. Do you think it's some sort of tummy bug?'

'I'm not sure, Sweetie,' Elli replied weakly. '*I think I'm going to...*' Elli suddenly said urgently.

Charles grabbed a small bin from the corner of the room just in time. 'Aww. Ell. Hold on,' he said, then ran to the bathroom, and returned with a cold, damp flannel. He placed it on Elli's forehead, whilst comforting her as she leant over the bin, retching.

Charles decided he would not leave it until the morning, he would call the doctor now. 'I'll just be a moment, Ell,' he said as he picked up the

135

telephone receiver, and started to dial. 'Hello, reception? Yes, this is Charles Watermere in the Sea Glass Suite. My wife is ill and I'd like a doctor to visit as soon as possible, please. Thank you.' He replaced the receiver and returned to his wife.

'Ell, they'll call the doctor and he'll be here as soon as possible.'

Elli nodded, but dared not speak. She was now attempting to take deep breaths.

'I'm just going downstairs to unlock the door for the doctor,' Charles informed her.

Elli nodded again.

Charles sped down the stairs, and had just unlocked the door when Lionel and Heather tapped on it. He opened it.

'We brought these,' Heather said, holding up some soda water and ginger snaps.

'Thank you. I'll try her with them in a while. I'm not too sure she's in a fit state for them right now —Ell's been vomiting. Sorry, but I need to go back upstairs. We're waiting for the doctor. Would you let him in?'

'Of course, Son.' Lionel replied.

Charles ran back upstairs to Elli, who was now sitting up taking deep breaths. 'That was Dad and Heather. They brought you some soda water and ginger snaps.'

Elli nodded, then said in a very shaky voice, 'Thank them for me.'

Charles sat on the edge of the bed and held Elli's paw. 'The doctor'll be here soon.'

She rested against her husband's shoulder, whilst he stroked her head.

A little while later, the doctor arrived, and Lionel and Heather sent him upstairs.

'Good afternoon, Mr and Mrs Watermere, I'm Doctor Jay Garrulus.' He was a bird dressed smartly in a tweed suit, with a white shirt.

Charles thought, *Is tweed some sort of doctor's uniform? He dresses just like Albie Tyto.*

'I believe you're feeling unwell, Mrs Watermere. If you would like to step outside, Mr Watermere, I'll examine your wife.'

Charles kissed Elli on the top of the head, then left, and went downstairs.

'How is our Elli, Son?' Lionel asked as soon as Charles stepped off the bottom step.

'I'm not sure. The doctor's examining her.'

'Sit down, my dear, and I'll make you a cup of tea,' Heather offered, as she stood up. As she passed his chair, she affectionately brushed the top of his head with her paw.

A cup of tea and half an hour later, the doctor made his way down the stairs. Much to everyone's surprise, Elli was following him. He helped her to a seat, and she sat herself down.

Doctor Garrulus said, 'I will leave you for now. Call me if you need me.'

'Thank you, doctor,' Elli said, as he headed to the door.

'Ell, my love, should you not be resting? Did he give you something for the vomiting?'

'Is it a virus, Petal?' Lionel asked.

'Let the poor girl answer!' Heather said firmly.

'Is it serious?' Charles asked fearing the worst.

137

'It's very serious,' Elli said flatly.

Their faces all dropped, and they sat there frozen, waiting for Elli to elaborate.

'It's very serious... because we're going to be parents,' Elli continued, a smile lighting her face.

'*WHAT*?' Charles screamed.

Lionel and Heather shrieked too. '*WOW*!'

A minute later, Ermgarde banged on the door then entered. Breathless, she asked, '*Is everything alright? I heard screaming.*'

Lionel and Heather looked at Charles and Elli, who were kissing.

'Uncle Squish, what's going on?'

Elli answered, 'I'm pregnant.'

Ermgarde shrieked '*CONGRATULATIONS*! How wonderful! Oh, wow!' She then hugged them both. 'When are you due?'

'February,' Elli answered.

'How exciting,' Heather cooed.

'How are you feeling, Petal?' Lionel asked.

'Tired and a little queasy, Daddy.'

'What you need is, some soda water and ginger snaps,' Ermgarde said. 'I'll go get you some.'

'It's alright, we bought some earlier,' Heather said, smiling knowingly.

'Did you suspect, Aunt Heather?' Elli asked.

Heather smiled, stood up, poured a little soda water, and put a couple of ginger snaps on a plate. She handed them to Elli with a gentle nod.

'I'm going back to let Rupe know everything's okay.'

'LP, Arch and Thia don't know yet—let us tell them, please,' Charles requested.

'Of course, Uncle Squish, Auntie Squish,' Ermgarde agreed, beaming. She hurried back to her suite.

Lionel was smiling broadly. 'I can't believe it... another grandpup!'

'It's wonderful news,' Heather said. 'If there is anything you need, just ask.'

'I do need something,' Elli said.

'What is it?' Heather asked.

'I need to know when I'll stop feeling like this.'

'How long *have* you been feeling like this?' Heather asked.

Charles looked at Elli, waiting for her to answer.

Elli shrugged, then said, 'On and off for a couple of weeks.'

'Ell, my love, why didn't you tell me?'

'It was on and off, so I thought it was just all the events of the previous months.'

'Sweet girl, hopefully, you're over the worst of it,' Heather said encouragingly.

Elli sipped her soda water and nibbled on a ginger snap.

'How's that going down, Petal?'

'So far, so good, Daddy,' Elli said cautiously.

There was a light tap on the door, and Charles answered it, to find Archie and Thia standing there. '*Come in, come in*!' Charles said, almost uncontrollable with excitement.

Archie and Thia gave Charles a sideways glance, then entered the suite. They immediately saw Lionel and Heather sitting there, and Elli sipping soda water. 'Oh! Full house, I see,' Archie said. 'Did the nap do you any good, Elli?'

'I didn't nap, Archie.' Elli replied.

'Are we missing something?' Archie asked, noticing the broad grins on all their faces.

'Well, Arch, you're going to be an uncle in February,' Charles announced.

For a second or two Archie looked blank, then the cuprum dropped.

'*How absolutely wonderful! How wonderful! A new Watermere!*'

Charles could not help but laugh at his friend's reaction.

'May I hug you, Elli?'

'Of course, Archie.'

Archie hugged Elli, then hugged Charles.

Thia said 'Congratulations, both of you.' She too gave them a hug.

'How fantastic!' Archie kept exclaiming.

Charles said, 'Sit down, Arch, Thia. I'll make you a cup of tea.'

'I'll make it,' Archie said. He obviously was getting overexcited and needed to calm down, and Charles felt making tea would be the way to do it.

'Darling Girl, you look a little stunned,' Heather said.

'Well, I am sort of, Aunt Heather. Like I said, I thought it was months of stress, the events, and all the changes.'

'Charles, my boy, you're quiet,' Lionel commented.

'I'm happy, Dad. I'm ecstatic! My gorgeous wife is having our pup!'

Lionel got up out of his chair, and kissed Elli on the cheek, then Charles on the top of the head.

Archie brought the tea tray in then served. He was humming a happy tune.

Charles smiled at Archie.

'I am sorry, I was humming,' Archie said.

'It's alright, Arch. I feel like singing,' Charles said.

'Do *not* sing, Charles!' Archie insisted. 'You may make it rain.'

Everyone laughed.

'Darling Girl, you may want to try eating a couple of ginger snaps or a piece of dry toast *before* you get out of bed in the morning,' Heather advised. 'Then take small sips of water throughout the day. Lolly ices also help.'

'Thank you for the advice, Aunt Heather. Did you hear that, Sweetie, I need breakfast in bed.'

'*Anything* you want, Ell. *Anything*!' an elated Charles responded.

'I'm sorry, I'm still wearing my nightgown.'

'You can wear whatever you want, my love,' Charles said.

They all sipped their tea and chatted. Elli rested her head on Charles' shoulder. A few minutes later, Heather grabbed Elli's teacup out of her paw and placed it on the table, because Elli had fallen asleep.

'Aww, she's exhausted. Time for us to leave, Lionel,' Heather instructed very quietly as she tugged on Lionel's arm.

Archie very quietly cleared the tea things, then the guests left.

Charles lifted Elli up, carried her upstairs, and gently set her down on the bed, then covered her over with a sheet. He grabbed his fountain pen and crossword book, then took himself to the balcony. He could not believe it—he was going to be a dad! His mind was racing at a million miles an hour. *Will I be a good dad? I don't know anything about having a pregnant wife. What will Ell need? Where will the pup sleep? We need a cot, a pram, and other stuff.* Charles mentally shook himself. *We have time.* He attempted to complete at least one clue in his crossword, but he could not concentrate. Finally giving up, he went back indoors and looked at his sleeping wife. 'I love you so much, Elli Watermere,' he said in a quiet voice as he passed the bed on the way downstairs.

He exited the suite via the patio doors and took a seat at a small table, which gave a great vantage point to see the whole courtyard and pool area. He espied Ermgarde, Rupert, and the pups in the pool.

Charles waved. Ermgarde waved, then got out of the pool with Charlotte. Ermgarde was wearing a red swimsuit, and Charlotte was wearing a delightfully cute pink one with white flowers all over. They approached Charles.

'Hiya, Squishy!' Charlotte squealed.

'Hello, gorgeous girl,' Charles replied.

Isaac, who was wearing blue shorts with smiling suns on, followed his mother and sister. 'Hello, Squish-Squish. You look happy.'

'I am, little man. We're on holiday!' Charles replied. 'Does he know?'

'Not yet,' Ermgarde said as she sat down, and lifted Charlotte onto her lap. 'Isaac, Uncle Squish wants to tell you something.'

Isaac took a seat next to Charles. His face

serious. He waited, his eyes fixed on his uncle.

'Auntie Elli is going to have a new person,' Charles told the young pup.

Isaac's eyes grew wide—so wide, the pup looked like nothing but eyes. Then he yelled '*YEAH*! A new person! *Yippee! Yippee!*'

Charles and Ermgarde could not help but laugh.

The pure joy on Isaac's face was adorable.

Isaac jumped off his seat, then did a little wiggly dance, singing, '*A new person!*'

'I think Isaac likes the idea, LP.'

'I believe you're right,' Ermgarde chuckled. 'Where's Auntie Squish?'

'Resting.'

'She should be over the worst of the sickness soon,' Ermgarde commented. 'Sweet Pea, go to Daddy.'

'Okay, Mummy,' Isaac responded.

'*No running!*' Ermgarde warned.

Isaac walked as fast as he could without running, then jumped into the pool right next to Rupert.

When Isaac was out of earshot, Ermgarde asked Charles, 'What's wrong, Uncle Squish?'

'I'm worried I won't be a good dad, LP.'

'Uncle Squish, come on! You're fantastic with Isaac and Charlotte. And before you say it, I know—you can give them back at the end of the day,' Ermgarde said, forestalling his comeback. 'You'll both be fantastic parents. You both have so much love to give. You honestly don't have *anything* to worry about.'

'Thanks, LP. I know Ell will be a fantastic mum.'

'How can you not be a good dad? Look at your role model.'

'True, LP. I hope I'm half the dad Dad is,' Charles said.

'You'll be just like him. Trust me.'

'Thanks for the chat, LP.'

'You're welcome, Uncle Squish. I should get this little one dried off, and give her a snack,' Ermgarde said. 'What are you doing for dinner?'

'Depends on how Ell feels.'

'We thought we'd go up the road, Archie and Thia said there's a nice restaurant,' Ermgarde said, as she stood up.

'It is nice, LP. Ell and I went, but left, because Ell didn't feel well. We'll see you later. Enjoy your meal.'

Ermgarde held Charlotte's paw, and they toddled back to their suite.

Charles sat back in his chair, and felt a kiss on the top of his head. He turned around, and there was Elli, dressed in a pale sage green, floaty dress, and flat strappy sandals.

'Hello, my love! You look better. Are you feeling better?' Charles asked.

She sat on his lap, and put her arms around him, before answering. 'I'm feeling a little better. I think part of it is because I'm not worrying what it's all about.'

'It makes sense, Ell. I wish you'd tell me when you're worried about things. You're not on your own. You have people who love you.'

Elli nodded.

'We're a family, Ell. A family that is about to

144

grow. Please talk to me.'

'I will, Sweetie. I love you, Charles Watermere.'

'I love you, Elli Watermere, and our pup,' he said, as he placed his paw on her belly.

The next morning, Charles served Elli some dry toast and a cup of tea in bed.

'Thank you, Sweetie,' Elli said, then she started to nibble on a corner of a piece of toast.

A few minutes later, Charles asked, 'How's the pup liking the toast?'

'Pup Watermere is liking it, I think,' Elli answered, then took a sip of her tea.

'That's good. Do you want to do anything today? Or do you want to spend time on the beach?'

'The beach I think, unless you want to do something,' Elli said.

'I want to do what you want to do. We're here to relax. Whatever we do is fine. I couldn't be happier,' Charles said. 'You rest a while, and see how that toast settles.'

They had a light lunch in their suite, which Elli managed to keep down, then they then decided to take a stroll on the beach. They walked paw-in-paw, and you could not have found a happier couple in Merashire—as far as they were concerned. They met Lionel and Heather, who were also strolling along the beach. Heather was carrying a basket.

'Hello, beautiful people,' Lionel beamed. 'You feeling better, Petal? How's our grandpup behaving?'

'I'm feeling better, thank you, Daddy.'

Heather hugged Elli. 'Darling Girl, you do look better. It's such an exciting time. If you need anything, please just ask.'

'Thank you. I'm sure I'll have a million questions. If you don't mind, Aunt Heather.'

'I don't mind at all.'

'Does your family know?' Lionel asked.

'No. I'm sure they won't be interested,' Elli said matter-of-factly.

Heather and Lionel looked shocked, and a little angry. 'How can they not want to know about their grandpup?' Heather asked, seething.

'If they don't care about their daughter...' Charles responded.

'Besides, they already have grandpups, and don't spend a huge amount of time with *them*,' Elli added.

'Oh, Petal, that's sad. Though, it does mean that *we* get to spend more time with our new family member,' Lionel said, then hugged her.

Charles smiled at how much Lionel and Heather loved his wife.

Heather, noticing the expression on Charles' face, smiled at him.

As Lionel and Elli let go of each other, Elli said in a thick voice, 'I have all the family I need, right here.'

Lionel patted Elli's cheek. 'We're glad you joined the family, Petal.'

'Have you been on a picnic?' Charles asked, referring to the basket in Heather's paw.

'No, we were collecting shells, pebbles, and sea

glass,' Heather replied, as she tilted the basket to show the contents.

'How lovely!' Elli trilled. 'I *love* sea glass!'

'Take some,' Heather offered. 'I have a lot of it.' Heather tilted the basket towards Elli.

'I couldn't take your treasures,' Elli replied.

'We can collect more. Take some,' Heather urged.

Elli looked in the basket for a second or two, then took one piece.

'You can take more,' Heather said.

'This is enough, thank you, Aunt Heather.'

'What are you doing for dinner this evening?' Charles asked.

'We hope we can celebrate with you one night, if you're feeling better,' Heather said with a smile.

'I managed toast this morning, and a light lunch,' Elli replied. 'I feel a lot better than I did.'

'That's good to hear. I think it's because you were getting worked up about being ill,' Heather said sagely.

'Glad you're feeling better, Petal. Let us know when you feel like joining us one night,' Lionel said.

'Will do, Daddy, but for now, I'm going to go take a nap, then a swim.'

147

GET LOST!

Archie and Thia were in town. They had visited The Natural History Museum, then decided they would buy Charles and Elli a gift, so, they made their way into the centre of the town. They came across a department store called Pickering's, entered and began to browse. They found a beautiful pale grey cashmere throw. They also came across a gorgeous cream silk maternity nightgown and robe set that had ties at the back, allowing the garment's size to change throughout the pregnancy.

'What do we buy Charles?' Thia asked Archie.

'I am not sure,' Archie replied.

'Then again, it is Elli doing all the work,' Thia chuckled.

'That is undeniably true, my love. Why don't we head to the bookshop to buy some books for new parents?'

'That is a brilliant idea. You are so excited about this pregnancy, Archie, my love.'

'I am, Thia. Charles is my brother from another mother. I could not love him more if he were blood.'

'That is so sweet,' Thia said, then kissed his cheek.

They left Pickering's and meandered back through the town towards the bookshop.

'Before Charles met Elli, he truly believed he would never find anyone who would love him for him,' Archie said, out of the blue.

'How so? He's a lovely, kind person. He's also very handsome,' Thia commented.

'Hey now!' Archie said jokingly.

'Not as handsome as you, my love.' Thia kissed him on the cheek again. 'I would imagine it would be hard for him to be sure people like him for him.'

'And not for his wealth,' Archie added.

'Exactly!'

'I am sure that would certainly be a concern. It would be mine,' Archie said. 'Elli met Charles before she knew who he was.'

'I'm sure I'm not in the same financial league as Charles, but I know the feeling,' Thia said. 'I've done nothing but work. As I became more successful, I spent less time socializing.'

'I was lucky you accepted Elli's invitation to the party then,' Archie said, as he squeezed Thia's paw.

'I couldn't have declined. Elli and I go back a long way, and she was so helpful when I first started in the business. As I've mentioned before, she'll always be my favourite model. She was my first model, but don't get me wrong—Elli is more than just a pretty face.'

'You should ask her to model for you some more.

Of course, if she has the time,' Archie suggested. 'She could model your clothing, and you could showcase her jewellery.'

'Archie, what a brilliant idea! Why didn't we think of that before?'

'You cannot think of everything, my love.'

Thia gave Archie a kiss on the nose. 'Though I'm sure she won't be up to modelling for a while.'

'Have you thought of doing a maternity range?'

'Archie, you're on a roll today! What an absolutely cracking idea. I love it! I hadn't thought about it, but why shouldn't pregnant ladies have gorgeous clothes?'

'No reason at all,' Archie replied.

'Most maternity clothes are smocks that look like tents,' Thia stated. She was now itching to get her paws on her sketchpad and start designing. 'I'll sketch a few designs and see what Elli thinks of them.'

'That is a wise idea. Elli does have great style and taste,' Archie said.

'Look at me. I'm on holiday, I shouldn't be working. Sorry, my love.'

'It is alright, Thia. I love how passionate you are about your creativity. When you have something new to work on, you are bound to be enthusiastic about it.'

As they reached the bookshop, Thia said, 'I can do it when I get home. I don't have any sketching stuff with me.' She laughed when she saw the name of the bookshop—GET LOST! In a Book. 'I like the name, it's clever.'

When they stepped into the bookshop, Archie said, 'Look, Thia! They have sketchpads and pencils.'

'That's great!' Thia exclaimed. 'You are a honey for spotting them. Thank you.' Thia gave Archie a big kiss.

Archie grabbed a basket, and Thia started loading it with pencils, pads, and a few other supplies. 'I wonder where we find books on parenting,' Archie asked Thia.

A salesperson (a rabbit), said, 'Congratulations, madam. They're just over there,' They're just over there,' pointing to a shelf a little way across the shop.

'I'm not pregnant!' Thia said indignantly.

'I'm sorry, madam,' the embarrassed rabbit came back. 'Please forgive me.' He then showed them the section with the books they were looking for. He apologised again, then made himself scarce.

Thia turned to Archie and asked, 'Do I need to lose weight? Do I look pregnant?'

'Thia, my love, you most certainly do not look pregnant or need to lose weight. You are perfect as you are,' Archie replied, irritated that Thia was made to question herself. 'Do not think about it for one moment.'

'I guess it was because we were interested in the location of the books for new parents, the assistant probably assumed I was pregnant,' Thia surmised.

'You are probably right,' Archie agreed. 'Let's get some books.'

They browsed the shelves and selected two books— *A Guide to Pregnancy* (*an Encyclopaedia*) and *The New Dad's Guide to Pregnancy*. Archie chose the one for Charles, commenting, 'That looks useful. I know he has not said it, but I suspect Charles is worried about being a good dad.'

'I can't imagine why he would worry. He's so kind. I mean look at how he and Elli are with Isaac and Charlotte. Besides, Lionel is such a good dad...'

Archie interrupted, 'He is, hence the reason I call him Dad.'

They paid for the books and drawing supplies, left the shop, and started strolling back to the hotel. On the way they chatted.

'I can understand Elli being anxious,' Thia said with a worried expression.

'How so?' Archie asked.

'Well, I'm not sure if you know, but Elli's parents aren't the nicest of people,' Thia admitted.

'You've met them?' Archie asked a little surprised.

'Once, and that was enough,' Thia said, shuddering slightly.

'That does sound bad.'

'They showed up one day at our flat when we were at university. I will never forget how they spoke to Elli.'

Archie stopped walking, and asked, 'It was *that* bad?'

'Imagine being told, "We wish we had never had you. You should have been a son." Or, in your case, told by your parents that they wished you had been a daughter.'

Archie looked like he was going to blow a fuse. If he were any angrier, he would have had steam coming out of his ears.

Thia continued, 'Elli worked hard, not only in university, but with her grandfather—learning the jewellery business. Her granddad was her true family— a lovely person. When he died, she was basically alone. Elli completely threw herself into her work. I was seriously worried about her. That's part of the reason I got her to model my collections—to get her involved with something that hopefully would bolster her confidence. I mean, yes, it helped me, but it also gave her a sort of family.'

'I see,' Archie said a little sadly. 'It explains a lot. Poor Elli. How could anyone not love her?'

'I don't know, Archie. She's lovely *in spite* of her family, not because of them.'

'Well, she need never worry about belonging again. The Watermeres adore her. You only have to see the way Charles looks at her. He loves every molecule of her.'

'That's clear the moment you see them together,' Thia stated. 'I know she feels the same way, about him.'

'Speaking of love... have I told you recently how much I love you, Thia?'

'I love you, Archie Erinac.'

'I also love Elli—because she introduced me to you,' Archie stated.

'Same here! As we've said, my love, meeting someone and not knowing their motives for getting to know you is hard,' Thia said.

'It is not as though I am after your money, Thia,' Archie stated bluntly.

'I'm not a pauper, Archie!'

'Thia, you misunderstood. I meant, I am not exactly cuprumless.'

'Then I'm after *your* money,' Thia laughed.

'You can have it all if you want it, Thia.'

'That's so sweet, Archie. You'd better be careful—some females would take you up on that offer.'

A very distressed Archie then asked, 'Why should I be careful? Are you breaking up with me?'

'*No*, Archie. You silly thing.'

Archie was relieved.

'I just meant, you're a very generous person, and there are some females who would have snatched your paw off with that offer. I am *not* one of them. In this world, there are givers and there are takers.'

Archie thought of Veraminta and shuddered.

'Are you alright, my love?' Thia asked, noticing.

'Yes. Just a horrid thought of the type of female you described,' he replied.

They arrived back at the hotel, where they deposited Thia's art supplies in their suite. They then went to the Sea Glass Suite to see Charles and Elli, but rfound they were not there. They returned to their suite, left the gifts, then headed out of the patio doors to the courtyard, where, to their surprise, they found Charles and Elli lounging by the pool. Elli was wearing a very elegant, black, one-shoulder swimsuit with a turquoise, silk sarong around her waist. Charles was wearing his favourite duck shorts. Archie and Thia approached.

'Hello, Arch, Thia! Had a good day?' Charles

asked in a buoyant manner.

'I was having one, until...' Archie glared at Charles' shorts.

'Arch, old man, I'm on *holiday*!'

'Yes, which means the general public *sees them*.'

Charles laughed. 'Arch, they won't be looking at me.'

'And why is that?' Archie enquired.

'I bought you some,' Charles said.

Archie sputtered, 'There is no way! No way, you or anyone else on this planet would see me in them.'

'Archie, my love. Charles is *joking*,' Thia said.

'Arch, it's not like you not to pick up on when I'm pulling your leg,' Charles said.

'My mind was elsewhere, brother. Elli, by the way, you look elegant as ever. You certainly make up for the fashion victim here.' Archie was back on form.

Charles laughed, looked at Elli, then said, 'Ell does look gorgeous.'

'So, did you have a nice day?' Charles asked again.

'We went to The Natural History Museum, then Thia picked up some art supplies.'

Charles stood up and offered Thia his sun lounger. 'I'll get another.'

Charles and Archie grabbed a sun lounger apiece and placed them either side of Elli and Thia.

'Sweetie, Thia just told me, she's thinking of designing maternity wear,' Elli said enthusiastically.

'How lovely!' Charles replied.

Thia looked a little sheepish.

'What's wrong, Thia? You look like you want to tell us something,' Elli said.

'I was wondering... if I design some... '

'Will I try them?' Elli asked.

'I was thinking... more of... model them,' Thia said gingerly.

'I'll be enormous!' Elli said.

'No, you won't!' Charles said firmly. 'You're gorgeous and will always be gorgeous.'

Archie gave Thia a look that said, *I told you he adores every molecule of her*.

Thia cut in, 'Charles is right. You are gorgeous, and still will be. I bought art supplies to sketch some designs. I would really appreciate your input.'

'I'm no expert, Thia. I've only known I'm pregnant for two days,' Elli gave a light laugh.

'But, that does not stop you possessing style and elegance,' Archie stated.

'Well said, Archie,' Thia cheered.

'Please excuse me one moment,' Archie said, then suddenly dashed back into his suite, returning with the books they had bought. He gave the encyclopaedia to Elli, and obviously, the new dad book to Charles. He had completely forgotten about the other gifts.

'How thoughtful. Thank you. I can read this each morning in bed when I'm eating my dry toast,' Elli said, as she opened the book to the first page.

'Thanks, Arch, Thia. I need this,' Charles said sincerely.

'Thia, when do you need input on the maternity wear?' Elli asked.

'As soon as you like. I mean, no use starting in

156

January,' Thia said, smiling.

'That's true,' Elli said looking down at her belly. 'Let's go indoors, I'm a little warm. We can start now, if you like, Thia.' Elli stood up, kissed Charles on the lips, then she and Thia entered the Sea Spray Suite, as that was where the sketchbooks were.

Charles and Archie stayed sitting poolside.

'Thanks again, for the book, Arch.'

'You are welcome, brother. I know if it were me, I would be in a state of pure shock and panic.'

'You would?' Charles asked, a stunned expression on his face.

'Oh yes,' Archie said, knowing that was what was on Charles' mind. 'I would be worried if I would make a good dad. After all, my father left and never returned.'

'I'm sorry, Arch.'

'Nothing to be sorry for, brother. I have a wonderful role model, Dad.'

Charles smiled.

'You still seem worried, brother.'

'Well, I think of Calista and Ermgarde's relationship,' Charles said reluctantly.

'But you and your sister are as chalk and cheese, and always have been. You and she are *nothing* alike, Charles. You know that. Stop torturing yourself. Read your book, and take Dad's advice, and you will not go wrong. I am sure. If you need a female's advice, I am absolutely positive Heather will oblige. I mean, Heather has become a lot like a mum to Elli.'

'You're right, Arch, she has. I know she loves Ell, by the way she calls her Darling Girl. I miss my mum, but I'm glad Dad met Heather. They seem to bring out the best in each other, and they do enjoy each other's company.'

'I could say the same about you and your darling wife, brother,' Archie smiled. 'Though she has not yet managed to curb your passion for questionable swimwear,' he said, raising his eyebrows.

'She knows they make me happy, brother,' Charles responded. 'I remember something, Dad said about Mum. He said Mum was too good for him. I think Ell is too good for me.'

'*Fiddlesticks*!' Archie blurted out. 'You are perfect for each other. It was fate, kismet, or whatever you would like to call it. The stars were all aligned for you to meet Elli. You met over the same crossword book.'

'Well, that was easy. There's only one bookshop in Mereland, Arch.'

'Yes, but… she was new to the village. Why had you not heard about a new otter in the village? Aunt Gerti did not even tell me, and she is like the local information centre,' Archie put forth.

Charles laughed. 'You're right, Aunt Gerti certainly knows what's going on in Mereland.'

'Exactly! And… you both went for the same book at the *same time*,' Archie stated.

'Yes, but, as I said, only one bookshop,' Charles countered.

'She could have gone for a novel, and you may never have met. Then you met again at Brass on the Grass.'

'By chance,' Charles said. 'And only for a minute or two.'

'See! *Chance*!' Archie said, feeling Charles was

proving his point for him. 'Then for her to be at Flynn and Willow's wedding.'

'Well, she did design their rings,' Charles argued.

'Brother, I do have to say...'

'What?' Charles asked.

'You are being a total and utter...'

'Plant pot?' Charles asked.

'Yes! *A gigantic one*!' Archie said, a little frustrated. 'Who invites their jeweller to their wedding?'

'Evidently, Flynn and Willow,' Charles replied.

'You are a total *pillock*!' Archie said exasperatedly. 'Would you invite your jeweller to your wedding?'

'Well... I married mine,' Charles said smugly.

Archie rolled his eyes at having painted himself into a rhetorical corner. He sighed heavily.

'It's okay, brother. I know what you mean.'

'Remember, she asked you out on a date,' Archie commented, not knowing exactly where he was going with the argument.

'Oh, I remember that,' Charles said.

'See! She too knew you were right for each other and was not after your money. She did not know who you were.'

'She's just perfect, Arch,' Charles said with a dreamy look in his eyes.

'She is, and that is my point. You are perfect for each other. Charles, I have to say something, and I am sorry to raise an unpleasant subject...' Archie started.

'Speak freely, brother,' Charles said, looking Archie straight on.

'Today, I realised fully what you must have gone through when Elli was...'

'Abducted?' Charles asked.

'Yes. How protective of her you were and are. It was only a small incident, and would not even register to some, but someone inadvertently made an assumption about Thia, and I wanted to jump all over him. I was incensed. I know it is nothing like what you went through, but it made me realise how hard it must have been for you. How much restraint it must have taken not to rip someone's throat out.'

Charles had never in all the time they had known each other seen Archie like this. 'I think that's why Dad punched Rook before I could get to him. I'm glad he did, because, had I wasted my time on him, Ell would not have made it. That thought haunts me, Arch.'

'Brother, she *did* make it, and she is here, because of you. And... she is going to have your pup. That is *wonderful*,' Archie beamed.

'Arch, old man. You sound like you wish it were you and Thia.'

Archie shrugged.

'Brother, if you love her, tell her.'

'I do, Charles. The problem is, she works and lives in Norchester, and I am in Mereland.'

'Arch, if you are trying to tell me you want to leave and move to Norchester...'

Archie cut Charles off mid-sentence, 'Certainly not! I love my life in Mereland.'

'You also love Thia.'

'I do love her. I am not sure if we can reconcile

the situation. I mean, she has her studio, workforce, and reputation as a designer in Norchester. All that is in Mereland is... me.'

'You *are* a match for all that, brother,' Charles said.

'Poppycock!' Archie exclaimed.

'Talk to each other about it. If you haven't, you should,' Charles advised.

'But what if...'

'She chooses Norchester?' Charles asked a downhearted Archie.

'Precisely,' Archie said, with a sigh.

'Cross that bridge when and *if* you come to it. Arch, I have said it before, and I will say it again... you are smarter than the average mammal. You'll work it out.'

'Thank you, Charles.'

'Remember, it's not whether you can live with each other, but whether you can live *without* each other.'

'I think your dad skills are starting to kick in, Charles.'

The two friends laughed.

Meanwhile, in the Sea Spray Suite, the ladies were discussing what type of clothing Elli thought mums-to-be would like.

'Thia, I'm no expert, but I would say a bit of everything, from wrap-over blouses, wide-legged trousers that have released pressure over the tummy, wrap-around dresses with ties at the back, so they can expand and contract. What about adjustable nightgowns and adjustable waist pyjamas? Some fabulously gorgeous underwear. Females still want to feel pretty, and it all starts with the undies,' Elli said, flowing with ideas.

Thia was attempting to keep up with her note-taking.

'I remember a friend asking me, "I wonder when you go into big knickers from skimpies.' Elli chuckled again.

'Probably when you're having your first child,' Thia joked. The two of them roared with laughter.

'Oh! Swimwear would be nice. I'm sorry, that's a lot.' Elli said, as Thia scribbled furiously. Elli grimaced.

'What is it, Elli?' a worried Thia asked.

'Evening clothes would be good. When we went to Heronpool, Ermgarde was pregnant with Charlotte, and didn't have much choice when it came to evening wear. I'm being greedy, but I would like some work clothes too, I think, Thia.'

Thia smiled as she finished her list. 'I have plenty to start with.' She then picked up her sketchpad and a pencil, and began sketching.

'Thia, I'll leave you to it. I'm going to take a nap before dinner. Thanks for the book.'

'Oh! Before you go, I have something for you,' Thia said, as she hopped up, and grabbed the department store bag and handed it to Elli.

'Thank you, Thia, but you already bought me a book,' Elli said, as she peeked in the bag. She pulled out the cashmere blanket, then held it to her face. 'Thia, this is gorgeously soft, and I love the colour. Thank you! I'll use it when I take my nap.'

'You're most welcome. There's something else in there.'

Elli looked in the bag again, pulled out the nightgown, and her jaw dropped. 'Thia, this is stunning! Sadly, I won't get to wear it for too long before the bump grows.'

'It's a maternity one! It's exactly what you asked for, an adjustable nightgown,' Thia replied smiling.

'Really?' Elli asked as she turned the garment to find ribbons to adjust it. 'Brilliant! Thank you, Thia.' Elli gave Thia a big hug. 'Now I'm all set for my nap,' Elli packed her items back into the bag, gave Thia a kiss on the cheek, then left her to her sketching.

On the way back to the Sea Glass Suite, she met Archie, and gave him a big kiss on the cheek, and thanked him for the wonderfully thoughtful gifts. On entering her suite, she found Charles sitting in an armchair reading his new dad book.

'Hello, gorgeous! What do you have there?'

'Gifts from Thia and Archie,' she said, as she took the items out of the bag to show him.

'Ooh! Lovely!' Thia knows you well, though I'm sure Arch does too, by now.'

Elli nestled herself on Charles lap, then gave him a kiss. 'How's the dad book?'

'Well, you'll be pleased to know, it's a dad's duty to give his partner back and foot rubs when needed.'

'That's good,' Elli said. 'What else does it say?'

'Apparently, lots of new dads are plant pots.'

Elli laughed. 'Surely it doesn't say that.'

'No. I paraphrase, but the gist is—all new dads panic, and wonder if they'll be good dads. It's normal for them to feel unsure of their role during the pregnancy. I mean, it's clear what the mother's role is.'

'I see,' Elli said. 'Well, your role is to be your wonderful self. Easy!' Elli kissed Charles on the nose.

'You mean, be a plant pot?' Charles asked. 'That's easy.' They both laughed. 'What shall we do for dinner tonight?' he asked.

'Dinner here tonight, I think. I'm a bit tired. In fact, I think I'll take a nap.'

GET LOST! In a Book

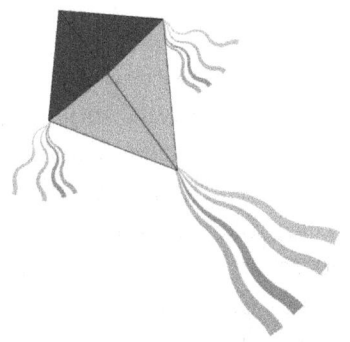

KITES AND FOSSILS

The next morning was bright and breezy. Isaac announced to his parents, 'It's windy! I'm going to teach Person how to kite!' So, the whole Staff family headed to the beach, Isaac's kite in his paw.

'Perfect morning for flying your kite, son,' Rupert said, as he started to untangle the tail of Isaac's shark kite.

'Daddy, please hurry! The wind will go!' Isaac pleaded as he did a little urgency dance.

'It's tangled quite badly. I'm going as quickly as I can. You really need to look after your kite if you want it to be ready to go straight away,' Rupert said, getting a little frustrated.

'I did look after it, Daddy. You're making it worse,' Isaac said, exasperated. 'Let Mummy do it.'

Hiding a smirk, Ermgarde asked Rupert to watch Charlotte, whilst she untangled the kite tail in a moment. 'There you go, Sweet Pea. All done!'

'See, Daddy! Mummy could do it!'

'Yes, but I loosened it,' Rupert quietly said to Ermgarde.

Ermgarde snorted.

Isaac turned to Charlotte and said, 'Come on,

165

Person! This is how you kite.'

Rupert set Charlotte down, and Isaac ran along the beach, releasing his kite at the perfect time so it took to the air. He was thrilled with himself. His dad was correct, it truly was a perfect day to kite. Charlotte, who was now sitting on the sand with Ermgarde, giggled. She did like the colourful thing flapping around in the breeze.

Isaac had been tugging and pulling on his kite for about five minutes when a sudden gust of wind caught the kite and almost pulled the pup over. A second later, the string snapped. '*MUMMY*! *DADDY*!' Isaac screamed as his kite was taken off by the wind. Isaac watched it fall a little way down the beach. He started running towards the area where he believed the kite had dropped, Rupert running behind him. 'Daddy, my kite has gone. *Where is it?*' a very unhappy Isaac wailed.

'It fell over there, by those rocks. Be careful! Rocks on the beach can be slippery,' Rupert warned Isaac, who was very eager to get his kite back. He followed his son, and being much taller than Isaac, had a better view to survey the whole rocky outcrop. 'There it is, son! Next to that big snail.'

Isaac, who was looking for a large snail, turned to his father and said, 'Daddy, you are silly! That's not a snail, it's an ammonite!'

'A what-on-ite?' Rupert asked.

'Ammonite,' Isaac repeated.

'What's an ammonite? A dinosaur?' a puzzled Rupert asked.

Isaac giggled. 'No, Daddy, it's a fossil. It's not alive now. Long, long time ago, it lived in the sea. It was like an octopus, but he had his house on his back.'

'So, I wasn't so silly saying it was a snail. Snails carry their houses on their backs,' Rupert retorted, feeling a little less stupid.

The father and son carefully made their way down the rocks, where Isaac picked up his kite. He then asked, 'Daddy, can we take the ammonite home?'

Rupert grabbed the edge of the fossil and pulled it forward, it came loose. 'That was lucky!' Rupert said. He had visions of a very disappointed son or a lot of digging.

Isaac was doing his wiggle dance, which he tended to do when extremely excited.

Rupert lifted the ammonite with some considerable effort. 'Wow! This thing is heavy! *Flippin' heck*! What did this chap eat? House bricks?'

Isaac giggled, then said, 'Of course it's heavy, Daddy. It's rock!'

'I thought you said it was a sea creature with a house,' Rupert said.

'It is, Daddy. That is his house, but it's all stone now.' Isaac said, as if his father should have known.

'It feels like I'm carrying a house,' Rupert groaned.

Very slowly, Rupert and Isaac made their way back along the beach, where Ermgarde was building sandcastles, and Charlotte was knocking them down.

'Sand!' Charlotte cried when she saw Rupert and Isaac. 'Sand, Daddy! Issy, sand!'

'Yes, Person, it's sand,' Isaac said.

Rupert dropped the ammonite on the ground

next to Ermgarde, then plopped himself down on the sand next to it, exhausted.

'What did you bring that great big rock back for?' Ermgarde asked.

Isaac sighed. He was going to have to explain again, which he did.

'Oh, that's interesting, but what are you going to do with it?' his mother asked.

'Keep it!' Isaac announced, then handed Ermgarde his kite. 'Mummy, can you fix my kite, please?'

Ermgarde untied the short piece of string dangling from the kite and securely reattached the spool of string.

'Thank you, Mummy.'

Archie and Thia approached and said their good mornings. 'Lovely morning to fly a kite, Isaac,' Archie said, then noticed the ammonite. 'My goodness! That is a very large ammonite.'

Isaac looked at Archie with wide eyes. He was incredibly impressed Archie knew what an ammonite was.

'Daddy and I found it, Uncle Archie.'

'It is a lovely specimen. They have some in the local natural history museum...' Archie was interrupted by Isaac.

'Uncle Archie, where is the museum?'

'In town, Isaac. Thia and I were looking at ammonites yesterday, but they have nothing nearly as nice as this.'

'Perhaps you should take it to the museum, Sweet Pea,' Ermgarde said. 'I think the museum would be the best home for your ammonite.'

Isaac was doing some serious thinking. 'But, Mummy, I love my ammonite,' Isaac said with a pained voice.

'I know, Sweet Pea, but if it goes to the museum, lots of people can love it.'

Isaac looked at Archie.

Archie answered Isaac's look, 'That is true, Isaac. Thia and I went to look at fossils, and we did not see anything quite like your ammonite. It would be a shame if people could not see something as wonderful as it.'

Isaac nodded. 'Uncle Archie, would you and Auntie Thia take me to the museum, please?'

Archie looked at Ermgarde. 'We could take you and your fossil to the museum tomorrow. If it is okay with your mummy and daddy.'

'That's fine with me,' Ermgarde said.

'We're going to have to go in the car, Archie,' Thia said. 'I'm sure we couldn't carry that heavy fossil all the way into town.'

'I agree, Thia,' Rupert said. 'Trust me, it's *heavy*.'

Isaac tried to move the ammonite, but could not budge it at all. He then wiped his brow, and said, 'Phew!' Which made the adults smile.

'How about we go to lunch afterwards?' Thia suggested.

'Then tea and biscuits, if I'm good,' Isaac said with a toothy grin.

'Isaac Lionel Staff! You cheeky article!' Ermgarde admonished.

'If you are good, we will take you for tea and biscuits. If you think it appropriate, Ermgarde,' Archie said.

'Okay. But...' Ermgarde was cut off by an excited Isaac.

'Only if I'm good,' Isaac said.

'Have you seen Uncle and Auntie Squish today?' Ermgarde asked.

'Not today. I think they have just been taking it easy. Elli was a little tired yesterday,' Thia answered.

At that moment, Charles and Elli exited their suite.

'They must have remarkably good hearing,' Rupert remarked.

The others laughed.

Charles and Elli approached the group on the beach. 'Is this a party?' Charles asked.

'We could have one,' Ermgarde said. 'We're just missing...'

Isaac jumped in, yelling, 'Pop-Pop and Gran-Gran Heather!'

'No need to shout, Sweet Pea.'

Isaac started waving. The group turned around, and there was Heather and Lionel a little way off down the beach. The couple appeared to stop, chat for a moment or two, then Lionel approached the group, whilst Heather unlocked their suite, and deposited a pile of shopping. She then returned to join the group.

'Hello, all!' Lionel said cheerily.

'Pop-Pop, Gran-Gran, we found an ammonite!'

Lionel and Heather looked at the spot on the ground where Isaac was pointing.

'That's a whopper!' Lionel exclaimed.

'Do you know what an ammonite is?' Isaac asked, thinking he would have to explain, again.

'I do, pup,' Lionel said, the others nodded.

'Uncle Archie and Auntie Thia are going to take me to the museum, so I can let them borrow my ammonite. Then everyone can like it.'

'That's a nice thing to do, pup,' Charles said.

'What's everyone doing here?' Lionel asked.

'We just met here,' Elli answered.

'We could all have dinner tonight if you're up to it, Auntie Squish,' Ermgarde suggested.

'How are you doing, Petal? How's the pup?' Lionel asked.

Elli rubbed her belly, then said, 'We're fine, thank you, Daddy.'

'That's good,' Lionel said.

'I'm okay, if you all want to do dinner tonight.'

'The big question is... where?' Charles asked.

'I guess that depends on if we want to dress for dinner,' Archie commented.

Heather spoke, 'There are a few restaurants in the town, the little one up the road, the hotel restaurant, which looks nice, or we could eat in the courtyard.'

Everyone looked at Elli.

'Why is everyone looking at me?' she asked, feeling rather self-conscious. 'I'll be fine. Where does everyone else want to go?'

'We can't go too late. The pups will be too tired,' Ermgarde said, as she grabbed Charlotte's sandy paw, which was about to go in her mouth.

'If nobody is going to decide, how about the hotel

restaurant?' Lionel asked the group.

'Sounds, like a plan!' Charles said. 'I'll book it. Six o'clock okay?'

'That's great, Uncle Squish,' Ermgarde answered. 'We should get back, and get these two showered.'

'Mummy, what about my ammonite?' Isaac asked.

'We're not going to shower that!' Ermgarde said.

'I'll put it in my car,' Archie said. 'It will be safe there.' Archie turned, and with some effort, hefted the ammonite off the ground.

'Need a paw, Arch?' Charles offered.

'I just need the car unlocking,' he mumbled.

'I'll do that, Archie,' Thia said, and taking the keys from his pocket. As they headed to the car park, they said they'd see everyone at dinner.

'I'm going to love you and leave you. I need to reserve our table. See you later!' Charles said as he and Elli started to walk to the Sea Glass Suite.

That evening, everyone met at The Beachcomber, the hotel restaurant. The decor was bright and white, with lots of navy accents. Charles and Elli arrived a little after the others.

'Sorry everyone. I took a nap,' Elli informed the others.

'Well, you look fresh as a daisy, Darling Girl,' Heather said.

'I took the liberty of ordering you a lemonade each,' Archie said.

'Perfect, Arch. Thank you.' Charles said.

'That's a pretty dress, Auntie Squish,' Ermgarde said. Elli was wearing a long, vibrant blue ombré, wrap-over dress. 'Thank you, Ermgarde. Hopefully, it will fit me for a while.'

'At least until you get some new pieces,' Thia said. 'I've been working on a few sketches. I should have something for you to look at soon.'

Ermgarde asked, 'Are you having a new dress designed, Auntie Squish?'

'No. Well... sort of. Thia is starting a new line in maternity clothing, and has asked my opinion on what to design.'

'That sounds wonderful, Thia. I wish they were around when I had our two,' Ermgarde responded, then she took a sip of her drink.

'I can show you them tomorrow, Elli. Perhaps after Archie, Isaac, and I return from the museum.'

'That sounds good, Thia. I'm sure they're lovely.'

Everyone perused their menu, although Heather was distracted by Charlotte who wanted to play peek-a-boo. Charlotte's big brother was sitting between Lionel and Archie. Isaac was telling Archie everything he could remember about ammonites from a book he had read.

A waiter (a curlew), arrived at the table. 'We do have a celebration family platter, if you would like to try that,' the curlew suggested.

'What is it?' Rupert asked, voicing exactly what was on the minds of all at the table.

'It is a platter of seafood—crab, king prawns, lobster, smoked salmon, and mackerel, with a leafy green salad, and vine-ripened tomatoes.'

The Watermere party looked at Elli. 'What's wrong?' Elli asked as soon as she felt them gazing at her.

'What would you like to eat, Ell?' Charles asked.

'I'll be fine with sharing the platter,' she said, a little embarrassed to be the centre of attention.

'Are you sure, Petal?' Lionel asked kindly.

'Yes, Daddy. I'll be fine, thank you.'

'Then a platter big enough for everyone, please,' Lionel told the waiter.

'Certainly, sir. Room number, please,' the curlew asked.

'The Sea Glass Suite,' Charles replied.

'Thank you, sir. Your food will be out shortly.' The curlew left and went straight to the kitchen.

'We're glad you're feeling better and we can celebrate your good news,' Heather said.

'Auntie Squish, when will your new person be here?' Isaac asked.

'After Papa Winter comes. At the beginning of next year,' Elli answered.

A disappointed Isaac turned to his mother. 'Mummy, will you be an auntie to the new person?'

'No, Sweet Pea. I will be a cousin to the new person,' Ermgarde replied.

'A cousin?' Isaac questioned.

'Yes, because my mummy and Uncle Squish are brother and sister. Just like you and Charlotte.'

Isaac looked at Charlotte then Charles. You could see the cogs whirring in the pup's head. He looked vaguely suspicious of the answer his mother gave him. 'What's the new person's name?'

'He asked what we were all thinking,' Rupert said.

Elli looked at Charles, then said, 'We haven't talked about it yet.'

'We've only just found out about it,' Charles added.

'Understandable,' Heather said.

A few minutes later, their food arrived. The platter was gigantic and took up most of the table. The waiter said, 'Enjoy!' then left them to it.

Everyone just sat there staring at the mountain of food before them. Nobody wanted to be the first to tuck in, until Isaac said, 'Mummy, may I have some crab, please?' After Ermgarde served Isaac some crab, everyone helped themselves. Ermgarde placed pieces of lobster, crab, and mackerel in Charlotte's bowl. Heather was having a hard time eating her food, because she was watching Charlotte, who was thoroughly enjoying her meal. The pup kept saying, 'Yum yum, fishy!' She tried her spoon, but got a little frustrated because her food kept falling off it. She decided to use her paws.

'What is everyone doing tomorrow?' Lionel asked. 'I know Archie and Thia are taking Isaac to The Natural History Museum. What about the rest of you?'

'We thought we'd have a lazy day, Granddad,' Ermgarde said.

'What about you and Heather? Where are you going, Granddad?' Rupert asked.

'We thought we'd take a boat to Lissof Isle,' Heather said.

'That sounds lovely,' Elli said.

'Come with us if you'd like, my dears,' Heather suggested as she looked at Lionel.

'I'm not sure I'm up to a boat trip. Sorry, Aunt Heather. I think I'm probably better on terra firma,'

Elli replied. Even the *thought* of a boat journey made her feel queasy.

'I do hope you enjoy yourselves,' Charles said. The group was making their way through the platter of food, with Elli managing to pick a bit here and there.

Charles leant over and quietly asked, 'Ell, do you want something else?'

'I know it's awful, but I would love some fresh strawberries and salt and vinegar crisps,' Elli said, then she bit her lip.

Charles gave her an odd look, then asked, 'You want them together or one after the other?'

'Together,' Elli replied a little shyly.

'Charles, your darling wife is craving. The pup wants them,' Heather said.

'They mention cravings in that book you bought me, Arch, but it didn't say it would be a mix of things.' Charles caught the attention of the waiter, who approached the table.

'May I help you, sir?'

'I would like a bowl of strawberries and a bowl of salt and vinegar crisps,' Charles requested.

'At once, sir. Anything else?' the waiter asked without batting an eye.

'Could you arrange for some to be put in the Sea Glass Suite, please?' Charles asked, thinking that this was not going to be Elli's only craving during their stay.

'Absolutely, sir,' the curlew replied, then left the table.

'I thought he would think it was an odd request, Sweetie.' Elli said, then thanked her husband.

'You're not the first to have cravings. I'm sure he's had many requests for a lot weirder things,' Charles retorted.

Everyone laughed.

When the waiter returned with the ordered items, Isaac watched Elli. 'Auntie Squish, you are silly. You have *crisps* with lemonade, not *strawberries*!' He giggled.

'I know, pup, but the new person asked me for some strawberries to go with the crisps,' Elli responded, then popped a crisp topped with a slice of strawberry. into her mouth.

Isaac watched wide-eyed, as she popped the bite into her mouth.

'Would you like to try some?' Elli offered.

Isaac thought for a moment, then nodded.

Elli handed Isaac some crisps and slices of strawberry on a side plate, then the pup made a tiny sandwich with the items just as Elli had, then took a big bite. Everyone waited for his reaction. Isaac licked his lips, then said, 'Yum!'

'You like it, Sweet Pea?' Ermgarde asked.

'Yes, Mummy. It's zingy and juicy. Have one, Mummy.'

'It's alright, Sweet Pea, you eat them,' his mother said, not fancying it at all.

'I think you've started something, Ell,' Charles said, a little amused by Isaac's reaction.

'Charles, dear, it could be worse,' Heather commented. 'Some females have cravings for soil, toothpaste, and other items.'

'Soil! Toothpaste!' Rupert blurted out.

'I craved oranges when I was expecting

Charlotte,' Ermgarde said.

'I'm not so odd' Elli said, as she took another bite.

'Does anyone want dessert?' Lionel asked the group.

'I don't think so, Granddad,' Rupert replied. 'I think someone will have to roll me back to our suite. I feel like a beach ball, I'm so full.'

'It was delicious. I'm full,' Charles answered.

Archie and Thia declined for the same reason.

Heather said that all she wanted was a nice cup of tea before bed.

'Speaking of bed. We should get the pups to theirs,' Ermgarde said, looking at Charlotte, who was nodding off.

'But, Mummy!' Isaac said. 'We're on holiday!'

'No buts! You're going to the museum tomorrow with Uncle Archie and Auntie Thia, and you need to get up early.'

'Okay, Mummy,' Isaac said, relenting.

After goodnight kisses were given and received, the Staff family returned to their suite. When Charles and Elli made it back to their suite, they found several packets of salt and vinegar crisps on the coffee table, and three punnets of strawberries in the fridge.

'Ell, you're all set for midnight cravings.'

'Thank you, Sweetie.'

'Do you need a back or a foot rub, Mrs Watermere?'

'Yes please, Mr Watermere. That would be *wonderful.*'

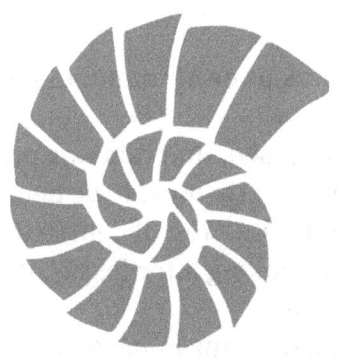

NATURAL HISTORY

Isaac was awake uncharacteristically early. He had washed and dressed himself, and when Ermgarde asked him why he was up so early, he replied, 'Uncle Archie will be up already. He's an early bird!'

Ermgarde had to bite her lip to prevent herself from laughing. 'Where did you hear that, Sweet Pea?'

'Squish-Squish said that Pop-Pop is an early bird, because he gets up very early in the morning. Uncle Archie gets up early too!'

Ermgarde had to agree; her son's logic was flawless. 'I know Uncle Archie will be up, but it's too early to go to the museum. Shall we have breakfast together, and let Daddy and Charlotte sleep?'

Isaac nodded. 'That's a very good idea, Mummy. May I have fish sausages and toast, please?'

Ermgarde smiled at her son, and thought, *My, how quickly you've grown.* Ermgarde called room service and ordered breakfast and tea for two to be served in the courtyard.

'Mummy.'

'Yes, Sweet Pea.'

179

'Will they look after my ammonite in the museum?'

Ermgarde realised, that this was probably why Isaac was up early. He must have been worrying about his ammonite. 'Yes, of course they will. They are the best at looking after fossils. It's a natural history museum.'

'A natural history museum. Why is it called that?' Isaac asked.

'It's a special museum that looks after things from nature. Things like fossils, dinosaur bones, and plants.'

Isaac's eyes grew huge. 'They have dinosaurs at the museum?' he asked.

'I'm sure they do,' his mother replied.

'Will they have a *Parasaurolophus* or a *Deinonychus*?'

'I'm not sure. You'll have to look when you get there.'

A while later, they saw Thia step out into the courtyard. She waved good morning. Isaac excused himself from the table and ran over to her. 'Hello, Auntie Thia. Is Uncle Archie awake?'

'He is. He's just had his breakfast.'

Archie stepped outside. 'Good morning, young Isaac. How are you?'

'I'm very well, thank you. I'm ready to go to The Natural History Museum.'

'That's good. We can leave in ten minutes. Does that suit you?'

'Yes, Uncle Archie.' Isaac then ran back to his mother, and excitedly said, 'Mummy, Uncle Archie said we can go in ten minutes.'

'Okay. Here's some spending money. Don't lose it,' Ermgarde said as she handed him five aurum.

'Thank you, Mummy,' the pup said, then gave her a kiss. 'I will ask Uncle Archie to look after it.'

'That's a very good idea. Now go brush your teeth.'

When he returned, Archie and Thia were waiting for him.

'Uncle Archie, please look after my spending money. I don't want to lose it,' Isaac said, as he held out his five aurum note.

'That is a lot of spending money!' Archie said.

'It will pay for his entrance,' Ermgarde said.

'Ermgarde, there's no fee to get in,' Thia informed her.

'Then he can spend it on whatever he wants, as long as it fits in the car to take home. I don't want a dinosaur tied to the roof all the way back to Mereland.' Ermgarde said.

Archie and Thia laughed, and Isaac joined in.

'That would be quite a sight,' Thia said. Imagine a dinosaur moving above the hedgerows. I'm sure it would quite unnerve some people.'

'Well, young sir, shall we go?' Archie asked.

'Yes, please! Bye-bye, Mummy! I'll be good,' Isaac said, then kissed Ermgarde. Thia took hold of his paw, and the three of them walked to the car.

When they arrived at the museum, Isaac was eager to get out of the car, but Archie stopped him. 'Young Isaac, we are going to have some rules. As your mummy and daddy are not here, it is important for you to stay with me and Thia. Do you understand?'

Isaac nodded. 'I'll be good, Uncle Archie.'

'Then let us go in,' Archie said.

The museum was, as you would expect, a stone building, with columns outside, and a rather grand entrance. As they went in, the first thing they saw was a dinosaur skeleton.

'Oh my! I wouldn't like him chasing me!' Thia exclaimed.

'It's okay, Auntie Thia, he's a brontosaurus. He's a veggie eater. He has a long neck to reach tasty bits of trees.'

'He certainly does have a long neck,' Thia said. 'I wouldn't like to knit him a scarf.'

Isaac giggled. 'It would be a very very very long scarf.'

They walked around, looking at exhibits, Isaac pointing out things he knew, and reading the plates of things he did not. 'This is a coprolite!' he announced.

'A coprolite? What is a coprolite?' Thia asked.

'It's dinosaur poop.' Isaac whispered, then giggled.

'Yuck!' Thia said.

'It's okay, Auntie Thia, it isn't smelly. It's a rock now.'

'Well, that is good to know,' Archie said.

The next exhibit was a large, fossilized pine cone with a label that said it was from Lissof Isle.

'This one is local,' Thia said, 'Lissof Isle isn't too far away. That's where Lionel and Heather are going today.'

'That's interesting,' Archie responded.

They walked into the next room, where a rabbit of about Archie's age was adjusting an exhibit. He was dressed in khaki shorts with lots of pockets, a khaki- coloured shirt, work boots, and a pair of glasses on a string.

'Excuse me, who would we speak to about an exhibit?' Archie asked the rabbit.

'Which exhibit?' the rabbit asked.

'I have an ammonite!' Isaac said excitedly.

'We have plenty of ammonites in that room,' the rabbit responded, then pointed to a room to their right. 'I am Doctor Anning Lapin, palaeontologist.'

Isaac froze and his eyes appeared huge.

'I'm sure you don't know what that is, young pup,' he addressing Isaac.

'I do! You're a fossil scientist! Are you a vertra-bit palaeontologist?'

'Yes, I am a *vertebrate* palaeontologist,' Anning Lapin responded, impressed by the pup's knowledge.

'Auntie Thia, vertra-bits are things with backbones.'

'Thank you, Isaac. I was going to ask,' she said.

'Yes, young pup, that is correct,' the rabbit said. 'Let me show you our ammonites,' he said as he led them to a display, which had eight ammonites of varying sizes; the largest of which was about the size of a dinner plate.

'They're not as big as *mine*!' Isaac announced, rather unimpressed.

'I am sure, young pup, these are the best specimens found locally,' Lapin said indignantly.

'Doctor Lapin, the pup is correct,' Archie stated. 'His ammonite is *considerably* larger.'

Isaac nodded frantically in agreement.

Doctor Lapin looked shocked. 'Then it wasn't local,' he said when he came too.

'It most certainly is local,' Archie stated, a little more forcefully than he had intended.

'Daddy and I found it on the beach!' Isaac informed the rabbit.

'Is there a way I could get to see it?' the doctor inquired.

'It's in Uncle Archie's car!' Isaac told Doctor Lapin.

'Oh, my word! Please may I see it?'

'Of course,' Archie said, then he, Thia, and Isaac walked back through the museum to the parked car, where Archie opened the boot. The doctor almost fainted when he saw the size of Isaac's ammonite, which was roughly the size of a car tyre.

'My goodness!' Lapin exclaimed. 'I have never found anything this *magnificent*! Would it be possible to display it?'

'Well, it is Isaac's ammonite,' Archie responded.

'Young pup, do you think you would allow us to *borrow* your ammonite? I will give you a smaller ammonite you may take home with you,' Lapin offered.

Isaac thought for a moment, then nodded.

'Oh, how fantastic!' the doctor said sounding quite giddy. 'I will go get a trolley to take it in.'

'That is a good idea, as it is rather heavy,' Archie said, relieved.

Lapin ran off into the museum.

'The doctor is very impressed with your fossil,' Thia told Isaac.

Isaac grinned.

When the doctor returned, Archie helped him move the weighty fossil onto the trolley, then the doctor proudly wheeled it into the museum. 'I must take it into the back so it can be prepared for display.'

'How long will it be before it goes on display?' Thia asked, hoping that Isaac could see his ammonite in an exhibit before he returned home.

'A day or two,' Anning Lapin replied, his eyes firmly fixed on the fossil.

Isaac looked a little deflated.

Anning opened a cabinet and took out an ammonite the size of a side plate. 'Here you go young pup.' Lapin said, as he offered it to Isaac, who took it. 'Where did you find the ammonite?'

'On the beach with my daddy.'

'Which beach?' the doctor asked.

'By the hotel!' Isaac stated, as if the doctor should have known all the best places to find fossils.

'What is your name?' the rabbit asked.

'Isaac Lionel Staff. I'm seven.'

'You know a lot about fossils for seven,' Lapin stated.

'I read,' Isaac said flatly.

'He reads *a lot*,' Archie said. 'He has had an interest in books since he could hold one.'

'I like *Parasaurolophus* and *Deinonychus* and trilobites,' Isaac announced.

Anning Lapin smiled at Isaac. He had never met a

young person quite like him. 'I am grateful you brought your ammonite to me, Isaac.'

'Mummy said lots of people should see it.'

'Your mummy is correct. Do you live in Trebmal Bay?' Lapin asked.

'No, we are from Mereland,' Archie answered. 'Thia is from Norchester. We will let you get back to work, Doctor.'

'Thank you, once again, Isaac,' Doctor Lapin said. Archie took the ammonite Anning Lapin gave Isaac to the car and placed it in the boot. Isaac stayed with Thia and looked at more exhibits. Only when Isaac got hungry did the trio leave the museum in search of a place to eat.

'Uncle Archie, can we go there?' Isaac asked, pointing to a building with the most garishly coloured front. The flashing sign said Patties Fish Burger Bar.

Archie looked at Thia, and the look on Archie's face said, *not somewhere I would enjoy eating.*

Thia squeezed his arm, then quietly said, 'It'll make him happy.'

Archie agreed. 'Of course, we can Isaac,' Archie said graciously.

They opened the door to Patties Fish Burger Bar and entered. The décor hit Archie and Thia like a smack in the face. There were fluorescent coloured walls, floors, and ceiling, with music blaring.

'I think I need sunglasses,' Thia said to Archie, who appeared to be stuck in place.

'I think I need earplugs!' he responded, but Isaac was beaming, and ran to look at the menu, which was on a big, illuminated board.

'Let's find a table,' Thia said.

Isaac came running over to the table Archie and Thia were now sitting at. 'Isaac, what would you like to eat?' Archie asked the incredibly excited pup.

'I would like a number five—a super fish burger. I would like it with chips and tartar sauce, please, Uncle Archie. And I would like a strawberry lemonade.'

'Okay. What about you, my love?' Archie asked Thia.

'The same, please. It sounds yummy,' Thia said, looking at Isaac.

Archie went to order at the counter, because, much to his shock, they did not take your order at the table.

He returned carrying a plastic tray of food. 'That was a very strange experience,' he told Thia.

'This sort of place not for you, hon?' Thia asked Archie, already knowing the answer.

'No. Most definitely not.'

Isaac was thrilled by the jarringly bright environment, whilst Archie and Thia felt they were being screamed at, but no matter, it was Isaac's treat.

'Uncle Archie.'

'Yes, Isaac.'

'Will Doctor Fossil look after my ammonite?'

Archie had to smile at Isaac's name for the professor. 'Most undoubtedly. He loves it as much as you do.'

Isaac thought for moment, 'Then why couldn't he

visit me to see it?'

'Because, your mummy said, more people should see it, and I am sure Mummy would not like lots of people traipsing through The Lodge.'

Isaac appeared satisfied with Archie's response. 'No, she wouldn't. They would have to wipe their feet. I have to when I've been outside, and I have to take my boots off when I've been gardening with Pop-Pop.'

Thia put her paw to her face to cover a small laugh, though Archie could see it in her eyes.

Archie smiled. 'Well, there you go! You do have a lovely ammonite to take home. That will remind you of your ammonite in the museum.'

They finished their food, and Thia asked, 'Where shall we go next?'

'Toy shop!' Isaac suggested. 'Please.'

Archie and Thia looked at each other, then both said, 'Okay.'

Outside Patties, Archie asked a passing stranger if the town had a toy shop, and was told there was one just a little way down the street. Isaac was eager to get there.

Glee was a pretty little toy shop, with a window full of entertaining board games. The three of them entered the shop, which felt a lot smaller than the outside, because there were mountains of toys and games everywhere. The shop owner, a marten greeted them, then asked if there was anything she could help them find. Archie told her they were just browsing for the time being and would let her know if they needed help. Isaac looked at sail boats, building blocks, cuddly toys, and board games. He spotted a pair of red roller skates.

'Uncle Archie, I want to buy *those*.'

'I am not sure your mummy would approve,' Archie said.

'She will.' Isaac said with his adorable toothy grin.

'What about a fun card game?' Thia asked. This one is called Zoomology. It says it's a fast-paced card game for all ages.'

Isaac looked at the cards, thought about them, but he could hear the roller skates calling his name. 'I want to buy the roller skates,' Isaac firmly told Archie and Thia.

'You'll need someone to teach you how to skate,' Thia told the enthusiastic pup.

Isaac picked up the red skates and handed them to the shop owner. 'Anything else?' she asked.

Isaac looked around the shop, and his eyes fell on a counting toy. 'Person will like this.'

Archie handed Isaac his five aurum note.

'Do I have enough money?' Isaac asked the shop owner.

'Yes, you do, and you will get some change.' The shop owner gift-wrapped the counting toy in very pretty paper, placed the roller skates in a bag, with the gift on top, and handed it to Isaac. She then gave him his change.

'Thank you, missus.' Isaac said, then waved as he followed Archie and Thia to the door. Sitting next to the shop door was a box with a sign attached— Please help feed hungry children. 'Uncle Archie, why are the children hungry?'

'They do not have as much as we do, and their

mummies and daddies cannot afford to feed them,' Archie said sadly.

'That's sad,' a pain-faced Isaac said. He took his change out of his pocket and dropped the lot in the box.

Archie and Thia followed the youngster's lead, putting money in the box. They then left the shop.

'Uncle Archie, can we help the hungry children, please?'

'We help everyone in Mereland when we know they need help,' Archie replied.

Isaac got into the back of the car, and they drove to the hotel. Isaac was silent the entire time.

When they got out of the car, Isaac had forgotten to take his ammonite, as he was deep in thought. Archie collected the fossil, and escorted Isaac to the Staff's suite. Ermgarde opened the door as they approached.

'Hello Sweet Pea. Did you have a nice time?'

'Yes, Mummy. Doctor Fossil is cleaning my ammonite,' the pup replied.

'Cleaning it?' Ermgarde asked.

'Yes, Ermgarde. Cleaning and preparing it for display,' Archie informed her.

'That makes sense. It's spent its life in the sand. Sweet Pea, you look sad, what's wrong?'

'Mummy, children are hungry,' he said painfully.

'Do you need afternoon tea?' Ermgarde asked, not understanding Isaac's statement. She looked at Archie and Thia. 'Which children, Sweet Pea?'

'Children,' Isaac replied.

Thia said, 'We saw a collection box for hungry

children, and Isaac put his change from his spending money in it.'

'That was most kind of you,' Ermgarde told her son.

'Mummy, can we take care of the hungry children?'

'I'm not sure where they are,' Ermgarde said to the sad-looking pup before her.

'Pleeease, Mummy.'

Archie said, 'I will attempt to find out who is organising the efforts to help hungry children, and will let you know, Ermgarde.'

'Thank you, Uncle Archie.'

Isaac brightened a little. 'Doctor Fossil gave me an ammonite!' Isaac informed his mother.

'Smaller than his one. Much easier to keep at home,' Archie said, as he handed the fossil to Ermgarde.

'That is good,' said a relieved Ermgarde. 'What else did you do?'

'We had fish burgers.'

'We went to a burger bar, Ermgarde,' Thia told her.

'Was it nice, Sweet Pea?'

Isaac nodded, Archie and Thia frowned and shook their heads. 'It was very brightly decorated, and plays *exceptionally* loud music,' Archie stated.

'If you like that sort of thing, it's nice, I guess,' Thia added.

'Then we went to the toy shop!' squealed Isaac. 'I bought roller skates!' He took them out of the bag to show his mother.

'Roller skates? Oh my! You'll need to learn how to skate before you use them on your own.'

'Yes, Mummy. I also bought Person a toy.' Isaac handed Ermgarde the gift-wrapped box.

'How thoughtful, and so beautifully wrapped. Charlotte is sleeping. We'll give it to her later. Did you choose the gift, Thia?'

'Isaac chose it himself.'

'We will see you later,' Archie said.

'Thank you, Uncle Archie, Auntie Thia.' Isaac said, then gave them both a kiss.

'Thank you.' Ermgarde called out, as Archie and Thia strolled to their suite.

The only way to get to Lissof Isle was by boat, so that morning, Lionel and Heather set off for a small dock, where they met two badgers, a male and a female, who too were making the trip. They greeted each other genially and found out that the badgers were also on holiday in Trebmal Bay.

The skipper, an avocet, soon arrived. He was dressed in navy trousers, a navy and white striped shirt, and a *very* off-white cap. He nodded a greeting as the two couples boarded the vessel. *Evidently, a person of very few words*, Lionel thought. After a relatively short journey, they reached the island, where they stepped off the boat onto a small dock near a beach.

The four tourists gasped when they got their first glimpse of the isle. It was stunning. There was a mountain in the middle, lush green trees and foliage, and the most beautiful white sandy beach.

'Does anyone live here?' Lionel asked the skipper.

'No. Nobody 'as ever lived 'ere,' the skipper said in a clipped tone. 'You go wander. I'll be waitin' 'ere.

I 'ave my book.' He waved his book airily.

'Oh, you like Salix Grouse?' Lionel asked.

'He's new to me. I met him in the town, and we got chattin'.' the skipper replied.

'He lives in town?' Heather asked.

'No, he's stayin' in the hotel.'

'We're staying in the hotel, we'll keep an eye out for him,' Lionel said.

'We'll let you get back to your book,' Heather said, as she tugged on Lionel's sleeve. She realised that the skipper was not really in the mood for chatting. Lionel and Heather strolled the entire island via the beach and stopped for a small picnic they had packed. When they made their way back to the boat, the other couple had not yet returned.

Lionel had an idea. 'Skipper, do you do private trips to the island?'

'I can do. Why do you ask?'

'I'd like to bring my family back here.'

'When?' the skipper asked.

'Tomorrow, possibly,' Lionel replied, then scratched his head.

'Give me a call,' the skipper said, handing Lionel a card with his phone number.

'Will do! Thank you. I'll check with the family when we get back, and let you know.'

The badger couple returned, and the five of them made the short journey back across to Trebmal Bay.

That evening, Charles and Elli took a drive to the town and had a romantic dinner in a very pleasant restaurant called, Sea Spray. Archie and Thia dined in their suite, and Lionel and Heather joined Ermgarde, Rupert, and the pups for dinner in the courtyard, where Isaac told them all about his day. In turn, Heather and Lionel told the Staffs about the day on Lissof Isle.

'Granddad, that island sounds idyllic!' Ermgarde said. It would be nice to go, but I'm not sure about Charlotte.'

'They do have a crèche here, Erm,' Rupert said. 'I noticed a sign for it.'

'In that case, we will go with you, Granddad,' Ermgarde said.

'We'll go ask the others,' Lionel said.

When Charles and Elli had returned from their meal, Elli decided to take a bath, put on a nightgown, and lounge on the sofa. They were both relaxing, reading their books when there was a knock on the door. Charles answered it. 'Dad, Heather! Come on in.'

'Hello, Petal,' Lionel said as he entered.

'Hello, Darling Girl,' Heather said.

'Take a seat,' Charles offered. 'Would you like a drink?'

'Only if you're having one,' Lionel replied.

'Sorry about the nightgown,' Elli said, a little embarrassed.

'Petal, you're in your own suite. You wear whatever
you want,' Lionel said, which made Elli smile.

'Thank you, Daddy. I always seem to be tired recently.'

'Darling Girl, you're bound to. You're growing a

pup. Besides, your hormones will be all over the place,' Heather said, as she patted Elli on the paw.

'That's true, Ell,' Charles agreed, as he poured three blackcurrant meads and one lemonade, then served the drinks.

'How was your day, folks?' Charles asked.

'Did you have a good time on Lissof Isle?' Elli asked.

'We did. It is an absolutely gorgeous island,' Heather said. 'The boat trip isn't that long, either.'

'At the moment, I couldn't imagine taking a boat trip,' Elli said shuddering.

'We were going to ask you if you wanted to join us tomorrow on a trip with the family, but, you've pretty much answered that, Petal. We just asked Erm and Rupe if they want to go with us. They're taking Isaac, but Charlotte will be looked after in the crèche,' Lionel said.

'We can look after Charlotte if Ermgarde wants to leave her with us,' Elli offered.

'We can let Erm know. I'm sure she'd prefer her to be with you than in a crèche,' Lionel said.

'What time are you hoping to go tomorrow?' Charles asked.

'Around nine,' Lionel and Heather said at the same time.

'We'll be here! Just get LP to drop Charlotte off when she wants to,' Charles said.

'Have you asked Archie and Thia if they want to go?' Elli asked.

'Not yet,' Heather said. 'They're our next stop.'

'Call them. The phone's behind you, Dad.'

Lionel called Ermgarde first, and she was sad

that Elli and Charles would not be joining them, but glad that Charlotte could spend time with them. He then called Archie and Thia.

'So, what have you done today?' Heather asked Charles and Elli, whilst Lionel was on the phone.

'We stayed here, swam, walked on the beach, then had dinner at a lovely restaurant called Sea Spray. A very romantic place,' Charles answered.

'You and Daddy should go there,' Elli suggested with a nod. 'It was quite elegant, and the food was delicious.'

Lionel returned from his phone calls, and Heather told him about the restaurant. 'We could go there tomorrow night, if we're back early enough,' Lionel suggested to Heather.

They finished their drinks, then Lionel said, 'Well, gorgeous people, we'll love you, and leave you. Night-night. I love you.'

'Night-night, darlings,' Heather said.

'Night-night,' Charles and Elli said as they stood at the door and waved.

BOATS AND BUCKETS

Charles and Elli were just finishing a breakfast of tea and toast, when Ermgarde knocked on the door. Charles answered it, and helped Ermgarde with the pile of things she was holding, apparently all items a toddler would need for the day. Elli took Charlotte.

'My goodness!' Charles exclaimed. 'That's a lot of stuff, LP.'

'Get used to it, Uncle Squish.'

'Hello, little one,' Elli said to Charlotte.

'Hiya Squishy,' Charlotte said.

Elli kissed the pup, 'You are clever,' Elli said, then tickled the little one.

Charlotte giggled, and repeated, 'Hiya Squishy.'

'Oh! She calls herself Lotti, so, we've taken to calling her it, too.'

'Will you be alright taking care of her, Uncle Squish?'

Charles gestured to Elli, who was now sitting on the floor reading to Charlotte. 'We'll be fine.'

'Everything you need is in that bag,' Ermgarde said, pointing to the holdall she had brought with her.

'I'm sure it's more than we need, LP.'

'She'll eat most things, so you *shouldn't* have any trouble with food,' Ermgarde said anxiously.

'LP, stop worrying. We've looked after her before,' Charles reminded her. 'Just enjoy yourselves.' As Charles had just finished what he was saying, Lionel, Rupert, and Isaac appeared at the door.

'Good morning, people! Ready for the off, Erm?' Lionel asked brightly.

'Yes, Granddad. Thank you, Uncle Squish, Auntie Squish. See you later!'

Isaac was extremely excited to be going on a boat. 'Pop-Pop, will we be going a long way on the boat?' he asked Lionel as they waited at the dock for the skipper.

'Do you see that island over there, across the water?' Lionel asked the pup.

Isaac nodded.

'That's Lissof Isle, and that's where we're going.'

'The skipper is here, dear,' Heather told Lionel.

'Do you have your bucket and spade, Sweet Pea?' Ermgarde checked.

'Yes, Mummy. Are we having a picnic?'

'Yes, later,' Rupert answered.

They all boarded the boat and departed; Archie held Thia's paw the entire journey. Isaac loved every second of being on the boat. Of course, he had been on Rémy's river bus, which went up and down the Cress River, but nothing as big as the boat they were on.

The craft bumped gently against the dock, and the skipper and Lionel helped Heather and Ermgarde onto the beach, whilst Archie held Thia's paw to guide her off the boat. Lionel and Heather suggested making a sort of base not far from the boat, so they could go their own way if they wished. Lionel chose a spot near a sandy cliff face to lay down a blanket, then Rupert placed the large picnic basket on top.

'Shall we explore, Sweet Pea?' Ermgarde asked Isaac.

'I want to stay here with Pop-Pop and Gran-Gran,' Isaac said, clutching his bucket and spade.

'Is that okay with you both?' Ermgarde asked.

'Of course! You four go wander,' Lionel told the two couples.

Ermgarde, Rupert, Archie, and Thia walked up the beach, whilst Isaac positioned himself next to the cliff face, and with his little spade started digging.

'What are you digging for, Isaac?' Heather asked. 'You going to make sandcastles?'

'No, Gran-Gran. I'm digging for ammonites!' said the very determined young pup.

'I do hope you find some,' she responded.

Heather lay against Lionel and relaxed. They watched the pup dig and dig, but not a single ammonite was found. About twenty minutes later, a great big clump of sand fell off the cliff face and missed Isaac by a hair. Lionel leapt forward and grabbed the pup just in time, as more sand fell.

'Oh my!' Heather cried. 'What's that?' It looked as though a face was grinning at her.

Lionel looked closely, as did Isaac.

'Pop-Pop, it's a *dinosaur*!'

'I think you're right, my boy!'

'What make is it?' Isaac asked.

'I think we'd have to ask someone who knows, and that isn't me,' Lionel admitted.

'Doctor Fossil will know,' Isaac said firmly.

'Doctor Fossil? Who is that?' Heather asked.

'Gran-Gran, he's the museum man. He's a fossil scientist, and he's looking after my ammonite.'

'Oh!' Heather said. 'He's a palaeontologist.'

'Yes!' Isaac said, very impressed by Heather knowing what a fossil scientist was called.

'He's a vertribit palaeontologist, Gran-Gran.'

'A *vertebrate* palaeontologist,' Heather corrected.

Archie and Thia approached.

'Uncle Archie, where's Mummy and Daddy?' Isaac asked.

'They are still exploring. They will be back in a while,' Archie replied.

'Uncle Archie, I found a dinosaur,' Isaac said.

Archie looked at the pup sceptically.

'He did find a dinosaur, Archie. Look!' Lionel said, pointing to the cliff face.

Archie leant forward to take a closer look. 'Oh my! That most certainly does look like a dinosaur. Not that I am any sort of expert.'

'We should take my dinosaur to Doctor Fossil,' Isaac said to his great-grandfather.

'I think Doctor Lapin should be brought here,' Archie suggested to Isaac. 'I do not think the dinosaur should be moved, Isaac. Doctor Lapin is the best person to remove it. I will go get him and bring him here.'

'I'll go with you, hon,' Thia said.

'Thank you, Archie,' Lionel said. 'We'll stay right here.'

After asking the skipper to take them back to the mainland, Archie and Thia left. All Lionel, Heather, and Isaac could do was wait, and have a picnic, but mostly wait.

Charles and Elli took Charlotte to the park, then returned to the hotel for a swim. They had lunch in the courtyard, then they all took a nap. It was not only Charlotte that was tired out.

Archie and Thia arrived at the museum and went in search of Doctor Anning Lapin. They were told he was in the back preparing an ammonite, and was escorted to the preparation room.

'Good morning, Doctor Lapin,' Archie said.

'Mr Erinac. Don't tell me you have another ammonite,' Anning Lapin said with a light laugh.

'No, Doctor. Isaac has found a dinosaur,' Archie stated with a straight face.

'A dinosaur? Surely not! What young children think are dinosaurs are quite often not dinosaurs,' Lapin said, and he continued working on Isaac's ammonite.

'I assure you, Doctor Lapin, it *is* a dinosaur. Isaac, as you well know, is not your usual seven year old. If you could come with us, we will take you to where it is.'

'Give me a few minutes. I need to speak to my assistant, and collect some items.'

'We will meet you outside at our vehicle,' Archie said.

Anning Lapin met Archie and Thia at the car. He looked as though he was going on expedition. Archie helped him haul his equipment into the vehicle, and they headed for the dock.

'Where are we going to?' Lapin asked. 'Are you taking me to Lissof Isle?'

'Yes, Doctor. That is where Isaac is.'

'You left a seven year old on an island alone?' a very shocked Lapin blurted out.

'Of course not. His mother, father, and great-grandparents are with him,' Thia said, slightly affronted, that he would believe they would do such a thing.

They boarded the boat, the skipper helping with the equipment. Archie slipped the skipper a bit of extra cash. 'Thank you, skipper!'

As soon as they landed at Lissof Isle beach, Isaac ran over. 'Hello, Doctor Fossil!'

'Hello, Isaac,' Lapin replied.

'I found a dinosaur!'

'So I believe. Mr Erinac said you did.'

'That's Uncle Archie and Auntie Thia,' Isaac said smiling.

'So, where is this dinosaur of yours?' Lapin asked, in at tone that wreaked of placation.

'Near Pop-Pop and Gran-Gran. They've been looking after it.'

Anning Lapin strode over to the cliff face, and Lionel and Heather were introduced to the palaeontologist. Isaac pointed at the section of cliff that he had collapsed, then turned to Anning Lapin, who was speechless.

'What's wrong, Doctor Lapin?' Lionel asked.

'I have never seen anything like this in this area. *Bloody hell*!' Lapin exclaimed, and immediately said, 'I do apologise for that outburst.'

'What dinosaur is it?' Archie asked.

'At first look, it appears to be a stegosaur,' Lapin said, as he stepped forward to inspect the specimen a little more closely.

Isaac was jumping up and down. 'I feel like doing the same thing, young Isaac,' Anning said. Just then, Ermgarde and Rupert joined the group.

'What's wrong?' Rupert asked.

'Nothing, Rupert,' Archie stated. 'Young Isaac found a dinosaur skeleton. Well, its skull, so far.'

'You did, Sweet Pea?' Ermgarde asked her extremely excited son.

'Yes, Mummy. I dug it out.'

'Well done!' Ermgarde and Rupert said at once.

'How long will it take to remove?' Lionel asked.

'Depends if it is just the skull or the whole skeleton. If you give me your contact information, I will keep you informed.' The doctor then started to erect a tent.

'You're staying here, Doctor?' Archie asked.

'Yes, of course! I would never leave the specimen exposed and unprotected.'

'Do you need anything?' Thia asked him.

'No, I have everything I need. Though, I will need the skipper to return in a day or two to check to see if I need to go back to the mainland.'

Archie said he would arrange that.

'Thank you, Mr Erinac. I should get to work, whilst I have light.' The doctor thanked Isaac and the Watermere party. As they felt they would be in the way, they packed their things. Archie, as good as his word, had made sure the skipper would return to check on Anning Lapin. He also gave the skipper some money, and asked if he would not mind delivering food and water to the doctor. The skipper said he was more than happy to oblige. They boarded the boat, and puttered their way back to the mainland.

The next few days were spent on the beach, by the pool, shopping, and dining as a family. Isaac was of course, eager to know how his ammonite and dinosaur were. He had to make one last visit to the museum, and everyone wanted to go see his ammonite on display. When the whole family arrived at the museum, they were greeted by Anning Lapin's assistant (a weasel).

'Doctor Lapin would have met you, but he is very busy preparing the skeleton of the stegosaur you found,' the assistant told Isaac and his family. She then escorted them to a room where Isaac's ammonite was in pride of place in a glass case all on its own. Inside the case sitting next to the fossil was a card, it stated:

Ammonite - undescribed genus and species

Trebmal Bay - Cretaceous

Found by
Isaac Staff (aged 7)

'Excuse me, but what does undescribed genus and species mean?' Elli asked the assistant. 'Sorry, if that's a stupid question.'

'Not a stupid question at all, madam,' the weasel replied politely. 'It means that it is a new kind of ammonite, and a paper is going to be written, where it will be given a new scientific name. Until then, we say it is undescribed.'

'Thank you,' Elli said.

Isaac looked puzzled.

'Sweet Pea, it's like when we were waiting for our new person to arrive, we didn't know what her name was going to be until she got here. Then we named her Charlotte,' Ermgarde answered, noticing her son's bemusement.

Isaac was happy with that answer, so the family looked at his ammonite a while longer, then wandered around the museum.

SHATTERED

The morning they were to return to Mereland, everyone was up early. The cars were loaded, and off they went. Isaac spent the entire journey reading, the ammonite Anning Lapin had given him on the seat next to him, whilst Charlotte was playing with the counting toy Isaac had purchased for her.

When they pulled up on The Holt's driveway, Charles said he would get the luggage, if Elli would unlock the door. The Staffs thanked Charles and then headed to The Lodge.

'Thanks, my boy, for a lovely break,' Lionel said.

'Yes, thank you, Charles,' Heather echoed, then gave him a hug.

'Do you need a paw with the luggage, Dad?' Charles asked.

'No thanks, Son. We're alright. See you later!' Lionel said, then he and Heather made their way down the lawn to The Cottage.

Charles and Archie gathered the luggage and entered The House, where they found Elli on the phone in the hall. Archie and Thia said they would

206

take the luggage upstairs. Charles thanked them, then made his way to the kitchen to make a pot of tea. Elli entered the room, and said, 'That was Doctor Tyto. I thought I should get checked out by him.'

Charles turned around so suddenly, he knocked a cup off the table, which dropped onto the floor and shattered.

Elli flinched, and cried, '*Oh no!*'

'Are you alright, Ell? Did it cut you? What's wrong?' Charles asked, a little panicked.

Elli was about to bend down and gather the broken pieces of china.

'No, don't Ell, I'll get it. Tell me what's wrong. Why are you getting checked out by Albie?'

'Sweetie, you are a plant pot. If you cast your mind back just a little way, you will remember that I'm *pregnant*. Albie is my general practitioner, and I thought it would be wise to get checked out by him.'

'Ell, I thought something was wrong,' a very relieved Charles said. He gave her a kiss, then grabbed a dustpan and brush, and swept up the broken pieces of crockery.

Archie walked in, and on seeing the contents of the dustpan, asked, 'Temper tantrum or clumsiness?'

'Clumsiness,' Charles answered.

'I will finish the tea, if you and your lovely wife would like to rest.'

'I'm okay, Arch. I'm not too sure about Ell,' Charles replied.

'Actually, I'm fine, Sweetie.'

'Ell, have you decided what you're going to do about work? You going back to three days a week?'

'Depends on how I feel, and whether I can fit behind the counter,' Elli said rubbing her belly.

'Well, I can take over if you need me to. I can't design anything, but I can sell stuff,' Charles offered.

'Yes, H, you did a good job when you last stood behind the counter.'

Charles smiled proudly.

'I still maintain it was because everyone wanted to see you work,' Archie said, as he put the teapot on the tray.

'I've decided I'm going to change the name of my shop,' Elli announced.

'What to?' Charles and Archie asked.

'It's a surprise, but I will need Ermgarde's help with the signage.'

'Okay, but I'll just ask LP what it's going to be called,' Charles said, then pulled tongues at Elli.

'*She's not going to tell you,*' Elli sang. 'Not if I ask her not to.'

'That's true. LP is good like that,' Charles stated resignedly.

'The tea is ready,' Archie said. 'Library or drawing room?'

'I'll take it, Archie,' Elli offered.

'If you insist,' Archie said, as he stood aside to let Elli take the tray. She started walking across the hall towards the drawing room when she slipped and fell. The tray and its contents flew in the air and came crashing to the floor, exploding extremely hot tea everywhere. Charles ran to Elli, who was slumped on the floor sobbing. 'Ell, Ell, are you alright? Are you hurt?' Charles asked as he attempted to check his wife for cuts and scalds.

Archie, seeing Charles was tending to Elli, started the job of removing broken bits of tea service. He then got to work mopping the floor.

Elli could not stop sobbing. Charles held her close. 'Ell, Ell, what's wrong? Are you and the pup okay?' Elli could not answer as she was crying so much.

Archie asked Charles if he needed any help, to which, Charles merely gave him a gesture and a look that said, *Call Albie Tyto*. Charles picked up a still sobbing Elli, carried her to their bedroom, and placed her on the bed. Elli held onto Charles and sobbed into his shoulder. 'Ell, my love. It's only some crockery. I didn't like it much. You can choose something new.' As soon as Charles spoke, he got the feeling, this was not about the tea service. Elli continued to sob, and no matter what Charles did or said, he could not console her. All he could do was hold her close.

A few minutes later, Archie tapped on the bedroom door and entered, Doctor Albie Tyto following.

'Hello there!' Albie said. Charles returned the greeting.

'Ell, Albie's here to check you and the pup out,' Charles said, and Elli reluctantly released her hold on him. She was still sobbing buckets.

Albie made a slight gesture telling Charles and Archie to leave the room.

'I'll just be outside, Ell,' Charles said, then he and

Archie left the room, closing the door behind them.

'Elli, I'm here to check on you and your pup,' Albie said very kindly. 'Let's start by taking a few slow, deep breaths. Let's try and slow your breathing down.' (Elli continued to sob.) 'Come on now, with me. One... two... three... deep breath,' Albie gently urged. Elli was now taking sharp gasps of breath between sobs. 'Elli,' Albie said quietly, but firmly. 'I need you to take *slow*, deep breaths. Gasping like that is going to make you light-headed and sick. It's not going to help your pup. Come on. One... two... three... deep breath,' he said soothingly. 'You can do it.' Elli inhaled deeply, then let it out slowly. 'That's good. Now another.' She stopped sobbing. 'Lovely!' Albie said as he handed her a tissue. 'Alright, alright. Now then, do you want to talk about what's upset you? Surely, it's not Charles' taste in swimming trunks,' Albie joked.

Elli gave a weak smile.

'Let's check you and pup out. If you want to tell me what's upset you, you can,' Albie said as he began to examine Elli for any injuries from her fall. 'Well, Elli Watermere, you're in one piece. Let's check on the wee one.' Albie checked. 'The pup is okay, and everything is as we would expect it to be.'

Elli sighed in relief, then took a deep breath. 'I feel so stupid, Doctor.'

'No need to feel stupid. You're pregnant, and you had a fall. It's normal to be frightened. You're carrying a very precious cargo,' Albie said with a warm smile.

'It's not that, Doctor,' Elli said, a little embarrassed.

'Okay. What was it? Do you want to tell me?'

Elli hesitated, then said, 'When the tea things smashed, it reminded me of my...'

'Incident?'

Elli nodded.

Albie patted her paw. 'It's normal to have things that trigger memories. Hopefully, with a bit of time, there'll be fewer triggers. It's only been a couple of months. You went through a lot. You almost died. That would traumatise the best of us.' Elli gave a little nod. Albie continued, 'You're not silly for feeling this way, and I would suggest you talk to Charles about it. He *absolutely* loves you to bits. We all know that! We were at your wedding,' Albie smiled. 'He'll understand, and won't think you silly, or weak. He'll think of you as nothing less than wonderful.'

Elli gave a weak smile.

'If you want to chat once a week, let me know. I think it would help. If you don't want to chat with me, at least chat with someone, as well as Charles. Perhaps a girlfriend,' Albie suggested.

Elli nodded, then said, 'I do need to talk about it, but I know it upset Charles so much when it happened, that I don't want to burden him.'

'Elli, married life is supporting each other in good times and bad. Don't block Charles out. I know it's a cliché, but a trouble shared, really is a trouble halved.'

'But he doesn't need my troubles,' Elli said.

'He may not need them, but he wants to help, and not knowing will make him feel helpless. To watch a loved one go through something is hard. To watch them go through something and not know what's wrong, is harder still. If you don't know, your mind goes to the worst possible place. It's just natural to do so.'

'I guess you're right, Doctor.'

'What exactly about the incident was your trigger, if it's alright to ask,' Albie asked carefully.

'The smash and fall. It's what happened when I was...'

'I get it. That's how you were injured?'

'Yes,' Elli replied.

'Then, your reaction today to the dishes smashing was completely understandable,' Albie said. 'I have an idea. I'll be back in a few minutes. You stay there.' He left the bedroom, spoke briefly with Archie and Charles, then returned to Elli. 'Okay, Mrs Watermere, let's go downstairs, have a cup of tea together, then... I will tell you my plan. Is that okay?'

Elli agreed, but was a little sceptical, though she did trust Albie.

Elli and Albie left the bedroom, rode down in the lift, then entered the drawing room, where Charles had set out a tea tray.

'Shall I be mum?' Albie asked.

'By all means,' Charles replied.

Albie poured three cups of tea, giving Elli the first.

Charles was sitting there, not sure whether or not he should ask what was wrong. On reflection, he decided it was up to Elli to tell him if she wanted to.

Albie broke the ice, 'Charles, mum and pup are

well. I think your pup is relaxing, probably doing a crossword.'

Charles smiled. 'That's good to know. Perhaps the pup can give me the answer to thirty across'

Elli smiled weakly.

They sat a few minutes in silence, then Elli said, 'Sweetie, I'm sorry.'

'What for, Ell?' Charles asked. 'You've done nothing wrong. As for the teapot and stuff, that can be replaced, you and the pup can't.'

Albie gave a little smile, then a slight nod, which meant, *Let her do the talking.*'

Charles took the hint, and held Elli's paw in silence.

All of a sudden, Albie said, 'Charles, do you mind if I use your telephone?' Albie did not need to make a call at all, he just wanted Charles and Elli to have time alone.

'Help yourself, Albie. It's in the hall.'

Albie left the drawing room, set himself down on the stairs, and waited.

In the drawing room, Elli turned to Charles and said, 'I'm sorry for getting so upset.' Even though Charles wanted to reassure Elli, he stayed quiet, because Elli was building up to telling him the real reason for the tears. 'When you smashed the cup, it made me jump,' Elli said. Charles simply nodded acknowledgement. 'But when the dishes smashed, and I fell, I had flashbacks.'

Charles had an anguished expression, and he squeezed her paw. 'I understand, Ell. I can't imagine how it feels, but I understand why you reacted the way you did.' He pulled her close to him. 'You're safe now, Ell.'

'Doctor Tyto said that I can talk to him about it, professionally that is. He also suggested talking to a girlfriend, but I'm not sure who to talk to. It's not that I can't talk to you about it, but I don't want our relationship to carry that burden. Does that make sense?'

Charles thought about what Elli had said for a beat or two, then answered, 'I understand, Ell. You know you *can* talk to me, but Albie has a point. As for who to talk to... how about Heather?'

'Why Aunt Heather?'

'One—she loves you to bits. Two—she was with you when you went missing. Sorry to bring that up, but I'm sure Heather was traumatized by the experience as well. I mean, when she got off the train, she blamed herself.'

'She did?' Elli asked, astounded by not knowing this. 'Poor Aunt Heather. It wasn't her fault.'

'I know, Ell. But perhaps she needs to talk about it, too.'

Elli nodded.

There was a tap on the door, and Albie entered. 'Elli, could you come with me, please? You too, Charles.'

Elli and Charles followed Albie across the hall to the front door. They exited the house onto the driveway, where Archie was standing with three large boxes.

'What's this for?' Elli asked.

'Therapy,' Albie replied.

Elli frowned with suspicion.

Archie opened the garage door.

'Has this got something to do with driving?' Elli asked Albie, still curious as to what was going to happen.

'Nothing to do with driving,' Albie responded with a little smile. 'Look in the garage.'

Elli peered into the garage. 'There's nothing there. Archie's car is on the drive,' Elli said, a puzzled look across her face.

'Put your hand in that box, and pull out what you find in it,' Albie instructed.

Elli did as she was asked. She was now completely confused, because what she had pulled out of the box was a dinner plate.

'Now, throw that plate at the back wall of the garage,' Albie instructed.

'*What*?' Elli exclaimed.

'You heard. Launch it at the far wall,' Albie reiterated.

Elli stood there holding the plate.

'Charles, you have a go,' Albie suggested.

Charles reached into the box, pulled out two plates and launched them as hard as he could at the back wall of the garage. *SMASH*! *SMASH*! Elli jumped when the plates made contact with the wall and exploded into hundreds of pieces. The look of disbelief that Charles actually threw them was written all over her face. 'Go for it, Ell. It feels great!' Charles urged. 'Arch, have a go!'

Elli looked on the verge of throwing the plate she was holding, so Charles and Archie stepped aside to give her a clear path. She threw the plate underarm, and the plate did not go too far, and broke into three pieces.

'Have another go, Elli,' Albie instructed her, handing her plate. 'Pull your arm right back over your head, and try to hit the back wall with that plate.'

Elli did as she was told. When Elli heard the loud smash, she jumped.

'Again, Ell,' Charles said. She hesitated. Charles handed a plate to Archie, who hurled it at the wall. *SMASH*! Charles then handed Elli one, and she threw it. *SMASH*! He handed her another, *SMASH*! He kept handing her them as soon as one had left her paw. *SMASH*! *SMASH*! When he had emptied one box, he opened the second one.

'Where did the plates come from?' Elli asked in between throws.

'I bought them,' Archie said.

'Oh, Archie, you didn't have to spend your money,' Elli said.

'It's okay, Elli. I put them on Charles' account,' Charles gave Elli a goofy grin, and Elli smiled.

'One more,' Elli said, and Charles handed her a plate. *SMASH*!

'Ooh, that was a good one, Ell!' Charles said. 'Wow! You have a good bowling arm. They should sign you up for the local cricket team.'

Elli chuckled, then turned to Albie. 'Thank you, but why did you get me to do it?'

'How did you feel when the first plate hit the wall?' Albie asked her.

'Scared, terrified, if truth be told. I felt lost,' Elli said.

'How do you feel now when you hear the smash?'

'It's just a noise,' Elli replied.

Albie smiled.

'Thank you, Doctor,' Elli said. 'Oh dear! I've smashed nearly all the plates.

Archie opened the boot of his car and showed Elli three more boxes inside it. 'We have plenty, Elli. If you ever feel like having a smashing time, we have more.'

'Just make sure Arch's car is out of the way first,' Charles said, winking at her.

Lionel and Heather came around the corner of The House. 'Is everything okay?' Lionel asked.

'Why, Dad?' Charles asked.

'We were sitting on the bench in the garden, and heard smashing,' Heather said.

'Hello, Albie,' Lionel said. He noticed a plate in Elli's paw. He looked in the garage, as the door was open. 'Heather, my dear, look at this!'

Heather took a look inside the garage.

'What's wrong with the plates?' Lionel asked.

'I didn't like the style of them,' Charles joked.

'No, Daddy. It was me smashing them. I needed to get something out of my system,' Elli answered. She put down the plate she was holding.

Lionel could tell Elli had been crying, because she sounded as though she had a head cold. Lionel stepped forward and hugged her. She held on tightly. 'We love you, Petal.' When they let go of each other, Heather wanted to hug Elli. As she did, she said, 'Darling Girl, Lionel is right, we love you.'

Elli whispered, 'Can we chat?'

Heather whispered back, 'Of course.' When they let go of each other, Heather said firmly, 'I think you boys should go inside, and make some lunch. I want to chat with my niece.'

'When you clean up that crockery, don't throw the bits away. I can use it in the bottom of my plant pots for drainage,' Lionel said.

'Don't worry, dear, we won't throw it away. You boys can clean it up later,' Heather smiled.

Albie said, he had to get back, and bade farewell to all. Elli thanked him again.

Charles led the way back into The House. Lionel followed his son to the library, as Archie went to the kitchen.

'Son, is everything alright with the pup? Albie was here,' Lionel asked with a furrowed brow.

'Ell had an accident earlier,' Charles stated.

'Oh no! Is she and the pup alright?' Lionel asked again.

'Yes, Dad. Albie said they're both fine.'

'That's good to know.'

'Ell slipped with a tea tray she insisted on carrying, and when she fell and the crockery smashed, it brought back...'

Lionel held up his paw to indicate, '*No need to say anything else. I know what you mean.*' Lionel scratched his head. 'So, Albie got her to smash plates to... what's the word?' Lionel asked.

'Desensitise her to the sound of smashing,' Charles replied.

'Yes.' Lionel responded. 'Did it help?'

'It did, but she may need another session. Albie told her to talk to a girlfriend,' Charles said.

'Ah! Hence them staying outside,' Lionel said astutely.

'Also, Heather went through the event on the train,' Charles said. He then answered his father's confused look. 'Heather was frantic when we met her at the train station, and she blamed herself for Ell going missing.'

'But it wasn't her fault,' Lionel stated.

'True, but... it may help both of them,' Charles commented with a shrug.

'I do hope so,' Lionel said, as he took the cup of tea

Archie, who had just walked in, had handed him.

Outside, Elli handed Heather a plate. 'Go on, Aunt Heather, throw it at that far wall,' Elli urged.

Heather did as she was asked, then turned to Elli. 'Darling Girl, what has upset you so much, it makes you want to smash crockery? Surely Charles isn't the reason you're smashing plates.'

'No, Aunt Heather. He's perfectly wonderful. It's just that earlier, I smashed a tea service,' Elli said, easing into the main reason.

'We all have little accidents, Darling Girl.'

'But, I slipped and fell,' Elli added.

'Oh dear! Are you and pup alright?' Heather asked with concern.

'Yes, we're fine. That's why Doctor Tyto was here. He was checking us out.'

'Good,' Heather said, most relieved.

'The problem was, I could not stop crying after it happened,' Elli confessed.

CHAPTER 23

Heather hugged Elli again. 'Darling Girl, you were bound to be shaken up. You're pregnant, and a fall...well...'

'No, Aunt Heather, it was the smashing of the crockery that gave me flashbacks of when I was... was... taken from the train' Elli said with great effort.

'How awful for you,' Heather said.

'Charles told me, that when it happened, you blamed yourself,' Elli said in a small voice.

'I did. I do. Darling Girl, if I had not wanted to leave that morning, you would not have been taken,' Heather said, her voice cracking a little.

Elli hugged her. 'Oh, Aunt Heather. No. Absolutely not. It wasn't your fault at all. I went for my dress fitting and lunch with...' She froze mid-sentence.

'Darling Girl, what's wrong?' Heather asked, because Elli was standing there with a fixed expression. 'Darling Girl, what's wrong?'

'I went to lunch with Crosby. There were two birds sitting at the table next to us, and one got really angry because Cros bumped into him.'

'Yes. I remember you mentioning them,' Heather said, not knowing where Elli was going with her thought.

'They were the ones who abducted me!' Elli said, the full realisation hitting her.

'Really?' Heather asked, astounded.

'Yes. They realised who I was, because they were eavesdropping. It must have been pure chance they found me. I guess they would have gone after Charles if they hadn't taken me.'

220

'I'm sure you're probably right, my dear.'

'Now, I'm glad they took me. Heaven knows what they would have done to Charles,' Elli said, looking quite faint.

'Darling Girl, you are both here, safe and sound. Don't torture yourself with those thoughts. It's over,' Heather said, then hugged Elli again.

Elli gave a watery smile, then said, 'So, you see, Aunt Heather, it really wasn't your fault. The fact you were there, helped Charles and the others know where I went missing.'

'My! That's exactly what your darling husband said.
Was it his idea to smash the plates?'

'No. It was Doctor Tyto who suggested it. He thought the smashing sound was the trigger that sent me back to being abducted, along with slipping on the floor, but mostly the smashing for some reason.'

Heather handed Elli a plate, and she pitched it at the garage wall. *SMASH*! 'You have a go, Aunt Heather!' Heather took a plate and launched it, *SMASH*! They threw a few more, *SMASH*! *SMASH*! Then started throwing them together. As they threw them, Heather asked, 'Do your parents know about your abduction?'

'No. They wouldn't care,' Elli said flatly.

Heather shook her head sadly. 'It is nice to have your mum around when you're going through things. Especially pregnancy,' Heather said, wistfully.

Elli shrugged. 'I wouldn't know. I only had my

grandma for a while,' Elli said.

'How old were you when she died?' Heather asked.

'Twelve,' Elli said.

'Darling Girl! If I had known you then, I would have adopted you,' Heather said sincerely. 'I'll adopt you now!' she exclaimed.

'I'm a bit too old now,' Elli chuckled. 'But... can I call...'

'Yes, Darling Girl. I would be honoured,' Heather said, then kissed Elli's cheek.

Elli hugged Heather as though she would never let go. 'Thank you, Mummy.'

A tear rolled down Heather's cheek. 'Oh, Darling Girl, I am so proud of you! Do you want to go inside The House? I think we could both do with a cup of tea. Throwing those plates is thirsty work.'

They both laughed, then entered The House arm-in-arm.

As they entered via the front door, Charles called out, '*Ell, we're in the library*!'

Heather and Elli smiled at each other then strode into the library, grins on their faces.

'You two look happy,' Lionel stated. 'You've been up to something!'

Elli and Heather giggled.

'We could hear you smashing plates,' Charles said.

'Yes, and you boys should clean the mess up later, and throw it all in the bin,' Heather instructed.

'NO!' Lionel exclaimed.

Heather looked at him fiercely.

'I meant, no, don't throw it in the bin.' Lionel

said. 'I can use it for the bottom of my plant pots for drainage.'

Elli and Heather giggled again.

Charles' heart lifted. To see Elli not only smiling, but giggling was a real tonic.

Heather announced, in a most un-Heatherlike manner, 'IT'S A GIRL!'

The three males all looked puzzled.

'Meet my daughter, Elli! I just adopted her!'

Charles, Lionel, and Archie's faces showed nothing but pure joy.

'CONGRATULATIONS!' they cheered collectively.

Heather and Elli sat themselves down on a sofa together.

'I am delighted for you both,' Archie said.

'How will it be explained in the village?' Lionel asked.

Archie cleared his throat. 'If I may make a suggestion. First and foremost, it really is nobody's business but your own. *If* you want to explain it to anyone, I see two possible explanations.' All eyes and ears were on Archie. 'The first is, you already call Dad, Daddy, and as Heather is his ladyfriend, she is your mother-in-law of sorts, therefore, it would not be unusual to call her Mummy.' Everyone nodded. 'The second explanation, though a little more complicated, could be, that you used to call Heather Mummy, before you arrived in Mereland, because she has always been more mother than an aunt. You merely called her Aunt Heather at first, so as not to confuse the issue, but since she now lives here, you wanted to give her back her rightful title, as it were.'

'I like *that* idea!' Elli said, then got up and kissed Archie on the cheek. 'You are ever so smart, Archie.' Elli turned to Heather, and asked, 'What do you think, Mummy?'

'Darling daughter, whatever makes you happy,' Heather replied. 'OH!' Heather bleated. 'I just realised! I'm going to be a grandma to your pup!' Heather squealed with delight.

'Yes, you will be,' Elli said, as Heather rubbed Elli's belly.

'Oh my!' Heather said as the tears started to flow. Elli started to sniffle.

'Please stop crying,' Lionel said. 'We'll all be crying in a minute.'

The ladies chuckled and dabbed their eyes with tissues Lionel handed them.

'I'm so happy for you, Ell,' Charles said with watery eyes and a great big smile.

'Anyone want a lemonade?' Lionel asked.

'I'll get them, Dad,' Archie said.

'It's okay, son, I'll do it,' Lionel insisted, then got up. Heather went to assist him. Lionel whispered something in Heather's ear, then kissed her on the cheek.

Charles went to sit next to Elli. 'Well, princess, how is our pup?'

'Princess? You've never called me that before,' Elli commented.

Heather interrupted, 'Darling Girl, if you are my daughter, technically, you *are* a princess.'

Elli chortled, 'I have a hard enough time with Duchess.'

'Don't worry, Ell, I'll only call you it at home,' Charles said, then kissed her.

'Charles, people would just think it was a term of endearment,' Heather said. 'Archie, where's Thia?'

'She is upstairs working on designs for the maternity range,' Archie answered. 'Thia wants them finished as soon as possible. She said she will head home tomorrow.'

'I'm sorry, Archie,' Elli said.

'Elli, Thia needs to go home tomorrow. She has been away from her business for weeks now. She will be back at the weekend. We have decided to see each other every weekend, alternating between Norchester and Mereland.'

'How lovely,' Elli said.

'Arch, why not take *every* weekend off?' Charles suggested. 'I mean, it can't be much fun for Thia to come here when you're working.'

'But...' Archie started.

'Arch, you can go to Norchester or spend it here, but take the time off,' Charles insisted firmly.

'But, with the pup on the way...'

'There's lots of willing helpers here for the two days you would be off,' Heather said.

'Yes, Archie. I have a daddy *and* a mummy now,' Elli said proudly. She smiled at Archie, and Charles knew the argument was done. Elli's smile charmed everyone.

'You look after that lovely lady of yours, Archie,' Lionel said, as he served the lemonade. 'Spend time with her. She's a keeper!' At that moment, there was a tap on the door, and Thia entered the room.

225

'Hello, my love!' Archie said brightly.

'Come on in, Thia my dear. Here, have this glass of lemonade,' Lionel said, as he handed her his untouched glass, then poured himself another.

Thia sat herself in an armchair next to Archie. They held paws.

'Is everything alright, my love?' Archie asked.

'Yes. I just finished the designs for the maternity range,' Thia stated. 'I'm going to head back tomorrow, and I should have some sample garments for Elli to try in a couple of weeks.'

'That fast?' Heather asked.

'Yes. I want Elli to have some to wear soon,' Thia replied.

'Thanks, Thia,' Elli said.

'Thia, my love, Charles has given me every weekend off,' Archie stated.

'That is fabulous! Thank you, Charles,' Thia said. 'I have a question,' she said sheepishly.

'What is it?' Everyone seemed to ask at the same time.

'I heard a lot of smashing earlier. Is that normal?'

'It was me relieving stress, Thia. Nothing to worry about,' Elli said. 'Oh, Thia. Just so you know, I've been adopted by Aunt Heather. She is now my mummy!'

'Elli, I am so happy for you. Both of you!' Thia corrected. Thia knew how desperately alone Elli had been growing up, and how much having a mother that loved her meant to her. 'Please forgive me if I am speaking out of turn, but whenever I've seen you together, you've always seemed more mother and daughter than aunt and niece.'

Elli and Heather smiled at each other, then at Thia. 'Thank you, Thia, my dear. What a lovely thing to say.'

Charles put his arm around his wife, who was chatting, laughing and joking. That was the Elli he knew and loved, but there was something else about her. She now seemed to glow. He thought, *Is it the pup? Or... is it having a mum and dad that love you? Probably both.*

Thia went home to Norchester the next day. Elli went back to work, where a customer or two gave her tummy a second glance but did not say anything. They probably thought it best not to ask a female 'When are you due?' just in case she was not pregnant. It would not be long before everyone in the village knew.

Elli stopped by Willow Tail Designs to chat with Ermgarde about the design and colour of the new signage for her shop, and of course, to tell her about Heather adopting her. Ermgarde thought it was a *wonderful* idea. She too thought the same as Thia, that Elli and Heather were like mother and daughter.

227

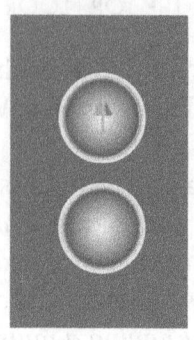

THE TOP FLOOR

One Friday evening a couple of weeks later, Archie greeted guests at the terrace doors — they included, Ermgarde, Rupert, Keen and Acanthus, Flynn and Willow, and Avril and Lyle Pica. When Archie directed the guests to the drawing room, they were greeted by Charles and Lionel. All asked why Elli, Heather, and Thia, were not present.

'They're upstairs. You'll see them soon,' was Charles' simple response, as he served them drinks.

The telephone rang and Archie answered it, then returned to the drawing room. 'This way, please, ladies and gentlemen.' He, Charles and Lionel escorted the guests to the top floor of The House.

'Ooh! I've never been up here!' Flynn said.

'Well, this is Arch's domain,' Charles said.

The guests noticed chairs set out on the very large landing outside Archie's penthouse.

'It looks like we're going to watch a show,' Ermgarde commented.

At that moment, Elli, who was dressed in a shapeless, black robe, stepped out of the door to

228

Archie's flat, and stood next to Charles.

Charles spoke. 'Well, family, as you know, it's been quite a year so far, what with everything that's happened.' There were some nods and mumbling. 'We got married, went on a cruise, and attended the coronation...'

'Really?' A couple of the guests asked.

'Uncle Squish and Auntie Squish *are* the Duke and Duchess of Mereland and Ashlowe,' Ermgarde responded, to stop any further questions.

Charles continued, 'We went on holiday for a couple of weeks, which didn't start off well, because Ell was sick.' There was a collective 'Aww' from the group. Elli took hold of Charles' paw, then said, 'But I saw a doctor, and he said, I was fine, and it was just morning sickness.' She paused, and when what she had said sank in, the roof of The House was almost blown off with the roar of congratulations. Everyone wanted to hug and kiss the parents-to-be.

'Thank you, thank you,' Charles said. 'But as LP suspected, you are here to watch something.' Charles gestured for them all to sit down. 'As some of you are aware, Arch's ladyfriend, Thia, is Thia Canire of Canire Couture. She and Ell have been friends for a long time, and she was the designer and creator of Ell's sensational wedding gown and the beautiful bridesmaids' dresses. Well, Thia has been *extremely* busy designing a new line of clothing, inspired by Ell. It's a maternity line, called Conception by Canire Couture. Thia has brought with her sample garments to show you, and they will be modelled by my gorgeous wife.'

229

Elli spoke. 'Thia would appreciate it, if you would be so kind as to make notes on those clipboards Daddy and Archie are handing out. Thia wants you to be honest. Don't write what you *think* she wants to hear, write what you really feel about the collection. Suggestions are welcome, but remember, other colours will be available. See you in a bit.' Elli then returned to Archie's penthouse.

'This is exciting!' Willow said as Heather stepped out of the flat, a clipboard in her paw.

'Good evening, all. I was asked by Thia to be your host for this little show, and I will be telling you a bit about each garment.' There was a tap on the flat door. 'That is to tell me, that our model is ready to step out in the first garment.' The door opened, and Heather said, 'Elli is wearing a pair of navy, linen trousers, with released pressure over the tummy, a hot pink, silk blouse, which has a tie back, enabling the wearer to let it out or cinch it in, depending on the stage of the pregnancy.' The guests wrote notes on their clipboards.

Elli walked around a little, turning here and there in front of the guests, then returned to the flat.

Heather heard another tap, then Elli again stepped out. Heather continued, 'Elli is wearing a turquoise, light silk, summer dress with wrap over top, and once again, a tie at the back.'

Elli stepped in and out of the flat a few more times. It took Elli a little while to get ready for the last garment, so Heather told the group, 'Thia will also be doing a range of intimate apparel and pretty swimwear, all stylish, and beautiful. All are specifically designed for pregnant ladies. Elli will notbe modelling those.'

When the door opened and Elli stepped out, there were gasps, and Lyle Pica whistled, then shouted, 'You look gorgeous, Duchess!'

'Lyle, I couldn't have put it better myself!' Charles agreed.

When the chatter died down, Heather said, 'Elli is wearing a sensational Canire Couture evening gown in black sparkles. It shimmers as the wearer moves. This garment has a secret, because it has hidden cinch ties, which means it can be worn through all stages of pregnancy, and afterwards. Ladies, it's also good if you overeat, just let it out a little.'

Lionel said, 'I need a pair of trousers with a waistband like that!'

Everyone laughed, and Elli smiled when Lionel winked at her.

When Elli had finished showing the gown, she stood there, and Thia joined her. Everyone gave Thia a round of applause. 'Thank you, all. That's it for our little show. I would like to thank Elli, my stunning model, and Heather for hosting.'

Everyone stood up, congratulated Charles and Elli, then mingled, chatting about the garments. Some were still filling in their comments on their clipboards.

Charles kissed Elli. 'Princess, you look stunning,' he said. Ermgarde heard, and said, 'You do, Auntie Squish. You should buy that one, and go somewhere special for the evening.'

'You're right, Ermgarde,' Willow commented.

'There was nothing like this when I was having Olive.'

As Charles wandered off to speak to Lionel, and let the ladies talk. Acanthus asked, 'So, what are the undies like?'

'*Beautiful*!' Heather replied.

'No big bloomers,' Thia said— The ladies all laughed. 'They're all silk and lace,' Thia added.

Avril Pica came over, and said, 'I am sorry, Elli, Thia, but we have to go. I have a friend calling over. Thank you for including us.' Avril and Lyle said their goodbyes, and Archie escorted them all the way through the side gates to the High Street, then returned.

Elli cleared her throat, then said, 'People, you know that my biological parents did not come to our wedding.' Everyone nodded. 'Well, the reason is because, frankly, they never thought or think much of me.'

'How awful!' Flynn and Willow said together.

Elli pushed on, 'I had my grandparents, which was enough for me, but I was twelve when my gran died.'

The guests looked pained.

Elli continued, 'I'm not telling you this for you to feel sorry for me. Trust me, I am getting to the point.' Heather took hold of Elli's paw. 'Growing up, I really didn't know how much families loved each other until I met you all,' she said, a catch in her throat when she looked at Charles and Lionel. Heather squeezed Elli's paw, then took over, 'I adore this darling girl. If I had known her years ago, I would have adopted her.'

'Aww!' Ermgarde and Willow said.

Elli sniffed, then said, 'From now on, you will hear me call this wonderful lady Mummy. If anyone asks you why I call her Mummy, tell them that she has been more mum than aunt, and is the mum I never had.'

'That's so lovely!' Willow said through tears. 'I know what it's like to have parents that are...' Willow left her sentence hanging in the air, but everyone knew what she meant.

'So, when Elli and Charles' pup is born, you'll be a *granny*!' Acanthus said to Heather.

'*Yes*!' Heather said, 'Though, I am already Gran-Gran to Ermgarde and Rupert's two darling pups.'

Rupert said, 'Lotti calls Heather, Gan-Gan.'

'Aww,' Acanthus cooed. 'I've heard her say "Where's Gan-Gan". Now I know what it means.'

'Well, I should get changed,' Elli said, turning to chat to Heather and Ermgarde. Charles crept up and kissed Elli on the neck. 'Ooh!' Elli said in surprise. 'Who's that?' she chuckled.

'Hey, now, princess! How many people kiss you on the neck?' Charles asked.

'Hmm?' Elli said. 'Let me think.'

The ladies all laughed. Elli gave Charles a kiss on the nose then went to get changed. She returned wearing a pair of white linen trousers, a white T-shirt, and an open, navy silk over-shirt.

'Elli, is that Canire Couture?' Acanthus asked.

'No. This is from my wardrobe.'

'You look lovely,' Willow said.

'Auntie Squish looks good in *everything*. She'd even make a paper bag look like couture,' Ermgarde stated.

'Ermgarde, why do you think I love her modelling for me?' Thia asked.

When the other ladies had stepped away, Elli spoke to Thia, 'I was wondering if I could commission you to make some of your garments and undies with silk Charles brought back from our honeymoon.'

'Of course I'll make them, Elli.'

'This is a *commission*, Thia,' Elli insisted.

'You're a good friend,' Thia countered.

'Please take it as a *commission*. You are a businesswoman,' Elli said firmly.

'I can afford it,' Thia said.

'*So can I*,' Elli argued.

'Besides, you just modelled for me. I should be paying you!' Thia said triumphantly.

Elli kissed Thia on the cheek.

'Hey, Thia! You could advertise that you design clothes for the Duchess of Mereland and Ashlowe,' Willow said. 'Hold on! If Heather is now your mum... aren't you a princess?'

Heather overheard this, turned and said, 'Willow, my dear, Elli has *always* been a princess.'

'Shall we go downstairs?' Lionel suggested.

'Actually, Lionel, we'll head out, and pick Lille and Acacia up from Mum,' Keen said.

'We should also head out,' Flynn said. 'Pup bedtime.'

Everyone met in the hall, some of the party leaving and some making their way to the drawing room.

'You will be seeing more of Thia around The Holt,' Archie said unexpectedly.

'That's nice, Uncle Archie,' Ermgarde said.

'Yes, Ermgarde. I will be visiting weekends, and working Fridays and Mondays in Mereland.'

'That's great news, Thia!' Lionel said.

'Thia, if you need some space, you're welcome to use upstairs above my studio,' Ermgarde offered.

'You need your space,' Thia said.

'No. I don't use it. There's a box or two up there, but nothing that couldn't fit in a cupboard downstairs,' Ermgarde explained. 'Use it if you like.'

'Really?'

'Yes. There are three rooms up there, and a bathroom,' Ermgarde said. 'It may need a bit of a dust, but it was painted a while back. Drop in to take a look when you're passing. Oh! Auntie Squish, your sign is ready.'

'Thank you, Ermgarde.'

'Sign? What sign?' Charles asked.

'I told you, plant pot. I'm changing the name of my shop,' Elli said.

'To what?' Charles asked, pushing his luck. He thought if he caught Elli off guard, she would slip up and tell him.

'Nice try!' Elli scoffed.

'And... I'm not telling you, Uncle Squish!' Ermgarde said defiantly.

'Sweetie, you will just have to wait.'

'Okay, I can wait,' Charles said resignedly.

'I could do with a brew,' Lionel announced.

'My love, you always need a cup of tea,' Heather chortled.

'I'll make it!' Charles offered.

'I can make it, Charles,' Archie said.

'Arch, you stay there with Thia,' Charles said firmly.

'None for us, Uncle Squish, we need to check on the pups,' Ermgarde said. Rupert and Ermgarde bade everyone a goodnight, then left.

Charles made the tea, and returned, placing the tray on the coffee table. Heather served it.

'We have the school opening soon,' Elli said, tiredly.

'We do,' Charles sighed. 'I wish someone else could do it.'

'Why, Son?' Lionel asked.

'You know I don't like fuss. Besides, it just feels wrong. I don't want the villagers to feel it's my village. If you know what I mean. I donated the land, because the village needed it, not for any recognition. I just want to be a villager.'

'I know *exactly* what you mean, my dear,' Heather said sincerely. 'I *love* being just a villager.'

'Are you alright, my dear?' Lionel asked a suddenly contemplative Heather.

'Yes, my love. I was just thinking about Mereland and the village, that's all.'

'You're a very talented young lady, Thia. And I must say, Petal, you did look very pretty in those clothes, Lionel praised.

Thia simply blushed.

'LP thought Ell should buy that gown, and we go for a night out.'

'We could all go!' Elli suggested.

'We could go to the city, and stay at the Norchester Regency,' Lionel said.

'We could go in two cars,' Charles said. 'Dad's and

236

Ell's car will make it to Norchester, and we can charge them at the hotel.'

'Where would we go in Norchester?' Heather asked.

'Oh noodles!' Elli exclaimed all of a sudden.

There was a collective look of panic. 'What's wrong, Petal,' Lionel asked, beating his son to the question.

'I just realised, I haven't told Crosby I'm pregnant.'

'It wasn't on purpose, Ell. You've been busy,' Charles said. 'How about we go to Norchester to see him? Or, we could invite him here.'

'We could go to see the play Crosby is starring in, if it's still running,' Heather suggested.

'Excellent idea, my love!' Lionel said, then he kissed Heather on the cheek.

'That is an excellent idea, Mummy. That could be the excuse to dress up,' Elli said with delight. 'I can call to see if I can get tickets.'

'Does everyone want to go?' Lionel asked.

'We do!' Archie and Thia said in unison.

Elli dragged herself off the sofa, went to the hall telephone, and dialled. 'Hello, yes. This is the Duchess of Mereland and Ashlowe, and I'd like to speak with Crosby Provo, please.'

'One moment, please, Your Grace. I will put you through to his dressing room.'

A few seconds later, Crosby said, 'Hello, sis! How's married life?'

'*Wonderful*, Cros.'

'That's good. Charles alright?'

'Yes, he's *fabulous*. Cros, I was wondering if your

play is still running. If it is, is there any chance of getting six tickets.' Elli asked.

'Yes, it's still running. They extended the run. You want *six* tickets?' Crosby asked. 'Who for?'

'Me, Charles, Daddy, Aunt Heather (she'd tell him about her calling Heather, Mummy in person), Archie, and Thia.'

'*Aunt Heather*?' Crosby exclaimed.

'Yes, Aunt Heather,' Elli confirmed.

Crosby gulped. He had just realised he would be performing before royalty. 'Sis, let me get back to you. I know we've been sold out. Let me see what I can do.'

'Okay, Cros. Thanks. I must go. Toodles!' Elli said. She hung up the phone, and returned to the drawing room. 'Cros said, he'd see what he can do, and get back to me. They've been sold out.'

'What play is it?' Lionel asked.

'*The Cloudburst*, by Guillaume Rattlepike,' Elli replied.

'I do like that one!' Lionel said.

'If we can get tickets, we could take Crosby out for a late dinner,' Charles put forth.

'He'd like that. He loved spending time with you all at the wedding.'

'Darlings, we should let you go to bed,' Heather announced. 'Let us know about the tickets.'

'Will do,' Elli said.

Hugs and kisses were exchanged, and Lionel and Heather left.

'Thia, I'd like to buy that gown for Ell,' Charles said.

'It's only a sample, Charles,' Thia replied.

'Then, can I commission you to make one for her?' he asked.

It's okay, I'll just make her one,' Thia replied.

'No, Thia! This is a *commission*,' Charles insisted.

Thia looked at Archie, and then back at Charles.'

'Very well. I'll do it as soon as possible, as we don't know what date the tickets will be for,' Thia said.

'Does Crosby know it will be in front of royalty?' Archie asked.

'He does, Archie, and is a bit freaked out by it, if truth be told,' Elli replied. 'I guess he'll be alright on the night.'

'Of course he will. He is a *professional*,' Archie stated. 'We are about to retire for the evening. Is there anything you need before we take our leave?'

'Nothing that I can think of, Arch. Have a good night,' Charles said.

'If you require strawberries and salt and vinegar crisps, there are plenty in the kitchen, Elli.'

'Ooh, goody! Thank you, Archie. You are so thoughtful. Night-night.'

'Come on, princess, time for bed,' Charles said.

The next day, Elli popped into her shop as she had a couple of items that she needed to work on, one being a commission a customer wanted fairly soon. Whilst she was there, Crosby called. 'Hey, Sis. I spoke with the box office, there's been a cancellation— a box, which is good, because you can fit six in there.'

'You are *wonderful*, Cros. Thank you,' Elli said. 'Everyone will be pleased. What day are the tickets for?'

'Friday. It's the best I could do.'

'Friday night is perfect! Cros, can you do dinner afterwards? Charles suggested we take to you for a late dinner.'

'I can do dinner afterwards. I'll leave the tickets at the box office for Mr and Mrs Watermere. Okay?'

'Thanks again, Cros. See you Friday.' Elli then called Charles, who told Archie, who told Lionel and Heather. '*No doubt, Archie'll take their evening suits out, and press them,' she thought*. Elli returned to what she was designing, which was a diamond and emerald ring.

When Elli got home, Charles told her that he had already spoken with Lionel, Heather, Archie, and Thia, and suggested they leave Friday morning. Elli agreed that this was a good idea, as it would give them time to do a little shopping in the capital. 'Are Mummy and Daddy shopping for anything in particular?' Elli asked.

'They thought you would like to do a little shopping for the nursery, Ell,' Charles said, setting down his crossword book.

'We don't have a nursery, Sweetie. Speaking of which, I hadn't actually thought about where it would be,' Elli said believing they had plenty of time.

'Ell, we could turn our private sitting room into one. We haven't been using it much recently.'

'Or...' Elli walked towards Charles' dressing room.

'You're not thinking of using west suite, are you, Ell?

'Why not?' She shrugged. 'I haven't designed my

dressing room yet, so it could be a nursery.'

'No, Ell. You should have your dressing room,' Charles said.

'That's because you don't want me stealing your dressing room, isn't it?' Elli joked.

'I hadn't thought of that, but that's as good a reason as any,' Charles replied. 'I think we should get Cendra in to redecorate the private sitting room. It isn't really needed now.'

'We could split my dressing room, it is excessive. I honestly don't need that much space. Even if we halved it, it would still be enormous,' Elli pointed out.

'Not a bad suggestion. If you're sure you don't need that much space.'

'Sweetie, I lived in a tiny flat, I can cope with a gigantic dressing room that's bigger than the whole of my old flat,' she responded with a light laugh.

'In that case, I'll get Arch to arrange it with the people who put the door in, and they can divide the space,' Charles stated.

'Do we need to buy stuff for the nursery this early?' Elli asked. 'My book says to leave it until about twenty weeks.'

'It's a bit early, but I think Heather is excited, and wants to take you shopping for pup stuff. New grandpup and all that,' Charles said.

'I think I'll ask her if she wants to go shopping for nursery stuff, then,' Elli said, a little excited.

'I think that will make her day, Ell.'

'Do you want to go shopping for nursery stuff with us, Sweetie? I mean, it is your pup, and I know you're excited.'

'I don't think I would be as much help as your mummy. It's not that I'm not interested, I just think you and she need time together.'

Elli kissed Charles. 'You are wonderful! Have I told you that?'

'Not today,' he said with a wink.

Thursday evening, Charles and Elli were packing for their trip. 'Sweetie, how about we go with Mummy and Daddy in their car?'

'Why? What's wrong?' Charles asked.

'Nothing. You said I needed to spend time with Mummy, and we can talk in the car,' Elli answered.

'What about Archie and Thia? Arch's car won't make it to Norchester,' Charles pointed out.

'They can use my car,' Elli suggested.

'They said that they'd be staying in Norchester the whole weekend and would get the train back here on Monday.'

'No problem. They just keep my car until they return,' Elli said.

'You won't have your car,' Charles stated.

'I'm sure Archie would let us use his car if we needed it,' Elli said. She seemed to have all the answers.

'Fair enough!' Charles agreed.

'You call Archie, and I'll call Mummy and Daddy on another line,' Elli said. Elli left the room before Charles could say another word. When Elli returned, she continued to pack.

'Are you nearly packed, Ell?'

'Just my evening gown and shoes to pack,' Elli said.

'Ooh! What gown are you going to wear?' Charles asked.

'The one Thia made me, you plant pot. I'm not likely to wear the one you bought me on the cruise, am I?' She said, rubbing her belly. If I could get in it and zip it up, you'd probably have to use a can opener to help me out of it.'

Charles laughed, 'That is true.'

'Don't worry, my love, I'll wear that gown again one day. I love it!' She kissed Charles on the nose. 'Okay, I'm all packed!'

SHOPPING

Friday morning was warm, and the smell of summer was in the air with a promise of a slight breeze—the perfect day to take a drive somewhere. At seven o'clock on the dot, Lionel and Heather showed up at the terrace doors, their luggage already loaded in Lionel's car. Lionel was wearing grey trousers and a white shirt. Heather had opted for black wide-legged trousers and a garnet red blouse. 'Good morning, Son, Petal!' Lionel said cheerily. 'You ready for the off?'

'Good morning to both of you,' Charles said. Elli waved, as she was rummaging through her handbag. 'Yes, sorry. Good morning, Mummy, Daddy,' she said when she had finished. 'We're ready.'

'You both look rather lovely today,' Heather said. Elli was wearing a pair of pale-yellow beach pyjamas. They were light, loose-fitting, and more importantly, comfortable. Charles was wearing navy trousers and a sky-blue shirt.

'My dear, saying they look lovely *today*, could mean they look like absolute scruffs most days,' Lionel joked.

'I may do, Dad, but Ell always looks gorgeous!'

Charles responded.

'Lionel, my love…' Heather said, as she turned to him, and gave him a look. 'These darling people know what I mean, don't you?'

'We do, Mummy. Thank you,' Elli said. 'As for you, Charles Hugo Watermere, you never look like a scruff.'

'I would beg to differ,' came a comment from Archie, who was descending the stairs, carrying his and Thia's luggage. Archie was wearing navy trousers and a white shirt, whilst Thia wore a long, dark green skirt, and a white sleeveless top.

'See, Ell, Arch knows the genuine me. The scruffy kid from Downthornton,' Charles said.

'You were never scruffy, Son. Mum would never have allowed it,' Lionel said. 'You and Archie always had grazed knees, because you got up to so much, but you were never scruffy.'

'With Archie as my best friend, it was amazing I didn't go to school in a bowler hat and carrying a briefcase.'

'No, Charles. You left the briefcase until you started work,' Archie stated.

'Enough chit-chat about growing up. Save that for later. We should get on the road!' Lionel said commandingly.

'Thank you, Elli, for the use of your car,' Archie said as he left his car keys in the hall table drawer.

'You're most welcome, Archie.'

All but Charles headed to the cars, Charles locking the terrace doors. After securing The House, he then joined his dad, Heather, and Elli in Lionel's car.

Thankfully, the journey to Norchester was uneventful.They only passed one or two cars on the road. Heather and Elli chatted most of the way, and they all noticed how Elli did not flinch when they went through Muttleby. Charles and Lionel were delighted by the chatter coming from the back seat.

'So, where are we going after we check in?' Charles asked.

'Mummy and I thought we'd start shopping for stuff for the nursery,' Elli's voice came from the back.

' You and I can find some mischief to get up to, Son,' Lionel said with a chuckle.

The ladies stopped chatting for a moment. 'I'm sure you can, Lionel, dear,' Heather cut in, rolling her eyes.

Arriving at the Norchester Regency, their luggage was unloaded, then a valet parked their cars, and plugged them in to charge. The party checked in, then Archie and Thia went off to pop in on Canire Couture. Afterwards they planned to do a bit of shopping, but would meet up with the others mid-afternoon at the hotel.

Elli and Heather said they were going to go into the city by taxi to start their shopping excursion.

'What shall we do, Dad?' Charles asked.

'Why don't you go to the SilentCart showroom, so you can look at the new models?' Elli suggested.

'Ooh! That sounds like a good idea!' Charles said excitedly. 'We can see what my new car will look like.'

'If you tell them your name, they'll show you the exact model you'll be getting,' Elli commented.

'That's a cracking idea, Petal!' Lionel said. 'Then we can meet back here this afternoon for tea.'

After kisses were given and received, Elli and Heather got in one taxi, Charles and Lionel in another.

Elli and Heather got out of the taxi in the capital, and the atmosphere hit them immediately. Even Heather, who had spent most of her life in Norchester found it quite jarring. The sights and sounds were quite overwhelming, the streets busy with shoppers darting in and out of buildings. After all they were both used to a quiet life in Mereland.

They decided to start at a shop called Parenting and the Pup, which sold pretty much everything you could think of, and many things you would not, for mother and pup. Heather was over the moon—not only to be shopping in Norchester in a regular shop, but to be helping Elli shop for the pup. The shop was bright, airy, and modern, with an overwhelming choice of merchandise.

'Good grief!' Heather exclaimed. 'There certainly wasn't anything like this when I had my pups. I mean, is all of this really necessary nowadays?'

Elli smiled. 'Mummy, I'm not sure. I'm new to all of this.'

A salesperson (a female fox) approached. 'Ladies, may I help you?'

Heather responded, 'My daughter... (she paused a beat, and smiled at Elli) is due in February, and this is our first visit to a mother and pup shop.'

247

The fox said, 'It can be a bit overwhelming at first. Here is a list.' She handed each of them a sheet of paper.

'A list of what?' Elli asked.

'Things you will need, may need, and would like to have,' the fox replied. Heather and Elli scanned the list and then gaped at each other.

'You're right. This is overwhelming,' Elli said, a little bemused. It was an unusual experience for Elli—she being a seasoned shopper.

The fox smiled. 'Most new mothers start with maternity clothing.'

'I'm all sorted with that, thank you,' Elli said.

'You may need to purchase different sizes as your pregnancy progresses,' the fox said.

'There's a new range of maternity clothing just launched, called Conception by Canire Couture, which is fully adjustable,' Elli told the fox.

'*Really*, madam? We should look into that! Then I would suggest you start in the furniture department, decide on a style for your nursery, and then work from there.' The fox showed them the way to the furniture department and left them to it.

Meanwhile, Charles and Lionel were entering the SilentCarts of Norchester showroom.

'Good morning, gentlemen. Are you new to SilentCarts?' a smartly dressed, female marten in a grey suit asked.

'No. We both own them,' Lionel replied.

'My wife has purchased a new one for me, and we're awaiting delivery.' Charles informed the marten. 'She suggested I come in and look at the model of car I'll be getting.'

'What model is it, sir?'

'To be honest, I'm not sure.'

'What is the name?' the marten asked.

'Charles Watermere, Mereland.'

'One moment, sir. I will check our records,' the marten said. A few minutes later, she returned, and asked Charles and Lionel to follow her. She escorted them to a back area, where a number of vehicles were parked. The marten handed Charles some keys, and said, 'This is your vehicle, Mr Watermere.'

'So, this is the same model as my new SilentCart?' Charles asked.

'No, sir. This is *your* vehicle.'

Charles and Lionel gasped, '*Wow*! *What a fantastic colour*,' Charles blurted out.

'Yes, sir. It is a custom colour, called midnight galaxy. It is black with dark blue sparkles,' the marten informed him.

Charles laughed.

'What's so funny, Son?' Lionel asked.

'It matches one of Ell's evening gowns!'

'Knowing our Elli, I'm sure it wasn't by accident,' Lionel said with a light laugh.

'You may take your vehicle with you, or we could deliver it,' said the marten.

'No reason not to take it today, Son. You could drive it home,' Lionel said.

Charles signed some papers, then he and Lionel got into the brand spanking new car, and drove out of the showroom.

'Do you think our Elli will be surprised, Son?'

'I think so. Let's go for a drive, then park up outside the hotel. See if Ell notices it,' Charles said conspiratorially.

'I just had a thought, Son. Perhaps our Elli suggested you go to the showroom because she knew your car was ready.'

Charles laughed, 'That does sound like her.'

'Then she's bound to notice it!' Lionel laughed.

They continued through Norchester and followed the road out to Briarheight Fields.

Elli and Heather were having a whale of a time. Elli had chosen some furniture, but said she would take the details of it, have a conversation with her husband, make a decision, and call them once the nursery was decorated. They did, however, buy nappies and a beautiful mobile with bumblebees. Heather bought a cashmere baby blanket and some baby booties.

The two ladies got out of the taxi at the hotel. As they did, Heather noticed a shiny new vehicle next to Lionel's SilentCart, and said, 'Ooh! What a *beautiful* car. It looks very special. I'm sure someone very important must own it.'

Elli smiled to herself, then said, 'I'm sure they are someone very special, Mummy.'

On entering the hotel, they headed straight to Charles and Elli's suite, knowing that was where everyone would meet.

'I would imagine, Lionel and Charles are having tea together,' Heather said. Lo and behold, Heather was shown to be correct. On entering the suite, they found Lionel, Charles, Archie, and Thia, teacups in paws.

Charles got up to greet Elli with a kiss.

Lionel said on noticing the packages, 'You've been busy, ladies. Did you have a good time?'

'I had a wonderful time,' Heather said.

'What about you, Ell?' Charles asked.

'A wonderfully exhausting time. Can I put my feet in your cup of tea, please?'

Charles laughed.

'I will get you both a cup of tea,' Archie offered.

'So, what did you gentlemen do?' Elli asked with a smirk.

'I picked up my new car!' Charles announced.

'I know. I saw it outside,' Elli said.

'That's *your* car?' Heather asked.

'The black sparkly one is mine,' Charles said.

'It's *gorgeous*!' Heather trilled.

'I wouldn't have expected anything else from our Elli,' Lionel said.

'I agree, dear. Elli has impeccable taste,' Heather said, as she patted Charles gently on the cheek. 'I was right, though. It certainly is someone special that owns that car, Darling Girl.'

'It certainly is, Mummy. Thia, what did you and Archie do today?'

'Dropped in at Canire Couture, did a bit of paperwork, and then went for lunch,' she replied.

'Shall I order tea?' Archie asked.

'Good idea, Arch!' Charles responded. 'We have a little while before we need to get ready for the theatre.'

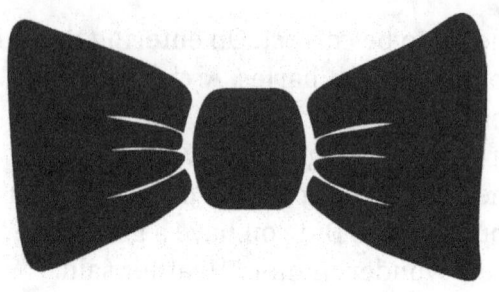

BOW TIES AND BUSINESS CARDS

As agreed, they all met in the foyer that evening. The gentlemen were wearing traditional black evening suits, white shirts, and black bow ties. Heather stood out in her full-length, black sleeveless gown, adorned with a delicate pearl neckline. Thia looked fabulous in a striking emerald green silk, off-the-shoulder gown, catching everyone's eye. Archie, captivated by Thia's beauty, couldn't take his eyes off her. As he stared, Charles quietly walked over to him and whispered in his ear, '*Breathe*, brother... breathe.' Turning towards his wife, Charles beamed with pride. Elli was the epitome of elegance in the black sparkly, specially commissioned Conception by Canire Couture evening gown—it shimmered with every movement. Charles gently took Elli by the paw and, with an adoring smile, asked, 'Shall we?'

They exited the hotel, where a limousine was waiting. The chauffeur got out, opened the doors, and the ladies got in first. Once everyone was seated comfortably, the driver pulled away.

'When did you arrange this, Charles?' Thia asked.

'The moment I knew when we would be going to the theatre, Thia.'

Arriving at the Norchester Royal Theatre, all eyes were on them when they exited the limousine. Everyone outside the theatre stopped in their tracks and started whispering. 'Oooh! Aren't those dresses lovely?' one person was heard asking a friend, and someone else said, 'They must be famous.' This made Thia giggle.

ROYAL THEATRE
NORCHESTER

THE CLOUDBURST
a play by Guillaume Rattlepike

starring

Crosby Provo   Bunny Fluffle

They entered the theatre. Charles went to the box office, where he paid for and collected their tickets, then returned to his group. He glanced at the tickets, then led the way to a door, which clearly stated 'Royal Box.' They all chuckled when they saw the sign.

'Well, Your Graces, lead the way,' Heather said.

'Surely...' Charles started.

'*No*, dear. *You* lead the way,' Heather insisted.

The box was large, comfortable, and had a great view of the stage, but what else would you expect of the royal box? Everyone appeared excited, Elli in particular.

'Ell, have you seen any of Crosby's other plays?' Charles asked.

'Only amateur stuff, but he was good,' Elli replied.

'I'm looking forward to seeing this,' Heather said. 'We were lucky to get tickets.'

'We do have *connections*, Mummy' Elli said with a cheeky smile.

'That is true, Darling Girl.'

'This is my absolute favourite Rattlepike play, and it's had *fabulous* reviews in the newspaper,' Thia stated. 'Archie and I were reading them the other day.'

'Yes, Thia is correct. They were all rave reviews,' Archie agreed.

The lights flashed to indicate the performance was about to commence, and Lionel whispered to Heather, 'They mustn't have paid the electricity bill.'

Heather chuckled.

The curtain rose, and the play began. The Watermere party was mesmerised by Crosby. At the end of the performance, the entire theatre audience gave a *ten-minute* standing ovation. When the cast returned for their final curtain call, Crosby bowed, looked straight up to the royal box, then blew a kiss.

'I'm no expert,' Lionel said, 'But, that was *terrific*! Crosby was *brilliant*!'

'I have seen many performances of that play,' Heather said. 'And without a shadow of a doubt that was *the best* performance I have *ever* seen.'

Archie said, 'Crosby's performance was a tour de force!'

They had decided to let the crowd disperse a little before heading downstairs, where Elli approached an usher (a hare), and said, 'I'm Crosby Provo's sister, Elli. We're supposed to meet him.'

The usher said, 'Let me show you the way.'

The Watermere group followed the usher down passageways, finally arriving outside a dressing room. The usher tapped on the door, and Crosby answered. He thanked the usher, as did Elli, and then Crosby invited his guests in. 'Hello, everyone! Hope you enjoyed the performance.'

Heather gave him a hug, and said, 'Crosby, my dear, we enjoyed it *immensely*.' The others nodded in agreement. 'My dear, it was *the best* performance of *The Cloudburst*, I have *ever* seen.'

'*Really*?' Crosby asked.

'Yes. I'm not just saying that,' Heather said.

'Thank you, Aunt Heather,' Crosby said. 'It means an awful lot to me.'

'You were great!' Lionel said.

'Most enjoyable!' Archie added.

'You all look very swish! Will I do in this black suit?' Crosby asked.

'Of course, Cros,' Elli said. 'You look sharp.'

'Where are we going?' Crosby asked the group at large.

'The Garden Room,' Charles replied.

'Ooh! Isn't that the rooftop restaurant?' Crosby asked, as he tied his burgundy-coloured tie.

'Yes, Crosby,' Thia answered, 'It's the rooftop restaurant, though I've never been there.'

'It will be an experience for us all,' Charles said. 'Thank you for getting us the tickets, Crosby.'

'You're welcome,' Crosby said, as he put his jacket on. 'Will I do?'

'You look very handsome, my dear,' Heather said, as she straightened his tie.

'Okay, let's go! I'm famished!' Lionel urged.

Exiting the theatre, they found their limousine waiting for them.

'Wow!' Crosby said.

'It's a special occasion!' Charles stated. 'We have a famous actor with us, after all.'

Crosby smiled, then got in the vehicle after the ladies. They drove through the dusky skied city; it being summer, the sky was not yet dark. They arrived at the tallest building in Norchester, the Merashire Skyline.

The Merashire Skyline was an office tower by day, with a restaurant located on top. As all the offices were closed, there was a concierge, a heron, at the front desk. His job was to greet diners and allow them entrance to a lift that would take them directly to the restaurant. He asked, 'Do you have reservations?'

Lionel thought, and was tempted to respond, '*Yes, we do, but we'll eat here, anyway,*' but decided against it, as the heron did *not* look like he had a sense of humour.

'Party of seven. Watermere,' Charles informed the heron.

The concierge pressed the button to call the lift, ushered the party in, pressed the button for the roof, and returned to his post.

The lift doors opened on what seemed like another world. The room was dark and moody, with what appeared to be thousands of candles. There were massive glass walls that had been slid back, so the inside and outside seamlessly blended. The maître d' (a rabbit) said, 'Watermere party of seven, this way, please.'

'*The heron evidently called ahead,*' Charles thought.

They were taken to the outside area, which seemed like a magical garden—with plants, lights, and the most glorious views of Norchester and beyond. As they were shown their table, the party was told that their waiter would be with them momentarily, and each of them was given a menu.

'You can see the palace from here,' Crosby said,

looking at Heather.

'I think you can see *everywhere* from here,' Lionel said. 'We're so high up.'

'It's a *spectacular* place,' Thia enthused.

Elli seized a moment in the chatter, and said, 'Before dinner is ordered, could we take a moment?'

'Of course, Petal,' Lionel said. The table fell silent.

'Cros, we've been really looking forward to seeing your play, which was incredible. But Charles and I wanted to talk to you about something.'

'What's wrong, sis?' Crosby asked, concern on his face. 'You're not ill, are you? Sorry, I didn't mean to pry, but I thought you looked healthy. Glowing in fact.'

'Cros, I'm fine,' Elli said reassuringly. ' I... *we*... wanted to let you know, I'm expecting a pup.'

'*What*?' Crosby cried out a little louder than he had intended, he then put his paw over his mouth, then quickly stood up and hugged Elli, and then shook paws with Charles. '*Congratulations*! I was going to say, you looked like you had put on a little weight, sis. I just thought it was happy and contented married life. You still look fab, sis! When's the pup due?'

'February,' the entire table chimed in almost in unison.

'*Wow*! A pup!' Crosby said, beaming. 'How *wonderful*!'

Just then the waiter came to take their order.

As they were eating their main course, a badger approached their table. 'Sorry to interrupt your meal, but are you Crosby Provo?' he asked.

'Yes, I'm Crosby Provo.'

'Mr Provo, I do apologise for interrupting your meal with your friends and family, but we (he gestured to the kestrel sitting at his table) were at your play this evening, and thought you were *sensational*! I'm Basil Brockton, Film Producer. We're going to be making *The Shaming of the Shrew*. It will be the first film shown in the new cinemas that are opening up and down the country. We'd like you to be the male lead.' He then handed his business card to a stunned Crosby. 'Call me tomorrow. Let's talk. Sorry for the intrusion, folks. Good evening,' the badger said politely, then returned to his table. Crosby sat there staring at the business card.

'Wow! Cros. That's *fantastic*!' Elli trilled.

'To tell you the truth, I'm somewhat...'

'Stunned, my dear?' Heather offered.

'Why, Crosby?' Archie asked. 'You were tremendous in *The Cloudburst*, and if that gentleman and his companion were at the theatre tonight, it is understandable why they would approach you.'

Crosby was only half listening, as he was still staring at the business card.

'Cros,' Elli said, attempting to bring her brother back down to earth.

Crosby stared at the card open-mouthed.

'Well, there's a first!' Elli said, laughing. 'My brother lost for words.'

'Well, it's a lot to think about,' Charles said.

'Sorry about that,' Crosby said.

'Nothing to be sorry for,' Lionel said kindly.

'Let's continue our meal,' Crosby suggested, after taking one more look at the business card before placing it on the table.

'I know how Elli is, but what about everyone else? Aunt Heather? Lionel?' Crosby asked buoyantly.

'We're well, thank you,' Lionel and Heather said in unison. 'I'm sure Elli has told you that, as you young people say, Lionel and I are "*an item*".' Heather chuckled.

'How lovely!' Crosby said warmly.

'How about you, Charles?' Crosby asked.

'I'm over the moon, elated, ecstatic, in love,' Charles replied as he looked at Elli.

'What about you, Archie, Thia?'

Archie and Thia looked at each other, then Thia said, 'We're fine, thank you.'

At that moment, the film producer and his dinner companion stood. As soon as they had left the restaurant, Crosby seemed to relax a little.

'So, what do you think, Cros— about the film?' Elli pushed.

'It's an enormous opportunity. Films are new, and this will be a big deal,' Crosby replied.

'So, what are you worried about?' Lionel asked.

'Whether I'll be good enough,' Crosby voiced, a little unsure of himself. 'I mean, it will be on *film*. A lot more people will see it.'

'Just do what you did on the stage this evening, and you will be wonderful, my dear,' Heather said in a motherly tone.

'Thank you, Aunt Heather.'

'No need for thanks. It's the truth.'

'So, are you going to call him, Cros?' Elli asked, excited for her brother.

Crosby glanced down at the business card once more. 'I think so.'

'Crosby, you have nothing to lose by calling,' Archie stated. 'It is only a phone call. Find out as much as you can, then you can make an informed decision.'

'Thank you, Archie,' Crosby said, putting the business card in his jacket pocket.

'Anyone want dessert?' Lionel asked, deciding Crosby looked a little stressed. 'Heather, my love, would you like dessert?'

'Yes, please. Raspberry and basil sorbet,' she replied at once.

'What about the rest of you?' Lionel asked. All but Elli said they would like the same. 'What about you, Petal?'

'Thank you, Daddy, but I think I'll give it a miss.'

Charles looked at Elli, with a twinge of concern. 'You alright, Ell?'

'Yes, Sweetie. It's just that I'm craving strawberries and salt and vinegar crisps.'

Crosby laughed. 'Sis, what did you just say?'

'Strawberries and salt and vinegar crisps,' Elli reiterated.

'That's weird!' Crosby mumbled.

'It's not that odd, my dear,' Heather cut in. 'When I was having one of my pups, I craved lemon curd and salmon.'

'At the *same time*?' Crosby asked, part amused, part disgusted.

'Yes, my dear. When females are pregnant, who

knows what we'll crave,' Heather replied.

'Ell, we can ask if they could do some strawberries with salt and vinegar, as I'm sure they won't have crisps here,' Charles said.

'It's okay, Sweetie. I'm not sure it will taste the same,' Elli said, as she sat back in her chair.

'We can get some when we get back to the hotel. I'm sure they'll have them. If not, I will scour the city to find you some,' Charles said firmly.

Elli kissed him on the cheek, then said, 'I'm sure the hotel will have them, H.'

Once dessert was over, Charles requested the bill.

'I will pay for our meal,' Archie said.

Charles, seemingly oblivious to the offer, handed over the payment along with a generous tip. He smiled at Archie and Thia, then stood to help Elli out of her chair.

Everyone thanked Charles, and he told them, 'It was entirely my pleasure.'

They made their way down to the waiting limousine, where Elli asked Crosby if he wanted to go back to the hotel with them for a nightcap. However, he declined the invitation, stating that he had a lot of thinking to do and an early morning. Outside Crosby's home, they all bade him a good night, and all the best with the telephone call. The rest of the Watermere party returned to the hotel, where Charles made sure Elli got her craving satisfied.

The next morning, the six of them met for breakfast, then Charles, Elli, Lionel, and Heather, hugged and kissed Archie and Thia goodbye, as they would not be returning to Mereland until Sunday night. Archie and Thia waved the two couples off—Charles and Elli in Charles' sparkly new SilentCart.

'I do love my new car, Ell,' Charles stated, as they pulled out of the hotel car park.

'I'm glad. May I turn the radio on?' Elli asked, as she reached forward.

'You don't need to ask, Ell.'

Elli turned the dial, and much to their surprise, their favourite song was playing.

'We danced to this at our wedding reception,' Charles said.

Elli smiled because he had remembered.

They drove all the way back to Mereland, happily singing along to the radio.

MELIS STUDIOS

Basil Brockton
Executive Producer

HIT AND RUN

Sunday evening, Charles and Elli had just finished a dinner of baked salmon, asparagus, and new potatoes, and were relaxing in the drawing room, when the telephone rang.

'It's probably Arch, saying he's staying an extra night or two,' Charles said to Elli, as he hauled himself off a very comfortable sofa, and made his way to the hall telephone. 'Watermere residence,' he said when he lifted the receiver. '*Oh no*!' Charles almost shrieked.

Elli ran to the hall. 'What's wrong? *What's wrong*?'

Charles said into the telephone, 'I'm leaving now!' Charles looked quite faint.

'Sweetie, tell me what's wrong,' Elli urged frantically. '*What's happened*?'

'*It's Arch*!' Charles blurted out, then he took a deep breath. 'He and Thia were in a nasty accident...'

'*Oh no*! When? Where? How are they?'

'Ell, I need to go to Muttleby hospital,' Charles said urgently.

'I'm coming *too*!' Elli said determinedly.

Charles did not have time to argue. '*Let's go*!'

'I'm going to call Daddy,' Elli said.

'Ell, I'll call Dad, you go put your shoes on.'

Charles called Lionel. 'Dad, Arch and Thia have had a nasty accident in the car.'

'*What*?'

'I don't know much, just that it's bad. We're heading to the hospital in Muttleby,' Charles said in a hurry.

'You said, "We". Is Petal going too?'

'Yes. She's insisting she go. Dad, I need to get going. I'll call you. I love you.'

'Take care, Son. I love you, too.'

Charles and Elli left the house then locked it up.

'Sweetie, give me the keys to the car,' Elli demanded.

'Why?'

'You're in no fit state to drive. That's why.'

'I'm okay,' Charles argued.

'No, you are *not. Give me the keys*!' Elli snapped.

Charles relented, and Elli got in the driving seat.

They left Mereland as quickly and safely as they could.

Charles was thinking out loud, 'What happened? Where did it happen? Why did it happen?'

'We'll find all that out when we get there, Sweetie,' Elli said, as she drove.

Charles, clearly on edge, started rocking back and forth, as though he was urging the car to go faster. The nearer they got to Muttleby, the faster he rocked. Elli got a glimpse of what he must have gone through when she was abducted and in hospital.

As they turned into the car park at Muttleby Cottage Hospital, Charles cried out, '*Pull up! Pull up! Park!*'

Elli threw Charles' new car into the first parking spot she found. She had barely come to a halt, when Charles launched himself out of the car and ran full pelt into the hospital. Elli locked the car, then followed him as quickly as she could.

Charles strode urgently up the hall of the hospital, and called out, '*Hello!*'

Nurse Purdy Cantrell (a kingfisher) appeared. 'Mr Watermere! Mrs Watermere!' she said, surprised to see them both so quickly.

'You called me. How is Archie? How is Thia?' Charles asked almost breathless.

Purdy Cantrell wore a grave look on her face.

'*NO*! Don't tell me, they're...' He could not bring himself to say it.

'No. They aren't dead, but it is *very* serious. Come into this room,' Purdy said, as she opened a door to an office. 'I'll get Doctor Allerton. Take a seat. Elli sat down, but Charles could not stay still, he was pacing back and forth.

Doctor Digby Allerton (a rabbit) entered the office. 'Charles, Elli, I wish we were meeting again under better circumstances.' (Charles and Elli were

266

on first-name terms with Doctor Digby Allerton, as he had become a friend, and had attended Charles and Elli's wedding.)

'Digby, how bad is it?' Charles asked.

'Apparently, they were driving along, and someone decided to overtake them on a bend, and Archie and Thia were pushed off the road, and the car rolled.'

'*Oh no!*' Elli exclaimed, horror-struck.

Digby continued, 'Luckily, there was a car following.
The people in it got out to help.'

'What's Archie and Thia's condition? What injuries do they have?' Charles asked.

'Archie's are worse...' the doctor started. (Charles gripped the back of a chair) 'Charles, sit down,' Digby urged. Charles lowered himself into a chair, and the doctor continued. 'Yes, Archie is unconscious. He must have hit his head. We're monitoring him. He has a linear fracture of the skull, which thankfully means, it isn't pushing in on the brain. He does however have some swelling, because as I'm sure you know, the brain is surrounded by fluid, and if there is a sudden stop, such as in a car crash, the skull stops when it hits something, but the brain keeps moving in the fluid, and collides with the skull. This causes bruising and swelling. Archie also has broken ribs and a broken leg. We *need* him to wake up. The sooner the better.'

'*Oh my!*' Elli exclaimed. 'How is Thia?'

'She has a broken arm and leg, and quite a

number of lacerations.'

'Does she know how bad Archie is?' Elli asked.

'Not yet. Besides, we really couldn't tell her much at first.'

'Can we see them?' Charles asked, eagerly.

'Archie is still unconscious, and we're closely monitoring him, but you may go and see Thia,' Digby said.

Elli could tell Charles had more questions for the doctor. 'Sweetie, I'm going to go see Thia, you stay here and chat with Digby. Digby, what do I tell Thia if she asks how Archie is?'

'Nurse Cantrell may be telling her, Elli. Thia's in the room opposite.'

Elli kissed Charles, left the office, crossed the hallway, and entered the room opposite. Thia was not surprised to see Elli, and thought Charles would be with Archie. After all, who else would be listed as Archie's next of kin? Poor Thia had cuts all over her face, a plaster cast and sling on her left arm, and her left leg was also in a cast.

'Aww, Thia. You poor thing,' Elli said, as she leant over and gently hugged her friend.

'Elli, how Is my Archie? How is he? They haven't told me,' Thia said, fearing the worst.

Elli sat in the chair next to the bed, and took Thia's right paw. 'We're not sure. We know he bumped his head, and he's unconscious, but they're monitoring him. He too has a broken leg. That's all we know so far.'

'Oh, Elli. It was bad. *Really*... bad,' Thia sobbed.

Elli handed her a tissue.

268

'I'm... sorry... your lovely car... is ruined,' Thia said through waves of tears and sniffs.

'I don't care about the car. That can be replaced. You and Archie can't. Don't give it a second thought,' Elli said, giving Thia another gentle hug. 'Are you in pain, Thia?'

'Mostly my face. Is it bad?' Thia asked.

The only thing Elli thought to say was, 'You'll heal. Do you need something for the pain?'

'They gave me something a little while before you came in. It should start working soon, I *hope.*'

'What happened?' Elli asked.

'We were driving along, and a lunatic overtook us on a sharp bend. They hit the side of the car, and we went off the road,' Thia told a stunned Elli.

'Did you manage to get the registration number?' Elli asked.

'No, but the people who helped us did,' Thia replied.

'Where are they?'

'They went to the police station,' Thia responded.

'Speaking of police, has Keen been told about Archie?' Elli asked.

'I don't think so. Should I call?' Thia asked.

'I can do that for you. Will you be alright for a few minutes?'

'Yes, I'll be fine. Thank you, Elli. Would you see how my Archie is, *please*?' Thia pleaded.

'I'll call Keen, then see what I can find out about Archie. I'll be back as soon as I can.'

Elli left the room, tapped on the doctor's office door, then entered. Charles was still chatting to Digby.

'Digby, how is Archie?' Elli asked. 'Thia wants to know.'

'No change as of yet,' the doctor replied.

'Sweetie, I'm going to call Keen. He doesn't know about Archie and Thia yet. I'll also call Daddy.'

'I should call Archie's brother, Oliver,' Charles said.

'Use this phone,' Digby said to Charles.

'Sweetie, I'll go use the payphone in the hall. I'll be back in a few,' Elli said as she opened the door. She then bustled up the hall, found the telephone and dialled The Cottage.

'Hello, Daddy.'

'Hello, Petal. How are they?' Lionel asked concerned.

'Archie's unconscious, has a fractured skull, broken ribs, and leg. Digby said it's serious. He also said, "The sooner he wakes up, the better." Thia has a broken leg and arm, and her poor face is *covered* in cuts. Daddy, I must go. I need to call Keen. He doesn't know yet. I'll call when we know more. I love you both.'

'We love you both, Petal. Love to Archie and Thia. Take care of each other,' Lionel said.

Elli hung up, then called Mereland Police House.

'Inspector Poddle speaking,' said the voice on the other end of the line.

'Keen, it's Elli.'

'Hello, Elli. Is everything okay? You sound a bit stressed.'

'We're at Muttleby hospital,' was all Elli could manage to say before Keen interrupted.

'Oh no! You're alright, aren't you? Is the pup

alright? Is Charles alright?'

'Yes, Keen, the pup and I are alright, so is Charles. It's Archie and Thia. They've been in a serious car accident.' The line went silent. 'Keen? Keen?'

'I'm here. Are they...' Keen started.

'No, they aren't. Thia has a broken arm and leg, and lacerations, but poor Archie hit his head, has a fractured skull, ribs, and leg. He hasn't woken up yet, and we *need* him to wake up soon.'

'Oh no!' Keen said painfully. 'How did it happen?'

'Lunatic overtaking on a bend hit them, and pushed them off the road,' Elli told him.

'Did the driver stop?' Keen asked. 'Did they get the number? Has anyone called Oliver?'

'No, the driver didn't stop, but there was a car following Archie and Thia, and they got the number, and went to the police station after they helped Archie and Thia. And... Charles is calling Oliver as we speak.'

'Okay. I'll be there soon,' Keen said urgently.

'I'm not sure what you can do here, Keen. We can call and keep you informed,' Elli said.

'I can go find the driver of the offending vehicle.'

'Okay, we'll see you later. Take care.' Elli hung up, went back to Thia's room, tapped then entered.

'How's my Archie?' Thia asked at once.

'No change, I'm afraid,' Elli replied sadly. 'I'm sure if there's any change, the doctor will let you know. I've told Keen, and he's on his way to Muttleby Police Station. He said he's going to try and find the driver of the vehicle that did this to you.'

'Elli, I want to see my Archie.' Elli believed,

because Thia had not seen him, she feared the worst.

'You rest. I'll ask the doctor if you can see him,' Elli said as she opened the door. She then crossed the hall, and tapped on the office door. On entering, she found Charles alone, pacing the room. 'Sweetie, what's wrong? You look agitated.' Charles was in a great deal of distress. 'Tell me what's wrong.'

'I don't know what's wrong. Digby rushed off to Archie. Nurse Cantrell said there were *changes*.'

'Changes? What changes?' Elli asked.

'I don't know, Ell. Changes, that's all I know.'

Digby returned to the office. 'How is he?' Charles asked, fearing the worst.

'Conscious,' the doctor responded.

Charles and Elli breathed a sigh of relief then they both asked, 'That's good, isn't it?'

'It's good that he's conscious, but it has been a number of hours since he was admitted. We need to watch him closely.'

'That's understandable,' Charles said.

'Has Thia been told?' Elli asked. 'She is desperate to see him.'

'She hasn't been told yet,' Doctor Allerton said.

'May I tell her? She's getting herself worked up, because I believe she fears he didn't make it, and nobody is telling her.'

'Yes, you may tell her,' the doctor replied.

'When can she see him?' Elli asked.

'In a while.'

Elli sped to Thia's room. 'I've just been told by Doctor Allerton that Archie is conscious.'

Thia looked half elated and half relieved. 'When can I see him?'

'Not just yet. The doctor is monitoring him. You'll see him soon,' Elli said, as she took a seat next to the bed.

Archie was groggy, and he had the mother of all headaches. Also, his sides hurt.

Nurse Cantrell was standing next to his bed, checking his pulse, blood pressure, and temperature.

'Where's Thia?' Archie asked the nurse hesitantly, as he too feared the worst.

'She's down the hall in another room,' Purdy Cantrell answered.

'I need to see her.'

'Not just at this moment, Mr Erinac.'

'Was she hurt?' Archie asked.

'She was hurt, but she'll heal. By the way, your brother is in the office,' Purdy informed him.

'My brother?' Archie asked, clearly confused.

'Yes,' the nurse said. 'Please excuse me a moment, Mr Erinac. I'll be right back.'

Purdy Cantrell left the room, and went straight to the doctor's office. 'Doctor, a moment, please.' The nurse and the doctor stepped out into the hall, as Charles was still in the office. 'Doctor, I told Mr Erinac that his brother was here, and he seemed confused, as if he didn't have a brother.'

'It could be because he has a biological brother, and calls Charles his brother. Let's just check,' Digby suggested, then led the way to Archie's room. 'Hello, Mr Erinac. How are you feeling?'

'My ribs hurt, and I have a pounding headache,' Archie replied, wincing a little.

'I'm afraid you're going to ache. You really banged your head and fractured your skull, but the headache will subside. If it doesn't subside, or if it gets worse, let us know straight away,' the doctor said firmly. 'Mr Erinac, could you tell me the name of your brother, please?'

'Which one?' Archie asked.

'How many do you have?' Digby asked.

'Two,' Archie replied, thinking it was either a cognitive test or perhaps, Digby knew Oliver.

Digby Allerton gave Purdy Cantrell a reassuring look.

'Their names are Charles and Oliver,' Archie added. 'Why do you ask?'

'Charles and Elli are in the office,' the doctor told him.

'Elli's here?' Archie asked, stunned.

'Yes. She's worried about you,' Purdy replied.

'Is she alright?' Archie asked most concernedly.

'Yes, she's fine. Why are you asking? You seem distressed by her being here,' Doctor Allerton said.

'Besides being back in Muttleby, *she is expecting a pup*,' Archie blurted out.

'I can imagine that being here again brings back memories she would rather forget. It is good news about the pup, though,' Digby said.

'May I see Thia, *please*?' Archie pleaded.

'You stay in bed. You are to be on *complete* bed rest for good while. Nurse Cantrell will bring Thia to you. But she can only stay for a few minutes. You both need your rest.'

'Thank you, Doctor Allerton.'

Purdy Cantrell left, and a few minutes later, returned with Thia in a wheelchair. She parked the chair next to Archie's bed, then left the room.

'Archie! My sweet Archie, how are you?' Thia asked as she reached out her good arm, to touch Archie's paw. Archie winced in pain as he sat up.

'My darling, Thia, your poor face, your arm, and your leg,' Archie said, his voice cracking, and a tear in his eye. 'I'm so terribly sorry, my love.'

'Archie, you have nothing to be sorry for. It *wasn't* your fault. It really wasn't,' Thia said, as she squeezed his paw.

'But I feel responsible. I was driving.'

'Archie, my love, I could have been driving. It was not your fault. Some maniac overtook us on a bend.'

'How's Elli's car?' Archie asked.

'Don't worry about that,' Thia said.

'I need to get home to look after the family,' Archie said, as Purdy Cantrell returned, overhearing the conversation. 'Mr Erinac, you are going *nowhere* for a while. You were unconscious for hours, have a fractured skull, broken ribs, and broken leg. We need to monitor you.' After she was satisfied that Archie and Thia were not in need of anything, she said, 'I will be back in a minute or two.' She then left, soon returning with Doctor Allerton.

'Okay, people, we are moving you, Mr Erinac to a

different ward,' the doctor stated, as he started to move Archie's bed.

'Why? What's wrong?' Thia asked.

'We'll be back in a minute,' Nurse Cantrell said, as she helped the doctor wheel Archie's bed up the hall. Once Archie's bed was positioned in a large ward, Nurse Cantrell returned for Thia.

'Why did you move Archie to this room?' Thia asked.

'Well, this room is for two patients, so you can share the room. The screens can be pulled around when privacy is needed,' Doctor Allerton answered.

Archie and Thia's moods lifted immeasurably at the thought of being together. They both thanked the nurse and doctor profusely.

'Charles and Elli are desperate to see you. Can I let them in?' Digby asked.

'Yes, of course,' Archie replied.

'I will be down the hall if you need me. Just press the button next to the bed,' Nurse Cantrell instructed, then she and the doctor left the ward. A minute or two later, Charles and Elli entered.

'Arch! Thia! How are you?' Charles asked.

'I have a headache, and my ribs hurt,' Archie answered.

'Brother, I was so worried about you,' Charles said, as he leant over to gently hug Archie.

Thia gestured to Elli to move her wheelchair, so as to give Archie and Charles a moment or two.

'Brother, it was scary,' Archie said, as he gripped Charles' paw.

'Arch, I really was worried about you,' Charles

said, a little choked by tears.

Archie sniffed, coughed a little, then said, 'Elli, I am sorry about your lovely car.'

'Archie, it doesn't matter about the car. You and Thia are all that matter,' she replied kindly. 'The car can be replaced, the two of you can't.'

'Have they moved the car?' Archie asked.

'We're not sure, Arch. I can ask Keen,' Charles said.

'Does Keen know about the accident?' Archie asked.

'Yes, Arch. Ell called him. He's on his way to Muttleby Police Station,' Charles replied. 'No doubt he'll come see you both.'

'I need to get home to take care of the family,' Archie said.

'Arch, brother, you're not going to be taking care of the family for a while. You need to recover,' Charles said firmly.

'Daddy sends his love to you both,' Elli said. 'I should go call him again. Let him know you're conscious. I'm sure he and Mummy are frantic. Do you want me to call your family, Thia?'

Nurse Cantrell was at the door when Elli spoke.

'I can bring the telephone cart in. That way, you can make your own calls,' she suggested.

'Thank you, nurse,' Thia said.

'You use the cart, Thia, I'll use the payphone in the hall,' Elli said, as she left the ward. Elli dialled the number for The Cottage. 'Daddy, he's awake!'

'That is good news! How is Thia?' Lionel asked.

'She'll heal. They've been moved into a two-bed

ward, so they can be together,' Elli informed Lionel.

'I'm so relieved he's awake. I'm sure they'll be happier being together in the same room.'

'They are. But Archie wants to go home, so he can take care of the family.'

'Typical! All bashed up, and still wanting to work,' Lionel responded. 'We may have to glue his bum to a bed or a seat.'

Elli chuckled. 'That'll do it! I'm not sure when we'll be back. You know Charles and Archie, Daddy.'

'I do, Petal. I do. There's a small hotel in Muttleby, if I remember correctly. Stay there the night, and come home tomorrow,' Lionel suggested.

'Not a bad idea, Daddy. I must go. Love to Mummy.'

'Give them our love, Petal. Bye.'

Elli hung up the telephone, grabbed the telephone directory, and found the number for Muttleby's only hotel, Muttleby Manor. After booking a room for the night, she returned to the ward.

'How's Dad and Heather?' Archie asked Elli.

'They're fine, but they're worried about the two of you. They send their love,' Elli informed them.

'Sweetie, I've booked us into a hotel nearby, Muttleby Manor.'

Charles laughed. 'It sounds like a haunted house.'

Archie also laughed, then cried, 'Ouch! Do not make me laugh, it makes my ribs hurt,' he told Charles. 'It reminds me of the ghost of Gideon Monarch.'

'That was my thought, too, brother.'

'Well, it's a bed for the night. It does mean we can come back tomorrow, if Gideon Monarch doesn't get us,' Elli said.

'You're right, Ell, and it's not worth driving all the way back to Mereland to drive back in the morning,' Charles said.

'Can we get you anything?' Elli asked a very tired- looking Archie and Thia.

'I just want to go home,' Archie said.

'I know, brother. There's nothing quite like your own bed,' Charles said. 'You'll be home soon, I'm sure.'

'Thia, did you get in touch with your parents?' Elli asked.

'There was no answer. I called my sister, Cassia, and she told me my parents are visiting friends in Barton upon Cress. Cass said, her husband Fiorello is working away, but they'll visit once he gets back.'

'We should let you rest. We'll see you tomorrow,' Elli said, noticing how drowsy both Thia and Archie were.

'Call us at the hotel if you need or want *anything*,' Charles added.

Elli kissed Archie on the cheek. As Thia's face was covered in lacerations and sutures, she kissed Thia on the top of the head. Charles gently hugged the two patients, then he and his wife left the ward, stopping by the office on the way out.

'We're just leaving. We'll be back tomorrow morning,' Charles told Digby.

'You're driving back to Mereland then coming back in the morning?' the doctor asked, surprised.

'No. We're booked into the Muttleby Manor,' Elli answered.

'That's a good idea,' Digby said.

'When will they be allowed to go home?' Charles asked.

'I'm concerned about Mr Erinac's head. I'd like to keep him here at least for another twelve hours for observation.'

'That's understandable, Digby,' Charles responded. 'We'll head out. Please call if you need us or if you want *anything*.' Charles and Elli bade the doctor and nurse goodnight, then left the office. As they were about to exit the building, they met Keen.

'Hello, you two! How's Archie and Thia?' Keen asked concernedly.

'Archie is conscious and eager to go home,' Charles responded.

'I guess that's a good sign,' Keen said.

'It is, but he needs to be monitored, at least until tomorrow,' Charles said. 'Keen, where are you staying tonight?'

'Hadn't thought about it. I just headed straight out and got on the first train I could.'

'I'll be back in a minute,' Elli said, then went back into the hospital. As promised, she returned in no time. 'Keen, you now have a room booked at Muttleby Manor.'

Keen smirked. 'It sounds haunted.'

'Yes! I thought the same, Keen,' Charles said.

'*Gideon Monarch*!' Charles and Keen blurted out together, then laughed.

'We'll wait for you if you're going to see Archie and Thia, though they may be asleep. That's why we left. They were both nodding off,' Charles said.

'I'll come back in the morning,' Keen said. 'Let's grab a bite to eat, then go to the hotel.'

They managed to find a small restaurant that was still open and ordered some fish and chips, and a pot of tea. After they had eaten their fill, Charles paid, and the trio got back in the car. Feeling much calmer than he had during the journey to Muttleby, Charles was now fit to drive to Muttleby Manor.

Muttleby
Manor

GRAPPLING HOOK

Muttleby Manor was much older than Bushelbee Manor, and as for the creep factor, well, that was off the charts. The building was a dark grey stone with a thatched roof. The doors and window frames, though painted black, were peeling, so the overall appearance was unkempt. Charles, Elli, and Keen looked at each other nervously.

'Oh dear!' Elli said with a gulp. 'I'm sorry, but it was the only hotel in the telephone directory.'

'Ell, it's okay. It's not haunted,' Charles said.

'We hope!' Keen added, with a laugh. 'It just looks it.'

'We either stay here, or we sleep in the car,' Charles stated.

'Okay, let's go in!' Elli said bravely.

Charles took a deep breath as he opened the front door.

They approached the front desk. The inside of the hotel looked as old as the outside. The walls were dark and rough, and overhead were heavy dark wooden beams. The curtains had seen better days,

282

about a hundred years ago, and the carpets were threadbare.

Charles hesitated to ring the brass bell on the reception desk, because he was having second thoughts about staying there. Elli reached over and rang it. A male raven appeared, dressed in a black suit. At that point, they all wanted to turn and run out of the place as fast as their legs would carry them. Before they could move, the raven said in a cheery manner, 'Good evening, folks. I'm Mr Sunny. Welcome to Muttleby Manor.'

The three guests all stopped in their tracks, and said, 'Thank you.'

'We have two rooms booked,' Elli said.

'Ah, yes! Mrs Watermere. A room for you and your husband, and a single for Mr Poddle. If you would like to sign the register, then I will show you to your rooms.'

Elli thanked Mr Sunny, whilst Charles signed the register and paid for the rooms.

'May I help you with your luggage?' Mr Sunny asked.

'We didn't plan this trip. We were just visiting friends in hospital, and it got too late to drive home, so we don't have any luggage,' Elli replied.

'Very well. This way, please.' Mr Sunny led Charles and Elli to one room, and Keen to the room next door.

When Charles and Elli opened the door, they stood there with their mouths wide open. The room was decorated in dark colours, with heavy wooden furniture. There was a massive wardrobe, an enormous four-poster bed with some seriously heavy brocade drapes, and there were about twenty candles sitting on practically every surface.

'Ell, have you seen how high the bed is?' Charles asked in amazement.

'You may need to give me a leg up,' Elli replied.

'I'd have to be able to get in it afterwards,' Charles said. 'I've left my grappling hook at home, Ell.' They both chuckled.

'We could use that chair as a step,' Elli suggested, pointing to a chair in the corner of the room. 'Though looking at it, it will take two of us to move it. Sweetie, turn the lights on. The room may not look as bad lit up.'

Charles looked on the wall for a light switch. 'Sorry, no light switch. No electricity, only candlelight.'

'*What*?' Elli asked. 'Okay. Fair enough.' Elli found a door and gingerly opened it, half expecting something to jump out at her, but it turned out to be a bathroom. There was a cord hanging from the ceiling, and Elli pulled it. The bathroom light came on. Elli called out to Charles, 'Sweetie, there's an electric light in the bathroom.'

'How odd,' Charles said. 'I wonder why there's none in here.'

'Perhaps it's for ambiance,' Elli mused.

'Okay, Mrs Watermere,' Charles said as he dragged the heavy chair over to the bed. 'In you get.' Charles helped Elli up onto the bed.

'This bed is *enormous*!' Elli said.

'To be honest, Ell, I don't care what it's like. I'm

so tired I could sleep on a washing line.' Charles blew out all but one of the candles, which he used to guide his way to the bed. Once he was in bed, Elli leant over, blew the candle out, then snuggled up to her husband. It was no time at all before they were fast asleep.

The next morning, when they awoke, they had quite a struggle to extricate themselves from the mattress. When they eventually managed to escape the clutches of the four-poster bed, they opened the curtains. The room did indeed look different in the daylight. It was actually quite grand, and not nearly as creepy.

Charles said, 'Look, Ell! The light switch was behind the door!'

'Who puts a light switch behind a door?' Elli asked.

'Evidently the mastermind who installed the electricity in this place.'

They freshened themselves up, best they could without toiletries or clean clothing, then went downstairs.

'Good morning, Mr and Mrs Watermere. Mr Poddle is in the dining room,' Mr Sunny informed them. 'I do hope you had a restful night.'

'Good morning, Mr Sunny. We did have a restful night, thank you,' Elli responded.

The raven directed them to the dining room, where they joined Keen at a table.

'Good morning,' Keen said.

'Morning, Keen,' Charles said. 'Did you sleep well?'

'I thought my bed was going to eat me. That was after I tried to find a ladder to get in it,' Keen said.

'Our bed must have been the same species. We had to fight it to get away from it this morning,' Charles said.

'Comfy though!' Keen added.

'No argument there!' Charles agreed.

'How did it go at the police station?' Elli asked Keen.

'I was a bit confused, to be honest. When I got there, they said that it wasn't Archie's SilentCart that was in an accident. They said it was registered to you, Elli.'

'Yes, Keen. It was my car. Archie borrowed it to drive to Norchester.'

'Now it makes sense. I went out to see the vehicle, as it was still at the scene. I collected the luggage and dropped it off at the police station. I can collect it later.'

'We can collect it later in the car,' Charles offered.

'Did you hire the one you drove here in?' Keen asked.

'No, it's new. Ell bought it. It was a wedding gift,' Charles replied with a smile at his wife.

'Lucky you! I wouldn't suggest you go with us, Elli, to see the vehicle, it isn't a pretty sight,' Keen said with a shake of the head. 'Archie's car would have been completely destroyed.'

'It's a good job you offered them your car, Ell,' Charles said with a shudder.

'Archie's car wouldn't have made it to Norchester on a single charge,' Elli responded. 'That's why I offered.'

'It was a good job it couldn't,' Charles said.

'Did you manage to find the person who ran Archie and Thia off the road?' Elli asked.

'The vehicle's owner was traced, but sadly, was reported stolen three days ago,' Keen replied.

'So, what are the chances of finding the driver?' Elli asked, hopefully.

'Not great, to be honest. Unless we catch the culprit with the vehicle, we really don't have much chance,' Keen answered.

'If you're both going to the police station and to see the car at the site, I'm going shopping,' Elli said.

'Shopping?' Charles asked, thinking it was a bit of an odd time to go on a shopping spree.

'Yes,' Elli said, as if Charles should have known what was on her mind. 'When Archie and Thia are discharged from hospital, they will need clothes to wear. With broken arms, legs, ribs, and a fractured skull, they'll need clothes that won't hurt getting on. I can get Thia a skirt, but Archie won't be able to get trousers over his cast, so I thought... if I buy some jeans, and unpick the seam of the leg, he can get them on. At home, he could wear shorts in bed.'

'Arch will not be best pleased wearing shorts,' Charles chortled.

'As long as he isn't wearing your duck shorts, I think he'll live with it. After all, nobody will see him in them. He'll be on bed rest,' Elli said.

'Are you saying, you're going to take the leg off the jeans?' Keen asked.

'No, Keen. Just unpick one seam on the leg, so it can fit over his cast,' Elli explained.

'That is *genius*!' Keen said. 'You're a smart lady!'

'I know she is! That's part of the reason I love her,' Charles said proudly.

'Okay, I'm going shopping!' Elli announced as she gave Charles a quick kiss.

'Do you want dropping off?' Charles asked.

'No, Sweetie. I'll walk. See you later!' And with that, Elli was out the door.

Charles drove Keen to the site of the crash. When Charles saw the state of Elli's car, he exclaimed, '*Good grief*! How they got out of that, is beyond me!'

'I know. That's why I didn't want Elli to see it,' Keen said. 'She already has a past with Muttleby, though, she seems to be getting through it.'

'I think it's because she's concentrating more on Archie and Thia,' Charles thought out loud. After visiting the site, and collecting Archie and Thia's luggage from the police station, Charles and Keen went to Muttleby hospital, believing Elli would be there. On discovering Elli was not, Charles looked concerned.

'Charles, my friend, she'll be alright,' Keen said, with a comforting pat on the shoulder.

'I guess you're right, Keen, but...'

'I know. You're having flashbacks. Let's give her a little time. Knowing Elli, she's buying up the whole of Muttleby,' Keen joked.

Charles chuckled. 'Ell is the queen of shopping. You're probably right, Keen.'

They walked up the corridor, and entered the ward, where they found Thia in her wheelchair next to Archie's bed.

'Cousin!' Keen crowed as he entered the room. 'How are the patients today?'

Thia said her face still hurt, but she was alright. Archie said he still had a bit of a headache, but his ribs hurt more than anything.

'How did you sleep?' Keen asked.

'Well,' the two patients answered.

'We chatted until we fell asleep,' Thia said. 'Where's Elli?'

'Not sure, be honest,' Charles said with a frown.

Archie looked at Charles with great concern. 'Why don't you know? Why? What's happened?' he asked, his panic rising.

'She said she was going shopping,' Charles answered.

'Well then, it could be days,' Thia jested. 'Let's face it, Elli could shop for Merashire.'

'True. I'll give her a while longer, then send out a search party.' Charles said, only half in jest. *Two hours* later, Elli arrived at the hospital and hurried up the corridor as quickly as she could, laden with bags. She entered the ward.

Charles exhaled, 'Ell! *Where have you been*? I was worried about you.'

'Sweetie, it's a long story, but I'm fine.'

'Elli, you have been busy,' Thia said, noticing the bags.

'I have,' Elli said. 'I bought you both some clothes to go home in. When they discharge you, of course.'

'Archie, my love, you won't be able to get trousers on over your cast. You may have to go home in a hospital gown,' Thia said.

'Thia, I thought we could unpick a seam on the

leg of these, jeans,' Elli said, as dragged a pair of denim jeans out of a Mallard's department store bag.

'That's a great idea, Elli! I can do that,' Thia said as she pressed the button next to Archie's bed.

Nurse Cantrell entered the ward, and asked, 'How may I help you?'

'I am so sorry to disturb you, but do you happen to have a pair of scissors I could borrow? We have these jeans, and we want to unpick a seam, so Archie can get them over his cast when we can go home.'

'Good idea!' the nurse said. 'I can bring you a suture cutter. That should make the job a little easier.'

'Perfect!' Thia said. 'Thank you.'

'Nurse, when can we go home?' Archie asked eagerly.

'After the doctor gives you the once over,' Purdy Cantrell replied. 'I'll be right back with the suture cutter.' Then she bustled off.

'Here you go, Thia,' Elli said, as she handed her a Fashion Mammal carrier bag.

'Elli, do they have a Mallard's and a Fashion Mammal in Muttleby?' Thia asked.

'No, Thia. I went to Norchester,' Elli replied matter-of-factly.

Charles gaped at his wife. 'Ell, you went to *Norchester by train*?'

'Yes, Sweetie,' Elli said nonchalantly.

'How was it?' Archie asked.

'I was a little nervous, but I made it there alright,' she replied, as if it were no big deal.

'That's wonderful, Ell!' Charles said. 'It's a big step.'

Elli smiled proudly.

Doctor Allerton entered the ward and asked the visitors to kindly step outside, which they did. As soon as they got outside the ward, Charles said, 'I'm sorry, how I reacted before. I was just worried about you and our pup. You said it was a long story, why?
What happened?'

'Follow me,' Elli said, and led the way out of the hospital's front doors, Charles and Keen in tow.

'*What's that*?' Keen asked, noticing a very large silver SilentCart parked in the car park.

'It's called a SilentCart Expanse,' Elli replied.

'It looks big,' Keen commented.

'It is big. It can take six people and luggage,' Elli added.

'Wow! How do you know so much about it, Elli,' Keen asked.

'You bought it, didn't you, Ell?' Charles asked.

'Yes, Sweetie, I did.'

'I like it!' Charles said enthusiastically.

'Well, we are a growing family,' Elli said, rubbing her belly. 'And, it will allow us to take Archie and Thia home in comfort.'

'Ell, you don't need to justify it, but everything you said is true,' Charles said, then kissed her on the nose.

'That is so thoughtful of you, Elli,' Keen said.

'Archie and Thia are family, Keen,' Elli stated with a warm smile.

'Who will drive the Expanse?' Keen asked.

291

'Which do you prefer, Sweetie?' Elli asked Charles.

'I do like the silver Expanse, Ell. Would you mind if I drove that?'

'That's fine, Sweetie. I'll drive the black sparkly one when I get home, but I'm sure Keen wouldn't mind driving it back to Mereland for me. That way, I can ride with you.'

'I'd love to, Elli! Let's go back, and see if they're being discharged,' Keen suggested, clearly eager to get on the road in Elli's car.

As they approached Archie and Thia's ward, Doctor Allerton opened the door and stepped into the hall.

'Can they go home?' Keen asked.

'They can, but...'

'Strict instructions,' Elli interrupted, having heard him say that to her when she was discharged.

'You got it!' Digby said with a smile.

'*Complete* bed rest, especially for Archie. If his headache gets worse, call me *immediately*. They both need rest, but Archie needs *total* bed rest.'

'If we have to, we'll staple him to the bed,' Charles joked.

'We may have to, Sweetie. You know Archie,' Elli said.

'If he won't stay on bed rest, he needs to be admitted again to be on bed rest under supervision. I'm *serious*. I've told him that, but he may need reminding.' Digby said. 'Nurse Cantrell will give you their prescriptions on the way out.'

'Thanks, Digby,' Charles and Elli said.

'Thanks, doctor,' Keen added.

'My pleasure, but we need to meet at happier times.'

'We certainly do,' Charles replied. 'You're always welcome to come to The Holt for a visit.'

'I'd love to, but I have so little time off. I'll keep that in mind, though. Thanks for the offer.'

They said their goodbyes to the good doctor, then entered the ward. As soon as they entered the ward, Archie cried, 'We can go home!' Both Archie and Thia were over the moon at the prospect.

'Well, you'll need to get dressed,' Elli said. 'I'll help you, if you need it, Thia.'

'Thank you, Elli. I'd really love some help.'

Elli stepped over to Thia's bed, drew the screens, and got to work helping Thia with a navy, shin-length skirt, and a white sleeveless blouse.

'Elli, you chose perfect clothes!' Thia said. 'I can fit my cast through the armhole.'

Meanwhile, Charles was helping Archie pull on his jeans with the side seam unpicked. Once the jeans were on, Charles got to work pinning the seam back together with the safety pins provided by Elli. Finally, Charles helped Archie into an overly large white button-up shirt. Elli felt that trying to squeeze a fractured skull through a T-shirt might be a bit painful.

'Thank you for helping me, brother,' Archie said.

'It's my pleasure, Arch. How many times have you helped me? I know, it's not the most elegant outfit you've ever worn, but...' Charles said.

'At least it fits over my plaster cast,' Archie said. 'I would not have liked to have travelled home in a hospital gown that did not close at the back.'

Charles chuckled at the thought. 'It would be a bit draughty, Arch. Well, sir, you are done!' Charles announced as he helped Archie transfer from the bed to the chair. He then pulled the screens back. When Archie saw Thia, he said, 'Thia, my love, you look *lovely*.'

'Thank you, hon. Then again, Elli did choose the clothes,' Thia said as she squeezed Elli's paw.

Keen said he was going to find Nurse Cantrell to get the prescriptions, and then they could leave.

'The doctor said, *complete* bed rest for both of you,' Charles reminded Archie. 'If you won't stay on bed rest, Arch, he wants you back here. It's time for *us* to look after you both for a change.'

Archie went to say something.

'*No arguments*! You're not going to heal overnight.'

'How about you use the north suites?' Elli suggested. 'Then you can open the sliding doors between, so you can see each other.'

'I know there's nothing like your own place, but... ' Charles said.

Archie and Thia looked at each other, then Archie said, 'Very well, we will stay in the north suites.'

'Good!' Charles said, feeling they were over one hurdle. The next would be keeping Archie on bed rest once he got home.

'Can we leave now?' Archie asked.

'We just need a wheelchair for you, Archie,' Elli said. As she spoke, Nurse Cantrell entered the ward with a wheelchair. Keen followed her.

'Okay, Mr Erinac, let's get you in this,' Purdy said,

as she helped Archie up out of the chair, and into the wheelchair. 'I have given Mr Poddle your prescriptions and your belongings.'

'Thank you, Nurse Cantrell,' Archie said as she pushed him towards the exit.

Charles pushed Thia's wheelchair, Elli still holding Thia's paw.

On the way to the hospital's front doors, Archie suddenly said, 'I have just had a thought! We will not all fit in Charles' new car.'

'Not a problem, brother,' Charles said, as they arrived at the car park.

Archie gasped, '*What a vehicle*!'

The patients were wheeled to the silver Expanse, where Charles helped Archie and Thia into the vehicle. They all thanked Nurse Cantrell profusely, then she returned to her duties. As Charles handed Keen the keys to the other car, he said, 'See you back in Mereland. Drive carefully.'

Charles and Elli got in the Expanse. 'Everyone comfortable?' Charles asked. His three passengers answered in the positive, so, Charles pulled out of the parking space. He thought Archie and Thia might be a little nervous being in a car for the first time after their accident, so he drove very slowly at first.

'Would anyone like to listen to some music?' Elli asked. 'There's a radio.'

'Some music would be nice, if it isn't too much for your poor head, Archie,' Thia responded.

'I'm sure I will be fine, my love. Music would be nice, Elli. Thank you.' Archie said.

Elli turned the radio on low and tuned the radio

to a station that played light music.

'This is quite relaxing,' Archie said.

'This is lovely, this piece,' Thia added, as she rested her head on Archie's shoulder. 'Am I hurting you, hon?'

'Not at all, my love,' Archie responded as he took hold of Thia's paw.

By the time they pulled up on the driveway at The Holt, Archie and Thia were sound asleep. Charles and Elli were loath to disturb them, so they got out, opened the door to The House, and Charles ran upstairs to get the wheelchair that had been stored there after Elli's abduction. When he returned, Keen had pulled up on the drive, and Archie and Thia were awake.

'Don't move!' Charles cautioned Archie and Thia. 'We have one wheelchair, so, I'll...'

Elli cut in, 'We have two wheelchairs, Sweetie. There's one in the back of the Expanse.'

'How?' Charles asked, somewhat perplexed.

'I bought one in Norchester,' Elli replied with a smile.

'Of course, you did. I hope you didn't lift it into the car, Ell,' a very concerned Charles stated.

'Of course not, plant pot! A very kind sales assistant did. I'm not a weakling, Sweetie, but I do know I'm pregnant.'

Charles kissed her nose, then said, 'I'm just being overly protective. I'm sorry, Ell.'

'It's okay. It's because you care.'

'I told you, you married a very smart lady, my

friend,' Keen said, as he helped Thia out of one side of the car, and Charles helped Archie out of the other.

Elli locked the car, then followed the two wheelchairs inside. She then took the stairs, whilst Charles and Keen took the invalids in the lift.

When the lift arrived, Elli asked Archie, 'Would you like me to buy some new pyjamas with wider legs, or would you prefer to wear shorts?'

'I think shorts will do. Thank you, Elli,' Archie said. 'As long as they aren't Charles' wild ones.'

'I can go up and get your stuff, Arch,' Charles offered. 'Ell, if you want to get Thia's things.'

'What would you like me to get?'

'If you could get me some toiletries, nightgowns, and...' Thia mouthed, *Some undies*.

'Will do!' Elli said as she and Charles headed to the stairs.

A SPOT OF OFFICE WORK

In Archie's penthouse, Charles collected some shorts, and a few pyjama tops, feeling that T-shirts would not be nice to be pulled over a fractured skull. Elli collected the items Thia had requested, along with some books she found next to Thia's bed. Charles had had the self-same idea. They made their way upstairs to the north suites. Elli closed the sliding doors between the rooms, and then helped Thia get into a nightgown. On the other side, Charles was helping Archie into his shorts and a navy blue and white striped pyjama jacket. Keen was waiting on the landing. Once Archie was in bed, Charles knocked on the sliding doors, and Elli opened them.

'Would you like something to eat?' Charles asked Archie and Thia. 'Don't worry, Arch, I won't cook.'

'I am a little hungry,' Archie replied.

'I could eat something,' Thia responded.

'We can order food from Enivid, but I can at least make you a cup of tea,' Elli said.

'We'll leave you in peace for a while. Call us if you need *anything*. Remember, *complete* bed rest,' Charles instructed.

298

'Please, call us. Don't do anything silly, like I did,' Elli pleaded, her face lined with pain.

'We will,' both patients said at once.

Downstairs, Elli made tea for everyone, and Charles took a tea tray upstairs for Archie and Thia. Keen carried another tray into the drawing room for Elli. Despite having had a smashing time with the plates in the garage, she just didn't trust herself to carry the tray. She had just dropped herself into an armchair when there was a knock on the terrace doors. Elli made to get up, and Keen said, 'Don't get up. I'll get it.'

Elli could hear Keen greeting Lionel and Heather in the hall.

'I take it Petal and my boy are back. We saw his car pull up,' Lionel said.

'Actually, that was me driving the car,' Keen said.

Lionel looked a little confused, thinking, *Why would Keen be driving Charles' brand new car?* He voiced his confusion, 'So, Charles and our Elli are still in Muttleby?'

'No. I drove it back, because, Elli bought another vehicle,' Keen explained.

'She did? Why?' Heather asked.

'Elli's in the drawing room, pouring tea,' Keen said. 'Ask her.'

They all made their way into the drawing room.

'Hello, Petal!' Lionel said as he kissed her on the cheek, then gave her a hug.

'Hello, Darling Girl. How are you and our grandpup doing? You do look tired, my dear.'

'I think it's tiredness and grubbiness,' Elli said.

'I need a bath.'

'Have a cup of tea first,' Heather said, encouraging Elli to drink her tea.

'My boy!' Lionel said as Charles entered the room. 'How are you? How's Archie and Thia?'

'I'm a little tired, but fine. Archie and Thia are on complete bed rest in the north suite,' Charles replied. 'We thought... Well, Ell thought they'd like to be able to see each other whilst on bed rest.'

'So, how are they, medically?' Heather asked.

'Arch still has a headache, due to his fractured skull. He has a broken leg and his ribs are broken. But, considering what they went through, he's doing pretty well. Thia has a broken arm and leg, and her poor face is covered in cuts and sutures.'

'*Oh, my word*!' Heather cried.

'To be honest, it's amazing that's all that happened to them,' Keen said, with a shake of the head.

'Did they get the son of a sea serpent that did this to them?' Lionel asked.

'Afraid not. The car was stolen,' Keen replied.

'*Stolen*?' Heather asked.

'Yes, Heather. The only way we'll be able to catch them... is if they're found with the vehicle.'

'Where was the car stolen from?' Lionel asked.

'Norchester, Lionel,' Keen replied.

'Speaking of cars, Keen just said you bought another one, Petal.'

'Yes, I did, Daddy.'

'Ell got the train to Norchester, and came back with a SilentCart Expanse,' Charles commented.

'You went to *Norchester* from Muttleby on your own, Petal?'

'Yes, Daddy,' Elli said proudly. 'I did travel in the main carriage with the other passengers, rather than a compartment.'

'That was a very wise thing to do, Darling Girl. I'm so proud of you,' Heather said, beaming. 'That was a huge step for you. Doing that on your own.'

'It was, Mummy, but we needed a way to get Archie and Thia home.'

'What exactly is a SilentCart Expanse?' Lionel asked.

'It's a six-seat family vehicle,' Elli replied.

'*Six seats*!' Heather exclaimed. 'That's gigantic!'

'Actually, Heather, it doesn't feel as big as it sounds,' Charles said. 'As Ell said, "We are a growing family", which is undeniably true,' Charles gently rubbed Elli's belly.

'Do you think Archie and Thia are up to visitors?' Lionel asked.

'Go on up. I'm sure they'd love to see you both,' Elli suggested.

'We need to call Enivid, unless you did it, Ell,' Charles said, remembering.

'Sorry, I forgot.'

'You going out to dinner?' Heather asked.

'No, Heather. Archie and Thia need feeding, and I don't want to poison them, and Ell works,' Charles said.

'I'll cook, my dears,' Heather offered.

'We can't ask you to do that, Heather,' Charles said, greatly surprised by the offer. Charles thought, *She's Queen Euphorbia! You don't ask The Queen to cook or do the dishes.* Although he had known Heather for quite some time, he still could not get his head around the plain and simple truth that she had been the reigning monarch not that long ago.

'You're not *asking*, I'm *offering*,' Heather said with a wonderfully warm smile.

'Thank you, Heather. That would be a great help,' Charles said, realising how much Heather truly loved taking care of the family. Charles mused, *I guess as The Queen, she never got the chance to do certain things. Things she now enjoys doing. Simple things, like, cooking, cleaning, gardening, and game nights.*

'Well, people, I should get home,' Keen said, draining his teacup. 'I called Acanthus last night and told her I'd be home today. Thanks for everything! I'll see myself out.'

Heather stood, and announced, 'I'm going to the kitchen to start some food.'

'I'll help, Mummy,' Elli offered, then followed Heather to the kitchen.

Charles and Lionel sipped their tea, and fell into conversation, 'What's wrong, Son? You look a bit worried. Was it our Elli going to Norchester?'

Charles shrugged, and Lionel knew Charles' goldfish bowl was a little low. 'Come on, now. It's me,' Lionel said.

'To be honest, Dad, I'm petrified,' Charles mumbled.

'Why, Son? What of?'

'Becoming a dad. It scares me. I mean, with so

much that has happened, and there's so much that could go wrong. What if I don't know how to be a dad, or I'm not able to handle things that happen?'

'You'll be a great dad, my boy! You love our Elli to bits, and she loves you. That's a good start! You know how to look after those you love. Just be yourself and stop borrowing trouble. I know you'll be there for our Elli and the pup.'

'Of course I will, Dad. I love her more than anything in this world,' Charles said with a sigh.

Lionel smiled at the look in Charles' eyes. 'That's clear to everyone, Son. None of us get a handbook when we have pups. We all fly by the seat of our pants. Stop worrying about not being a good dad, and enjoy the journey together.'

'I love you, Dad,' Charles said.

'I love you, Son.'

Heather had cooked and served baked salmon, broccoli, and a few new potatoes to Archie and Thia, much to their delight. After checking on their condition, Heather returned downstairs to have dinner with Lionel, Charles, and Elli.

'I've just remembered something,' Charles said, a forkful of salmon halfway to his mouth.

'What is it, Sweetie?' Elli asked.

'We have to open the new school in September,' Charles said with a heavy sigh.

'Oh dear!' Elli said. 'I'm too tired. Can't someone else open it? I know it's an honour, but, so much has gone on, and I'm *exhausted*.'

'I know, Ell. I'm with you on that one,' Charles said.

'What if I could get someone else to open it?' Heather asked.

'No, Heather. We don't want everyone to know who you really are, unless of course, you do,' Charles said at once.

'No, my dear. I was thinking of someone else.'

'*Very* mysterious,' Elli said.

'I'm sure I could arrange for *someone*. Leave it with me,' Heather said.

'Very well,' Charles agreed. 'Thank you.'

The weekend before the school opening, Charles went upstairs to visit Archie. When he tapped and entered Archie's room, the dividing doors were closed. 'Is Thia asleep, Arch?' Charles whispered.

'No, she is changing her clothes.'

'How are you doing, brother?' Charles asked.

'I want to do something to help the family. I cannot sit here all day doing nothing,' Archie stated exasperated.

'Well, there's one thing that you could do, if you'd like to help,' Charles said.

Archie looked excited to be put to work. He was eager to help the family again.

'Have you told Thia about the GM Trust?' Charles asked.

'*No, Charles. Certainly not!*' Archie stated, quite affronted that Charles would believe he would betray his confidence.

'Brother, it's not an accusation. Thia is part of the family, she should know. You may want to tell her.'

'It is not my place to tell her,' Archie said stiffly.

'Why not, Arch?'

'It is your business, and your secret to divulge to whomever you wish to divulge it to,' Archie stated.

'Fair enough. She obviously knows who Gideon Monarch was, because we mentioned him in the hospital, and she didn't ask who he was.'

'Yes, Thia knows who Gideon Monarch was,' Archie said, as Thia tapped on the dividing doors, and wheeled herself into the room.

'Charles! Nice to see you,' Thia said.

'You look well, Thia,' Charles said.

'My face is healing, but I'll still have scarring,' she replied.

'You are beautiful, my love,' Archie said.

'Thank you, hon.'

'Thia, my love, remember we were both saying that we wished we could do something useful?'

'Yes, Archie Bug.'

'Well, Charles needs some help with something,' Archie said, paving the way for Charles to take over the conversation.

'Before I tell you what I or *we* need help with, I need to tell you a bit of a story,' Charles said.

Thia leant in, intrigued.

'A few years back, a couple of crooks were snooping around the estate...'

'*No!*' Thia blurted out.

'Yes. They did a bit of late-night digging in the lawn, and then headed across the flower field to Bushelbee Manor.'

'The house you can see from the penthouse living room window?' Thia asked.

'The exact one! Well, they were in there, because they had heard there was treasure on the Bushelbee estate,' Charles said.

'How exciting! Did they find it?' Thia asked. Archie was watching Thia, who was spellbound by the story.

'Anyway... Arch spotted some lights coming from the manor, and the next day we went to investigate. We found signs of inhabitants, who should not have been there.'

'As you know, Thia... ' Archie cut in. 'Charles owns the manor.'

'Yes, of course,' she replied.

'To cut a very long story short, we set a trap for them, and caught the ringleader,' Charles said. 'The other one was harmless and was dragged along pretty much against his will. The thief had nearly cleared out the manor of all the valuable items. Granted, I didn't know the items existed...'

'But still...' Thia added.

'Exactly! So, we brought all the valuables back here.' Charles took a deep breath. 'All that was left in the manor was an ugly looking coat rack. Arch thought LP would like to see it, because she likes unusual things.' Charles smirked a little, then continued. 'LP couldn't see it clearly, because the hall was dark, so Rupe told her to move the coat rack, but she couldn't. She asked Rupe for help, the two of them couldn't move it.'

'Was it bolted to the floor?' Thia asked.

'That's what Rupe thought, but no. It was just so flipping heavy. We all lifted it out of the corner, and that's when we discovered it was solid gold covered in paint.'

'*WHAT*?' Thia exclaimed.

Both Archie and Charles laughed at her reaction,

then Charles continued. 'We finally managed to get it back here, and we cleaned it up. We discussed it, and decided that all the valuables the thief was going to take should be auctioned off. The money was donated *anonymously*, to the village school, and the coat rack was auctioned off and the money was used to set up the GM Trust.'

'I hear people talking about the GM Trust, but nobody seems to know anything about the origins of it,' Thia said.

'That's good!' Charles said, relieved. 'We want it to stay that way. If people found out we were behind it, we would never get a moment's peace or be able to get to our front door.'

'I'm sure you're right,' Thia agreed.

'I decided, as we consider you family, it was time to tell you. Please don't be angry with Arch for not telling you.'

'I understand. He did what you asked him to do, and didn't tell anyone,' Thia said, smiling at Archie.

'*Precisely*! Another little bit of information you will need to know… the office for the GM Trust is upstairs in the other side of The House from the penthouse.'

'That's what's there!' Thia exclaimed. 'I've thought it was just storage.'

'Well, it is. It's storage for the GM Trust, in a way. I'm getting to a point, I *promise*. The applications for the GM Trust fund are sent to a box outside the Mereland Mirror. Rupert collects them, and brings them home. He recently put a chute in the wall, so the applications go straight into a locked filing cabinet that is bolted to the wall. The applications are brought back here, and we meet to discuss them. Then one of us types a response letter, and it's put in a locking mail wallet, and taken to the post office.'

'Locking mail wallet?' Thia asked.

'It has a lock on that's only opened when it gets to Norchester. That way, the mail is not postmarked Mereland, but Norchester,' Charles explained.

'Clever!' Thia praised.

'That was Rupe's brilliant idea,' Charles said. 'So, if you two are feeling up to a spot of office work, we have a stack of applications that need responses. I can bring down a typewriter and any other things you need. You both have rolling bed tables to work from.'

Thia and Archie looked at each other.

'Don't decide now. I know it's a lot to ask. Think about it,' Charles said.

'We don't need to think about it,' Thia replied.

'We will do it!' Archie and Thia said in tandem.

'*Fantastic*!' Charles cheered.

'Charles,' Thia said tentatively. 'If I do a good job...'

'I'm sure you will do an excellent job, Thia,' Charles interrupted.

'I may like to do it on a more permanent basis. I'm not sure if you know, but a company has been looking to buy Canire Couture. If I sell, it would be nice to move to Mereland and have something to do with my time. Besides, you and Elli will be a little busy with the patter of tiny paws soon.'

'That would be wonderful, Thia! You could be the director of the GM Trust. It would still have to be hush hush, you understand,' Charles said, delighted.

'Of course. I would just tell people that I'm working on other projects.'

'Speaking of other projects, weren't you working on one recently?' Charles asked.

'It didn't pan out, Charles,' Thia said with a shrug.

Elli walked into the room. 'Is everything alright?' she asked.

'Yes, Ell. I thought it was time to tell Thia about the GM Trust.'

'Good! Now we all know.'

'Thia and Arch are going to deal with the pile of applications waiting for responses. Also, Thia said she would like to work on the GM Trust, on a more regular basis if she decides to sell Canire Couture.'

'Great news! Let me know if I can get you anything,' Elli offered.

'I'm going upstairs to get a typewriter and some stationery,' Charles said, then he beetled off.

'I was going to make a cup of tea, would you like one?' Elli asked.

Archie and Thia responded in the positive, so Elli headed to the kitchen.

By the end of the week, the rest of the family were told that Thia was now privy to the GM Trust secret, and she and Archie had waded through all applications.

The morning of the sixteenth of September was clear and bright, with a slight breeze. After Charles and Elli had helped Archie and Thia to dress, they dressed themselves. Charles wore a navy suit, a white shirt, and a lavender tie. Elli wore a very pretty navy, Canire Couture dress. Elli had to admit, her bump was showing now, and soon the whole village would know.

Lionel and Heather, Ermgarde and Rupert with their two pups, and Keen and Acanthus all arrived at the terrace doors at the same time.

'That's good timing, folks!' Charles said.

'Who will look after Archie and Thia?' Lionel asked.

'The doctor has given them permission to attend the opening ceremony, as long as they stay in their wheelchairs,' Elli informed the group.

'They are dressed and ready, we just need to go get them,' Charles said.

'I'll help!' both Keen and Rupert offered.

'Why don't you boys take a wheelchair each?' Heather suggested.

'Will do!' Rupert said, then he and Keen headed upstairs to collect the last two members of their party.

'Squish-Squish, this is my new school opening,' Isaac said.

'I know. Isn't it exciting?' Charles asked.

'It is!' Isaac squealed. 'Auntie Squish, can I feel the pup kick?'

'Not yet, pup. Soon, perhaps,' Elli replied.

Ermgarde said, 'He used to love feeling Lotti kick.'

'When the pup starts kicking, I'll let you know. Okay?'

Isaac nodded and smiled.

Lionel and Heather also looked keen to know

when the kicking would start. Elli noticed the look on their faces, and said, 'I will let you *all* know when the pup starts kicking.'

Rupert and Keen arrived in the hall with Archie and Thia.

'Are Flynn and Willow not going?' Heather asked.

'Yes, but they'll meet us down there. Honeysuckle is down from Norchester,' Charles replied.

'Are we ready?' Lionel asked.

'Ready as I'll ever be,' Charles said, resignedly. Heather had not mentioned anything about someone else doing the opening of the school, and Charles had not pushed the issue.

BUSHELBEE
ACADEMY

BENIGNITAS
PRAE OMNIBUS

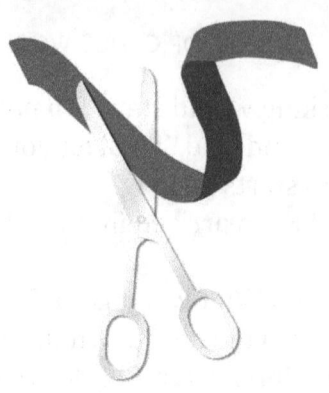

PROMISE KEPT

They all walked slowly down Bushelbee Lane, Charlotte sitting on Thia's lap so she could get a ride. Thia loved every minute of it. When they turned up the newly named School Lane, Charles gave a heavy sigh. Elli knew what that meant. It meant Heather had not kept her word about finding someone else to open the school. Elli took hold of Charles' paw.

The new school did look incredible. You could tell the architect who worked on The Holt had designed it. It was white, smooth sided, modern, clean lined, with lots of big windows that seemed to bring the outside in.

As the Watermere party arrived, everyone started to cheer. Charles anxiously took a deep breath. As he went to step forward towards Athena Tyto, Heather patted him on the shoulder. He turned around to see two black limousines approaching. The vehicles stopped, and much to the entire community's and Charles' surprise, King Maldon and Queen Angelica got out of one of the vehicles. There came a deafening roar from the villagers. The King and Queen could not

312

have wished for a warmer welcome. Everyone, including Charles, Elli, Lionel, and Heather, bowed or curtsied. Archie and Thia bowed their heads, as they were sitting in wheelchairs.

Isaac asked, 'Are you The King?'

Maldon smiled, and responded, 'I certainly am.'

'Do you live in a palace?' Isaac asked.

'Your Majesty, I am sorry,' Ermgarde said, a little embarrassed by her son's boldness. 'Sweet Pea, The King is here to open the school. Stop asking him questions.'

'I don't mind answering questions. Certainly not from an inquisitive young pup like you,' Maldon replied. 'And, yes, I do live in a palace.' Maldon shook paws with Isaac, then he and Angelica approached Athena Tyto, who almost fainted, but managed to steady herself enough to curtsy.

'Your Majesty,' Charles said, to gain Maldon's attention. 'May I present, Doctor Athena Tyto, headmistress?'

Maldon spoke directly to Athena, 'Doctor Tyto, the Duke informed me of your school opening (Maldon fibbed. He certainly was not going to tell her, that his mother, Heather had told him). The Duke thought you would not mind if I opened it in his stead.'

'Your Majesty, of course I don't mind!' Athena said wide-eyed with surprise.

'Then let us open your school,' Maldon said pleasantly. At that moment, Athena Tyto gave Charles a look that clearly screamed, *You could have warned me*!

Maldon stepped up to the big blue ribbon that

was tied across the front doors of the school. 'People of Mereland, I was told all about your school, the old and this incredible new one, and the struggle you went through. I was also informed of how the whole community pulled together to make a temporary school to educate the fine young people of this beautiful village. It takes a lot to keep going in the face of adversity, but you did, and I applaud each and every one of you for that. As your king, it is important to me to get to know the wonderful people and villages in Merashire, so when the opportunity arose to come here, I jumped at the chance. This is such a *special* place, with a *lot* of heart. I wish you all the very best.'

Athena Tyto held a pair of scissors, offering them to King Maldon. He took them, his gaze shifting to the blue ribbon stretched across the entrance. With a proud glance at the school's name, he declared, 'I, King Maldon of Merashire, hereby officially open Mereland Academy.' As he cut the ribbon, the crowd roared and cheered.

Athena guided the King, Angelica, their security, Charles, and Elli through the school. Once they had finished, Maldon turned to Athena, Charles, and Elli, and said, 'Thank you,' his voice filled with genuine appreciation.

'Your Majesty,' Charles said. 'Would you care for some refreshments at our home, The Holt?' This was Charles' way of asking Maldon if he would like to visit with his mother.

'That would be delightful. Thank you, Duke.' Maldon then thanked Athena Tyto for allowing him to open her school. The King said, 'Duke, if you and the Duchess would like to join us in the cars.'

'Certainly, Sir,' Charles replied. As they walked towards the vehicles, they stopped at the Watermere family. 'Sir, may I introduce our family and extended family?'

'Of course,' Maldon said.

Charles introduced *everyone*. Of course, Maldon had already met *some* of them, one being his own mother, but Charles was attempting to protect Heather's identity in front of the watching villagers. Charles told his family that he and Elli were joining Maldon in the car, and would meet them back at The Holt. Maldon suggested that Lionel and Heather could join them in the car, which they did. The rest of the family made their way back up Bushelbee Lane, Rupert and Keen pushing Thia and Archie in their wheelchairs.

Back at The Holt, the two limousines pulled up, then the gates were closed. Everyone got out, and Charles unlocked the front door. Once inside The House, Maldon hugged his mother, then shook paws with Lionel and Charles. He then gave Elli a hug, and whispered something in her ear. Elli dabbed away a tear. Angelica hugged them all.

'Gentlemen,' Maldon addressed his security. 'Please relax. I am safe here.'

'If you would like to make yourselves comfortable in the library, I will make you some tea,' Elli offered. The two badgers in dark grey suits, followed Elli to the library, then she bustled off to the kitchen. At that moment, Archie and Thia were wheeled into the hall, then Rupert and Keen

315

excused themselves and left.

'Archie!' Maldon exclaimed, 'What happened?'

'Someone ran us off the road, Maldon,' Archie responded.

'How awful!' Maldon responded. 'I do hope you are both on the mend.'

'Yes, thankfully,' Archie said. 'May I introduce my ladyfriend, Thia Canire?' Thia just looked stunned.

'Of course, of course, Archie. Lovely to meet you, Thia,' Maldon said.

'Canire? Not Canire Couture?' Angelica almost squealed.

'Yes, Your Majesty, I am Thia Canire, designer and owner of Canire Couture,' Thia replied, completely totally, and utterly stunned that The Queen would know of her work.

'You are a most wonderful designer! Maldon's sister, Marjy introduced me to your brand,' Angelica said, answering Thia's surprised expression.

'Thank you, Ma'am.'

'Thia, please relax,' Maldon requested. 'I believe you know who my mother is.'

'Yes, Sir,' Thia said, looking at Heather.

'I am Maldon in this house. Please relax.'

'Yes... Sir... I mean, Maldon,' Thia said a little uncomfortably.

'Thia, we've all been where you are, and felt how you're feeling,' Charles said kindly. 'If you would like to go to the drawing room, I will help Ell with the tea.' Charles headed to the kitchen, and the others entered the drawing room, Lionel and Maldon pushing the wheelchairs. A couple of minutes later, Charles and Elli entered the room, Charles pushing a tea trolley.

'I would have helped, Charles,' Archie said.

'I know, Arch, but you're incapacitated at the moment. Just relax, brother.'

Heather offered to serve the tea.

'Maldon, thank you so much for opening the school. It made everyone's day,' Charles said. 'But, I think Athena Tyto believes I kept you a secret from her.'

'Sweetie, you're lucky she was so stunned,' Elli commented.

'It was all Mummy's idea. She felt, if I opened the school, it would be given a royal charter.'

'A royal charter is very special,' Lionel said.

'You're right, Lionel. The school would be protected, because as you know, in Merashire, a royal charter is registered. Before the building could be re-purposed or demolished, it would first have to get *my* approval. And, of course, there is no way I would allow your school to be at risk. A copy of the charter will be filed at the land registry with the original deeds to the school.'

'What a brilliant idea!' Elli said.

'It was all Mummy's idea, of course,' Maldon admitted, smiling at Heather.

'Thank you, Heather,' Charles said.

'Well, my dear, it is *my* village's school. How can I not want it protected,' She beamed.

'I believe congratulations are in order,' Angelica said. 'I heard there will be an addition to the Watermere family.'

'Yes, Angelica,' Elli said, rubbing her belly.

'When are you due?' Angelica asked.

'February,' Elli and Charles answered.

'By the way, you have a *spectacular* home, Charles, Elli,' Maldon gushed.

'Thank you, Maldon. If you and Angelica would like to look around, please feel free,' Charles offered.

'If you would like the guided tour of The Holt, Lionel and I could take you,' Heather offered proudly.

'You're welcome to stay. The Guest House is always ready,' Charles said. Archie gave Charles a stern look that said, *I have not been able to freshen it*! 'Your mum has a key,' Charles added.

'Thank you. That is most kind of you,' Maldon said.

After they had finished their tea and chatted about life in Mereland, Heather and Lionel took Maldon and Angelica out into the grounds via the terrace doors. As soon as the doors were closed, Thia asked, 'You call The King and Queen Maldon and Angelica?'

'Yes. So do you, now, Thia, my dear' Archie said.

'It takes a bit of getting used to,' Charles added.

Archie and Thia chatted amongst themselves.

Charles turned to look at Elli, who appeared pensive. 'You okay, Ell?'

'Yes, Sweetie, I'm fine.'

Charles spoke in a low voice, 'You don't have to tell me, but what did Maldon whisper to you?'

'Maldon said, "Mummy told me. Welcome to the family, princess." Which I found quite touching.'

Charles kissed Elli.

Meanwhile, Maldon and Angelica were being

enchanted by The Cottage, The Lodge, and The Bower. Maldon could not believe Charles had had a home built for his mother. He and Angelica loved the location of her waterside home with its beautiful orchard. Maldon felt it just oozed serenity. 'Mummy, I can feel myself unwinding,' Maldon commented.

'That's The Holt effect,' Lionel said.

'It certainly is, Lionel, dear,' Heather agreed.

'Let's show you The Guest House,' Lionel suggested, as they strolled across the lawn.

'My! What a guest house!' Maldon exclaimed, as they stepped foot inside. 'Angelica, darling, we could stay here. There are two bedrooms, which means, the security could use one.'

'Though, to be honest, Maldon, dear, you probably won't need it. I didn't,' Heather stated.

'It was so kind of Charles to make the offer,' Maldon said. 'He is such a...'

'Special person?' Heather suggested.

'Yes, and he's so down to earth,' Maldon added.

'And Elli is the *sweetest* lady,' Angelica praised.

Heather smiled. 'She certainly is, Angelica, dear. If you ever need or want fashion advice, that young lady is the absolute best.'

'Is that who helped you and Marjy?' Angelica asked.

'Yes, Angelica.'

'I do love your new look. Or should I say, your Mereland look?'

'My "Mereland look", Angelica?' Heather queried.

'Yes. You never looked like that at the palace.'

'Ah! Now I understand. You're quite right, my

dear, Mereland has changed my life in a number of ways,' Heather said, as she took hold of Lionel's paw.

'Well, you're welcome to stay whenever you like,' Lionel said.

'We can't stay tonight, but we will visit again soon,' Maldon promised.

'Perhaps come in a plain vehicle, my dears,' Heather suggested. 'It worked for me.'

The four otters strolled back across the lawn, and up the terrace steps, where they met Charles, Elli, Archie, and Thia.

'Thank you, for a lovely warm welcome,' Maldon said.

'Our pleasure,' Charles and Elli said at once.

'We need to head back to Norchester, but would love to visit again, and perhaps stay a night or two. Mummy was right about The Holt, it really is the most relaxing place I have ever been to.'

'Just arrange the date with your mum. She has guest house keys,' Charles said.

'Well, we will say farewell,' Maldon said as he hugged his mother first, then Lionel, and then the others. On the way through The House, Maldon collected the two badgers who were still in the library. Once the guests were in their vehicles, Charles opened the gates After a final farewell wave, The King and Queen were on their way home to Norchester.

change

EPILOGUE

One Saturday morning after the opening of the Bushelbee Academy, Elli said it was time for her shop's new name to be revealed, so the inhabitants of The Holt made their way down to the High Street. Charles and Rupert pushed the wheelchairs, and parked them outside Elli's little shop.

'Ell, your sign is blank. Did you decide not to give it a name after all?' Charles asked, with a wink.

'No, plant pot, it's covered with a dark cloth,' Elli said, knowing that Charles was just being silly.

'This is exciting,' Heather said.

'It is. Our Elli making the shop her own,' Lionel added.

Elli smiled broadly. She then asked Lionel to pull a string, which tugged the dark fabric off the new signage. As the fabric dropped, a large rectangle in Elli's favourite colour, turquoise, was revealed. In black letters was the new name of her shop.

321

OURELLI

For a second or two they all just stared at the sign, until Archie cried out, 'Our Elli!'

Lionel laughed, then kissed Elli's cheek. 'Our Elli! Our Elli!' Lionel kept saying. 'I mean, it is our Elli's shop!' Lionel loved the new sign.

'That's *perfect*, Ell,' Charles said with a smile.

'Darling Girl, you clever thing!' Heather praised.

'Actually, Ermgarde suggested putting the two words together. She's the clever one,' Elli said, smiling at Ermgarde.

'Lovely job on the sign, LP,' Charles raved.

'I like the new sign,' Isaac announced. 'It's *happy*!'

Everyone gathered outside the shop. Archie and Thia's wheelchairs were positioned in the front, with Charlotte and Isaac sitting on their laps. Rupert set the timer on his camera, then ran into position. They just had to have a photograph of the moment.

THE END

Ashlowe Announcer

News From Ashlowe and the Surrounding Area

CAR THIEVES IN FATAL CRASH

Two suspected car thieves died on Friday morning after the stolen vehicle they were driving left the road.

According to witnesses, the thieves attempted to overtake another vehicle on a blind bend with fatal consequences.

'This was a preventable tragedy,' said Deputy Chief Constable Falco. (More details page 3).

Mallard's

New!

MAC & MONTY

BOLD AS BRASS
ASHLOWE

BRASS ON THE GRASS

Support your local brass band at Brass on the Grass in Mereland next weekend!

LIST OF IMPORTANT CHARACTERS

Charles Hugo Watermere - Otter

Duke of Mereland and Ashlowe, and Lord Bushelbee of Mereland. Inherited a vast sum of money from his great aunt Harriet. Home is The Holt, Bushelbee Lane, Mereland, Merashire. Called Uncle Squish by his niece, and Squish-Squish by his grandnephew and niece.

Elli Sapphire Watermere - Otter

Charles' wife. Master jeweller to the crown. Owns a little shop on the High Street. Estranged from her family, except for Crosby, one of her brothers. Spent most of her childhood with her grandparents. Grandfather was a master jeweller.

Lionel Watermere - Otter

Charles' widowed father, retired landscape gardener. Lives in The Cottage at The Holt. Known as Pop-Pop by his grandpups.

Queen Euphorbia of Merashire (Retired) - Otter Also Known as Heather Birkdale

Retired to Mereland after nearly thirty years as reigning monarch of Merashire. Called Aunt Heather by Elli. Lionel Watermere's ladyfriend.

Archie Erinac - Hedgehog

Charles' best friend from kindergarten. Insisted on working for Charles as his valet when Charles inherited his wealth. Spent so much time with Charles' family that he calls Charles brother, and Lionel Dad. Father left one day and never returned. Mother died a number of years back. Has a biological brother, Oliver.

Thia Canire - Hedgehog

Archie's ladyfriend. Went to university with Elli. Met Archie at a party thrown by Charles and Elli. Famous fashion designer, her brand—Canire Couture. Lives in Norchester.

Ermgarde Staff - Otter

Charles' niece. Lives in The Lodge at The Holt with her husband, Rupert, and her two pups, Isaac and Charlotte 'Lotti'. Commercial graphic artist. Has a studio named Willow Tail Designs on the High Street. Called LP (Little Pup) by Charles.

Rupert Staff - Otter

Ermgarde's husband. Editor of the Mereland Mirror. Father of Isaac and Charlotte. Loves music.

Isaac Lionel Staff - Otter

Ermgarde and Rupert's first-born. A whirlwind. Loves reading, dinosaurs, and science. Calls Charles—Squish-Squish, Lionel—Pop-Pop, and Elli—Auntie Squish. Best friend to Pippo Rohan. Calls his sister Person.

Charlotte Nola Staff - Otter

Isaac's younger sister, whom he calls 'Person'. Also known as Lotti.

Keen Poddle - Hedgehog

Archie's cousin. Local police inspector. Lives in the Police House in the village with his wife Acanthus, and twin daughters, Lille and Acacia. Mother is the local grocer, Gerti.

Dear Reader,

If you're reading this, then you've made it through—not one, not two, but seven whole books chronicling my escapades, mishaps, and the occasional tea-related accident, all accompanied by a healthy dose of well-placed sarcasm. For that alone, you deserve a medal. Or at the very least, a Garibaldi biscuit and a cup of tea.

Now, I must make a humble request — and no, it doesn't involve tackling crooks or rescuing anyone. (Though if it does turn into that, I'm sure Arch will provide snacks.) Would you consider leaving a review?

Truly — a few kind words, a thoughtful observation, or even a quietly enthusiastic note on Amazon, Goodreads, or wherever you feel moved to share makes a world of difference. My author is an indie — no marketing team, no publicist, not even a personal tea-brewer (which frankly seems like an oversight). Just her, doing it all herself. Your review helps new readers discover the series and keeps the story alive — which, she assures me, isn't quite finished yet. (I'm bracing myself.)

So whether you laughed, cried, gasped, or simply shook your head and muttered, 'Oh, Charles...' — I'd be honoured if you'd share your thoughts.

With appreciation (and a fresh cup of tea),

Charles

P.S. If you love my books — tell everyone!